THE WITCHES OF PENDLE

THE
WITCHES
OF PENDLE

YVETTE FIELDING

ANDERSEN PRESS

First published in 2023 by
Andersen Press Limited
20 Vauxhall Bridge Road, London SW1V 2SA, UK
Vijverlaan 48, 3062 HL Rotterdam, Nederland
www.andersenpress.co.uk

4 6 8 10 9 7 5

British Library Cataloguing in Publication Data available.

ISBN 978 1 83913 318 3

Printed and bound in Great Britain by Clays Ltd, Elcograf S.p.A.

For all the *Most Haunted* fans who have loved and supported the show for over twenty years. You're amazing!

CHAPTER 1

A Haunted House and an Eerie Song

The little farmhouse stood abandoned in the middle of the countryside. It was obvious that no one had lived there for some time. The windows were grimy and cracked, and a square piece of splintered wood lay on the ground near the weathered front door. It was a sign, its black letters faded and the words *Malkins Cottage* just visible. An ancient, twisted oak tree tapped its long, bony fingers against the dark glass, *tap . . . tap . . . tap*. The sound was ominous in the December bleakness.

It was a small house, one storey. Originally the building had been just one room, the occupants of old sleeping and eating together. Over the years, people had come and gone, building in an extra room here and there, trying to live a happy existence in the place. But for some strange reason, no one had ever managed to stay for very long. The locals said the place was cursed, haunted even, by the ghosts of a family.

Now the snow was coming down thick and fast; big powdery blobs slowly twisted and tumbled towards the muddy ground. The little cottage and the land it sat on were starting to look pretty.

Along the dirt track leading up to the cottage, a four-wheel drive rumbled slowly to a stop. Its doors opened and excited voices broke the wintery silence.

'Oh, look, Steve, doesn't it look perfect?' A woman with blonde hair pulled back into a ponytail clapped her hands together, her face lighting up like a Christmas tree.

She opened the back door of the car and helped a young boy climb out. He was about seven years old and looked just like his mum. He'd obviously been asleep in the car, as his hair stuck up at odd angles; he rubbed his eyes and stared at the house, his new home.

'Well, we knew it needed some work. But d'you know what, Moll? I reckon we'll have it looking lovely for Christmas.' Steve was a big man, tall and muscular. He smiled over at his wife and son. 'What do you think, Jamie? Just look at the size of your new garden! C'mon, let's go and explore.'

Steve and Jamie ran together towards the cottage while Molly brought some bags and a box with food provisions inside.

The rest of the day was spent cleaning and unpacking. The removal van arrived some hours later, bringing the furniture and the young family's treasured possessions. And at the end of a long, exhausting day, the family settled down for their first night's sleep in their new home.

Jamie woke with a start; the lightning cracked loudly above the house. The noise was so deafening, he thought the roof was about to split open. Thunder rumbled around like an angry giant, crashing and stomping about. Lightning splintered above again, and Jamie screeched, throwing himself under the duvet.

Slowly, he counted to three, then whipped the cover back, hurtled out of the dark room and crashed into his parents' bed.

'I'm scared,' he announced.

His mum cradled him to her and kissed the top of his head. 'It's all right, it'll be over soon. It's just a storm. *Shhh, shhh.*' Jamie relaxed in the comfort of his parents' bed and fell back to sleep.

The storm raged all night. The thunder and lightning died down eventually, but were followed by an angry wind that whipped and bellowed through the countryside. The following morning, Jamie crept out of bed, trying not to disturb his sleeping parents. Still in his pyjamas, he slipped on his boots and ran outside to the back garden.

Everywhere was a mess. Trees, branches, bricks and slates scattered the slushed-up lawn. The ancient tree, which had reminded Jamie of an old, twisted woman, had fallen over. Its branches lay crumpled and broken on the wet ground. The tree's trunk and roots seemed so vulnerable lying there.

Jamie picked up a stick and began to whack it against the trunk, and as he did so, he started to sing out loud:

> '*Witches in the garden,*
> *Witches in the tree,*
> *Turn around, turn around, one, two, three.*
> *Look inside the bottle,*

You will see,
Five witches in the garden,
Will come to you and me.'

Jamie didn't know why he had just sung that strange song; he'd never heard it before. He began to spin around, slowly at first, but then faster and faster, and as he went, he sang louder and louder.

Suddenly he stopped and, after the dizziness had subsided, he walked over to the bottom of the fallen tree. The roots sticking out reminded him of his gran's knitting, all messy and knotted. Gnarled claws of twigs entwined each other, like hair that had never been brushed.

Jamie felt an urge to touch the roots; they were wet and slimy. He pushed his hands in between the stringy threads and plunged his fingers deeper and deeper down into the cold. He wasn't sure why he was doing this, but he found he couldn't stop himself. Suddenly his little fingers recoiled as he touched something cold and hard. Feeling curious, he took a breath and pushed his hands back in again. His fingers touched something, something that seemed out of place in a tree. It felt like glass. He pulled at the object, scratching his hands as he yanked them backwards. Placing one foot on the trunk of the tree, he leaned back and pulled as hard as he could.

Unexpectedly he felt himself falling backwards, landing with a gentle thud on the cold, wet ground, and to his delight the object he had pulled from the tree's roots lay on his chest.

Wiping away the mud and slime he could see he had found an old glass bottle. Around the neck, wound tightly several times, was an old cord of some sort, and hanging from the material were little white figures that jangled and danced about. At first Jamie thought they were teeth but upon closer inspection he could see that they were miniature carvings of men and women.

The boy was excited to have found some treasure. Just wait till he showed his dad! He ran inside, his cheeks rosy, his head brimming with mysteries and magic.

His parents were making coffee in the kitchen. Jamie plonked the bottle on the table and grinned.

After his mum had cleaned it up as best she could, they all sat around the table staring at the strange object.

'What do you think it is?' asked Jamie.

'I've no idea,' answered his dad. He picked the bottle up and turned it slowly one way then the other. 'It's sealed at the top with black wax. Very odd.'

'Well, I think it's weird. I don't like it,' said his mum. 'It gives me the creeps, all those little figures. What on earth is that all about?' She shivered and rubbed her arms as if someone had suddenly opened a door and let in a cold draught.

'Can I have it in my room?' asked Jamie.

'Let's just keep it here in the kitchen for now. When we've got the place straight, I'll do some research and see if we can find out what it is. OK?' Molly smiled at her son.

'Who knows, it could be worth millions,' laughed Steve.

The rest of the day was spent unpacking and then clearing

up the debris the storm had left outside. Molly and Jamie raked up all the broken twigs and branches, and Steve began to chop up the fallen tree for firewood. They worked happily together in their new garden, little knowing that in a few hours their lives would take a dramatic and terrible twist.

CHAPTER 2

The Possessed Child and a Ghost

As darkness fell across the Lancashire countryside, the lights in the little cottage were turned off one by one, and the family settled down for a well-deserved sleep.

At about 2 a.m. Molly thought she was dreaming. She could hear Jamie singing. The tune was lovely but, in the dream, Molly was scared, she didn't like the words. She snapped her eyes open, only to realise that she wasn't dreaming at all and that the singing was coming from the kitchen.

Confused, she got out of bed and padded down the hallway, following her son's voice. She stopped short when she saw Jamie sitting with his back to her in the middle of the floor.

He swung from side to side as he sang. Molly had never heard the song before.

> *'Witches in the garden,*
> *Witches in the tree,*
> *Turn around, turn around, one, two, three.*
> *Look inside the bottle,*
> *You will see,*

Five witches in the garden,
Will come to you and me.'

'Jamie?' She placed her hand on his little shoulder.

He stopped instantly but didn't turn or respond.

Molly walked around to face him and as soon as she looked at him, she recoiled in horror. His eyes were marble white, and his face had a sickly greenish tinge to it. She tried to pick him up, but he viciously slapped her away with one hand while clutching the strange glass bottle to his chest with the other.

Then, in an eerie woman's voice she didn't recognise, Jamie spoke: *'We are coming, we will have our revenge.'*

In that terrifying moment, Molly knew they needed help. She screamed for Steve. As she called his name over and over, she noticed that the strange blue bottle had been opened, the wax seal snapped off.

Steve ran into the kitchen and instantly saw what the matter was. To his horror he saw that Jamie's face, body and whole demeanour had changed. 'What the hell?' he whispered.

Molly had begun to cry. 'I don't know what's happened to him, but he's not right, Steve. We have to get him to the hospital or something.'

'It's all right, Moll, it'll be all right.' Steve went to pick Jamie up but was met with punches and kicks. The strange bottle fell from the boy's protective grip and landed on the floor. The little figures danced up and down as they clattered and banged against the coloured glass. It rolled across the wooden floor, disappearing into the dark shadows.

'No! Leave me!' screeched Jamie. His voice was low and guttural. Steve recoiled in shock.

Then loud menacing banging noises began to vibrate throughout the house.

'What's that?' screamed Molly.

'I don't know! C'mon, let's get Jamie and get out of here.' Steve and Molly both made a grab for their son. The little boy screamed, kicked, bit and scratched. Terrified, his parents eventually managed to get him to the front door, but he kicked and screamed the whole way.

'It won't open, Steve!'

'Here, let me. Keep hold of Jamie though. Hold him tight.' Steve pulled at the door, but nothing happened. The knocking noises were getting louder and louder, and suddenly Jamie stopped fighting.

'It's here!' he growled in his new sinister voice.

Jamie slipped through his mother's grasp and fell to the floor, his breathing coming in rasping waves. The knocking was now happening at a terrific pace, so much so that Molly could feel the walls beginning to vibrate — and then she saw it!

Steve followed his wife's shaking finger. A dark shadowy figure had come silently towards them. This thing, whatever it was, loomed over them all. It looked like an old woman, but Steve couldn't be too sure. He suddenly felt a pressure on his throat, it felt like someone was crushing his Adam's apple.

He stood up, choking, and grasped at his throat, trying desperately to breathe. He managed to pull in some air and staggered his way to the window. Taking a lamp, he threw it with as much force as he could muster and the window splintered into a thousand pieces.

'This way!' he gasped to Molly.

She picked up their son, and after Steve had climbed out first, Molly passed the boy to him. She took one look back and saw that the shadowy figure had disappeared. The family left the little cottage for the last time that night. They all knew they would never be coming back.

CHAPTER 3

Something Wicked This Way Comes

'Take the prisoner down.'

The judge took a sip of water and watched over the top of his half-moon spectacles as the convicted criminal was led, handcuffed, down the steps from the court into the cells.

It had been a long trial and Judge Bromley couldn't wait to take off his itchy wig and give his balding head a good old scratch. He was looking forward to getting home and taking his wife out to the golf club for a Christmas drink. Now that this case was over, and another useless waste of space was off the streets, he could look forward to a relaxing weekend. He picked up his paperwork, nodded to the court and went through the door into his private chambers. Once inside, he sighed with satisfaction as he scratched away at his shiny pate and hung up his black gown on the back of the door.

Suddenly, a drinking glass from his desk whizzed through the air and smashed against the closed door, narrowly missing his head.

'Good God!' He jumped with shock and whipped round, confused as to what had just happened.

His eyes stared in absolute disbelief as his chair now moved from his desk, seemingly unaided, and slid sideways across the floor, stopping directly in front of him. He was aware of a knocking noise and realised it was his personal assistant trying to get into the room.

'Your honour, is everything all right?'

'Come in, Sylvia,' he shouted, never taking his eyes off the chair. He hadn't imagined it, had he? And the glass? His shoes crunched over the broken crystal. No, it had definitely smashed.

Then the eeriest of voices whispered in his ear, a woman's voice. 'Guilty!'

The word was said slowly, and the judge could hear the malevolent tone behind it. His blood ran cold.

The door handle turned erratically, this way and that, the personal assistant's concerned voice could be heard from the other side.

'Your honour? . . . Hello? I can't seem to get in, is the door locked? . . . Are you all right?'

Judge Bromley spun around, desperately trying to find where the vile whispering was coming from. The more he turned, the more confused he became, and now the woman's frightful murmurs had multiplied, more voices ringing in his head. The noise was getting louder and louder. He shouted out, 'Stop it!'

A pain shot through his head, like a red-hot knife searing into his brain. Then a terrible sizzling, burning sensation exploded within his stomach. The judge screamed out in terror. He couldn't stand the noise inside his mind, nor the pain, and his whole body buckled and fell to the floor. Suddenly a feeling of being squeezed took over him, everything began to feel tight inside him. All his muscles began to constrict and throb and the sensation rose to his throat. It felt as if it were tightening. He began to kick out, struggling to get air into his body. He grappled with his throat, something was still there, tightening, squeezing, crushing his windpipe.

Without any warning the door splintered open, the personal assistant and two security guards discovered the judge, clawing at his throat, gulping for air like a stranded fish out of water. He was surrounded by shattered glass and his shirt was torn open to reveal the most horrific-looking burn. The judge's eyes rolled around in his head as he managed to gasp two words to his appalled onlookers: 'I'm guilty!'

The police constable was having a good day, she had made two arrests so far. Her sergeant would certainly be pleased with her progress.

The odious toad she had pinned to the bonnet of a parked car had managed to evade her for a few months, but thanks to a sly tip-off she'd been able to, at last, apprehend the creep. His sole occupation seemed to be to break into pensioners' homes and steal their life savings. She'd had to chase the scumbag on foot for a mile but her visits to the gym had paid off. She patted down the apprehended young villain, brought his wrists together and clicked on the restraints.

But as she began to read the prisoner his rights, she stopped suddenly when she heard a woman's voice whisper in her right ear.

'Guilty!'

'Did you say something?' she asked the young offender.

'Me . . . ? Nothing, not a word.'

'Right,' she continued, shaking her head, pulling herself together, 'you have the right to remain silent . . .'

There it was again! . . . 'Guilty!'

This time it was louder, and it was definitely a woman's voice. Immediately she grabbed the back of her head as she felt what could only be described as a terrible burning sensation, sizzling through her skull.

'Arghh!' The police officer turned around, expecting to see someone else standing behind her, but to her surprise no one was there, just a few curious onlookers on the other side of the road.

'Hey, what's going on with you, yeah? You ain't right!' The young burglar watched open-mouthed as the policewoman clawed at her neck with her nails before her eyes bulged and rolled back in her head.

'Oh, my God!' The burglar looked about him, panic rising. 'I didn't touch you,' he shouted at the police officer, who was now kneeling on the floor, desperately clutching at her throat. 'I never touched her,' he shouted, so the onlookers could hear. But he didn't stay to help; he ran off as quickly as his stolen Nikes would carry him.

The PC was taken by ambulance to the hospital, fighting for breath. The paramedic noticed deep red marks around her neck and also a peculiar pattern that had been branded onto her stomach.

'Come and get your lovely fresh veg, look at these potatoes. Dug up first thing this morning, they were. Perfect for Christmas dinner.'

Dave had always been a market trader and his family had owned a market stall as far back as he could remember. He was one of life's happy people: content with his lot. His stall was his pride and joy, although this morning had proven a little difficult. His bed had been so cosy and warm, his wife's full figure especially lovely to cuddle up to on a winter's morning. As soon as his big toe had touched the floor he had shuddered and shot straight back under the covers until his wife had pushed him off to work.

A few hours later, here he was, where he loved to be, standing behind his stall, chatting away to his customers. He stomped his feet to get the blood pumping and hopefully radiate a little heat. He blew into his hands, which were layered with the fingerless gloves his wife had knitted for him.

He called out to people passing by: 'Get your lovely fresh vegetables, I got spuds, carrots, parsnips. How about some grapes, love?' Dave laughed and winked at an old lady, who shook her head and waddled by. He looked up at the pink clouds in the sky and his eyes followed the light flakes of snow that had begun to tumble down.

'*Guilty*!' The word spat in his ear.

'What?' Dave spun round, expecting to see one of his mates standing behind him, but there was no one nearby.

'Guilty!'

There it was again. This time said with even more venom. He could feel the icy breath on his neck.

Suddenly he grabbed at his throat, as he felt a pressing sensation.

'*Guilty!*' The word was now being screamed at him, not by one voice, but many.

He tried to breathe, tried desperately to get some air as the realisation hit him: he was being strangled! But by what?

He grabbed hold of the edge of his stall, trying to steady himself, but instead he brought the whole table of fruit and veg crashing down. Fellow stallholders ran to help, calling out his name.

'Quick, someone call an ambulance, I think he's having a heart attack!'

But Dave wasn't having a heart attack. He was, however, under attack from an invisible power.

Dave was admitted to hospital with a strange burn and strangulation lesions.

CHAPTER 4

The Falling Woman

Being the week before Christmas, Lancaster was as busy as any other town at this time of year. The snow was falling on an already blanketed white city. The busy roads had turned the snowy powder to a dirty brown sludge. Cars drove slowly through the streets, their red brake lights flashing on and off as Christmas shoppers dodged and weaved their way from shop to shop.

Maisie Shaw was one of these shoppers, a young mum who pushed her sleeping baby Alex through the throngs of carol singers and Santas jangling their charity buckets for change.

Her bags swung from the handles of her pram as she made her way through the crowds. Maisie had spent the morning buying presents and had just finished a quick coffee with her friend in the Castle Café.

She began the walk back home and sighed inwardly at the thought of a hot luxurious bath. She hoped Alex would stay asleep long enough for her to enjoy a little 'me' time. She pushed on up the road, which was proving to be more difficult with every passing second.

Lancaster Castle loomed ahead. Maisie had grown up in

Lancaster, it was a place she loved, but whenever she passed the castle, she always had to squeeze her eyes shut tight and count to ten slowly, breathing deeply as she went by. She'd never known why she behaved this way. It was just a feeling she'd always had; a sensation of absolute dread and fear. So deep was this emotion, she'd never been able to go anywhere near the building.

She remembered a school trip to the castle when she was fourteen. Maisie had tried desperately to get out of it, but to no avail. Taking a brave stance, she'd decided to confront her demons and go. That day she had stood shaking with abject fear, no reasonable or logical explanation for her bizarre reaction. She had only managed to walk up to the main entrance. When the rest of her friends had gone inside the building, Maisie had rushed off and thrown up in the bushes. The teachers, much to Maisie's relief, and sent her back to the bus, where she'd remained for the rest of the morning.

What was it about the castle that affected her so much? Maybe because she knew it had been a place where many men, women and children had met a grisly fate? Possibly the tales of such atrocities had subconsciously impacted upon her over the years. Of course, there were all the stories of the Pendle witches too. Living in Lancaster, it was hard not to know all about their story and their sad demise. Wrongly accused and imprisoned at the castle before being hanged over four hundred years ago. Whenever they were mentioned, Maisie felt so emotional. She didn't tell people about her fears of the castle, she kept that to herself, not wanting people to think she was strange. Only her mum knew of her adverse reaction to the foreboding place, and she had never understood her daughter's odd behaviour either.

As Maisie pushed on, for some odd reason, and for the first time, she felt her face being pulled towards the castle. Almost against her will, her eyes robotically looked at the big stone structure. She didn't know why, and she wished to God she hadn't. Fear rushed through her body like a train whistling through a dark tunnel. Her hands shot with the sharp sensations of pins and needles. Her throat went dry, eyes wide with terror: because, standing on one of the turrets, was a woman. As her long dark hair whipped about her face, she appeared to be wearing a long, dirty tattered dress and a trailing black cloak that buffeted backwards in the wind.

Maisie threw her hand to her mouth as she watched the poor woman fall forwards, arms outstretched at her side, her cloak billowing above her. Maisie screamed so loud, poor baby Alex woke with a start and screamed too.

'Oh my God!' Maisie began to run towards the castle, stopping other pedestrians as she went. 'Did you just see that?' she shrieked.

'See what, dear?' asked an old woman. Maisie shook her head in confusion and ran up to a group of young lads laughing together.

'Did you see that woman, up there?' Maisie pointed to the castle, aware her voice was shrill and shaking.

'No, love, didn't see no woman. Here, you all right?'

Maisie yelled out in frustration and tears streamed down her face as she pushed the pram through the slippery snow.

Within minutes she was in the castle grounds and sprinting to where she thought the woman's body should be. But there was nothing there! She looked about her in confusion. There was no body, no blood, in fact it looked as if no one had been in the area since the fresh snow had fallen. Maisie rocked the pram and shushed the baby, with the slow, dawning realisation that she was within the walls of the place that filled her with fear.

Had she imagined it? She was sure she had seen a woman falling to her death. She closed her eyes and tried to remember what she had just witnessed. The falling woman. She had definitely seen it. So where was the body? She decided to walk around the castle, just in case the woman had somehow survived the fall and was looking for help. She was just about to push the pram off again when she heard a polite cough behind her.

She spun round to find a teenage boy smiling at her.

'Erm, hello, sorry. I didn't mean to scare you, but I wanted to let you know, I saw her too.'

Maisie watched him, aware that her mouth was hanging open in astonishment.

'You won't find her,' he continued, 'but if you ever want to talk about it, please feel free to call this number.'

He handed her a card; she took it cautiously, not really knowing what to make of the whole situation. The card he'd given her was very plain, just an image of a snake in the figure of eight, eating its own tail, and under it a number to call.

'Pleased to meet you. My name's Tom.'

Maisie couldn't speak, she didn't know what to say. And yet she had so many questions. For now though, all she could do was nod and tuck the card into her coat pocket.

Tom watched the young woman push her pram away. He felt sorry for her; he knew only too well what she was feeling. It had been a frightening spectacle to witness. The poor young mother must have been terrified and confused, especially when she discovered there was no body on the ground. He kicked his boot into the thick snow in the place where the falling woman's body should have landed. Wrapping his arms tightly around himself, needing to feel some sort of comfort, he sniffed in the chilly air and shivered. It was getting colder.

He made his way towards the main entrance of the castle. His parents were in there somewhere; they had decided to visit the famous landmark before heading back home. He had enjoyed visiting his dad's old barracks and meeting his dad's old army friends, but now he just couldn't wait to get home to London and back to his friends, Clovis and Eve.

While his parents had been looking inside the castle, Tom had watched the woman falling from the turret. He had shouted out but quickly realised he was seeing an apparition, a ghost that was replaying its terrible demise. Over the last few months, Tom had encountered a few of these awful apparitions, where spirits played out their deaths in some kind of loop, too terrified to go into the light.

You see, Tom had acquired a gift, an unusual gift that he loathed and loved in equal measure. It had started during a paranormal investigation he'd done when he and his friends had contacted the spirits of two murdered children. Tom had been terrified to discover that he could talk to dead people. Sometimes he could see them, which wasn't very nice, especially when they woke him up, sitting at the end of his bed. But most times he could just hear their voices.

The only people who knew of his secret were his best friends, Eve and Clovis, Eve's uncle — Professor Rufus Pepper — and Detective Inspector Rutherford, head of the Society of Paranormal Investigations, or SPI for short.

The professor had been delighted to find out about Tom's ability, and asked him all sorts of questions. He had really helped Tom to understand that this was a true gift and he had spent many an hour teaching him how to control it.

The apparition Tom had just witnessed falling was yet another frightful scene he was having to get used to. His mind went back to the young mum who had also witnessed the apparition. Hopefully she wouldn't have any nightmares, and with any luck would get in touch with the SPI. They would be able to help her and give her some answers.

As Tom pondered his bizarre gift, he suddenly felt a strong pulling sensation to enter the castle. Such a sensation usually meant that a spirit wanted to communicate. Was it the falling woman he had just seen?

He walked under the portcullis and across a square courtyard. The feeling of being pulled was becoming more intense, as if a rope had been wound around his waist, and someone was yanking on the other end. He didn't fight it; he knew by now there was no point. He took a huge gulp, relaxed and went with it.

'I'm in here, come to me.' The voice was gentle and soft. He didn't feel threatened. He rarely did when spirits spoke to him. Tom went through a large door and instantly found himself inside what looked like a stately home. A grand staircase wound itself around the edge of the room and disappeared up into a dark mezzanine. The voice lulled him through another door, where he found himself alone in an old courtroom. Rows of wooden benches lined the room and a huge ceiling bowed over him, its wooden beams and struts all on show like the bones of an old skeleton. The judge's bench loomed high and threatening and Tom instantly wanted to leave. He didn't like this place. He could feel at once all the anger, the sadness and despair of it.

He looked around to make sure he was still alone and then whispered quietly, 'I'm here. Come and speak to me, show yourself if you can.'

Instantly he felt a cold blast of air hit his neck, a tell-tale sign that a spirit was close.

'My name's Jennet . . . Jennet Device.' A small voice tickled inside his head.

'Hello, Jennet,' replied Tom nervously. 'Was that you I saw falling from the castle?'

'Yes . . . it was me. I just couldn't live with the torment any longer. She makes me so mad, she's always there, in my head, always threatening, always wanting her revenge. She was so angry with me, you see; she won't let me forget;

she won't forgive. You must help me. She's so angry and so are the others. They're coming . . . they are coming, rising to get their revenge. You must warn . . .'

As quickly as Jennet's voice had come, it vanished.

Tom took a deep breath to calm his nerves. He knew she was still there; would he be able to see her?

He turned around slowly and instantly felt as if he'd been winded. For there, floating a couple of feet away from him, was the ghost of a young woman. She was hovering above the seats, slightly transparent, withered, her body covered by a long dirty dress and cloak that hung about her brittle frame. Her face was emaciated and gaunt, her body stick-thin and grey. She was a pitiful sight.

Tom felt her sorrow. 'Jennet, is that you? Who is angry with you?'

Suddenly, Jennet's ghost rushed at him. He stepped backwards, terrified, misplaced his footing and fell. A terrible pummelling and pounding sensation squeezed inside his head, and voices, lots of different ones, began to scream from within.

'Guilty!'

'Witch.'

'Hang them all!'

'Guilty.'

'Witchcraft!'

'Devil.'

'Cursed.'

'Witch.'

'Show me the mark!'
'Burn in hell!'
'Eleven shall hang.'
'Curse you, Jennet!'
'Pedlar.'
'Point at the witches, Jennet!'
'Curse you, Jennet.'
'Damn you, Jennet.'
'Damn you to hell!'

Tom held his hands to his ears, the pain was so intense, the voices so loud. He could feel many awful emotions rolling around inside him. He slowed his breathing down, attempting to get the emotions under control, all the time trying to put what the professor had taught him into practice. He could see that Jennet's ghost had disappeared, but he knew she was still in the ether.

The voices were ringing in his ears, but he knew what to do to make them stop.

'I promise I'll help you, I promise, Jennet.' Straight away the noise abated, and Tom slumped back down, relieved and exhausted.

He whispered, 'I will come back and bring my friends; we will help you.'

Jennet's soft voice sighed back inside his head. 'The little boy, he's released them. You must stop them, they are so angry, they are rising for their revenge. Help me. I've waited so long to be saved.' Then just like that, she was gone.

Tom stood up and ran as fast as he could outside.

'Tom?' It was his mum, Ange. 'Whatever's happened, are you all right?' she said, coming over and rubbing his back.

'Sorry, Mum, I got lost. I'm all right now.'

'You sure?' Ange looked concerned and placed a hand on her son's forehead. 'Come on, we'll get your dad and go back to the hotel for a few hours before the train home. Looks like you could do with a lie down.'

Back at the hotel, Tom grabbed his phone and sent an urgent message to Clovis, Eve and the professor. Then he went into the bathroom and called Inspector Rutherford. In hushed tones he explained what he had experienced earlier at the castle.

The inspector listened carefully. 'Everything you have told me fits with some other cases that have come in over the last couple of days; all within that area. Mmm . . .' Tom could almost hear the cogs in her brain turning. 'Right, leave everything to me, young man, just stay where you are.'

'But my mum and dad want to go back to London now. Our holiday's over.' Tom was a little worried.

'As I said, leave everything to me.' Inspector Rutherford's voice was firm but kind. 'Your parents will shortly get a call from the professor, and all will be well.'

CHAPTER 5

A Flushing Good Time

The Bow Bells Pub in East London had become known in the paranormal world for having a most unusual ghost.

A particularly mysterious spirit loved nothing more than to scare the pants off poor unsuspecting occupants of the female toilets. Just when a lady had got comfortable upon the seat, the chain would suddenly be pulled by some invisible force and . . . whoosh! A great avalanche of water would drench an unfortunate pair of buttocks, followed by the poor victim running screaming whilst desperately trying to pull up her undergarments.

This unsavoury and impolite ghostly behaviour had been occurring for nearly fifty years and even though many people had tried to find out the identity of the mischievous spirit and why it haunted the pub, no one had ever got to the *bottom* of it. Eve, Clovis and Uncle Rufus had high hopes that they might be the ones to finally crack the mystery of the elusive loo flushing ghost.

They had decided to check the whole building out first to see if they could uncover any clues as to who the ghostly resident might be and, so far, all was quiet. Eve and Clovis were the first to enter the ladies' toilets, whilst Uncle Rufus did a final look on the upper floor. He had left them to set up the equipment and take the baseline tests, something his new apprentices had picked up quickly. Once the readings of the temperature, air pressure and electromagnetic field were taken, and their EVP watches were turned on, it was just a case of switching on the night-vision camera and hoping that the ghost could be cajoled into appearing with the help of a trigger object, which in this investigation happened to be a very reluctant Eve.

Clovis spoke quietly into a night-vision camera as he panned slowly around the room. It was quite a large space with three cubicles sitting side by side. Opposite them, three sinks ran across the wall and a huge mirror reflected the room behind them.

'It's seven o'clock on Sunday the twentieth of December. Continuation of The Bow Bells Pub investigation. We are now in the ladies' loos.' Clovis emphasised the word 'loos' with a slightly comical voice. He zoomed in on his friend Eve, who looked very unimpressed. She had been volunteered as the sitting duck. She checked the temperature gun and spoke in an unhappy voice.

'The temperature is still sixteen degrees Celsius, which is normal.' She let out a huge sigh and manoeuvred herself into a more comfortable position. 'I can't believe you're actually filming me sitting on the toilet. Thank God you didn't want it to be *too* realistic, and at least the lid is down.

Clovis bit his lip, trying to stop himself from laughing.

There sat his best friend, on a toilet, trying to communicate with a ghost. Just wait till he showed Tom.

'And if we don't capture anything, you're not showing this to Tom, do you hear me, Clovis Gayle?'

'Of course, cross my heart.' Clovis drew an imaginary small cross over his heart and grinned. 'You know I'd take your place if I could, but it's the *women's* toilets, and if I'm not mistaken, you are a girl. The toilet wouldn't flush if I sat on there.'

Eve smiled sarcastically at the camera, sucked in her breath and decided to call out to the ghost that had been stalking the toilets for years.

'Hello, if there's anybody here, can you perhaps . . . show yourself . . . make a noise, or . . . flush the loo I'm sitting on.' Eve squeezed her eyes shut in anticipation.

Clovis slowly zoomed out so that the whole cubicle was in frame. He jumped suddenly as the main door to the room slowly creaked open. Quickly he whipped the camera around, hoping to catch some paranormal action, but was disappointed to see the professor's head peer around the side. 'Sorry, chaps,' whispered Uncle Rufus. 'Everything is quiet upstairs and young Boris here didn't seem to detect anything.'

Boris the British Bulldog was Uncle Rufus's beloved pet, and he accompanied the investigators on all their spooky missions. Although manners were not his strong point, on the other hand detecting ghosts was his forte. Sadly, his grunting, burping and farting could sometimes upset the most hardened of stomachs.

The sturdy little brindle-coloured dog waddled into the

toilets, walked over to Eve's feet and flung himself down with exaggerated exhaustion onto the tiled floor.

Uncle Rufus spoke in hushed tones: 'Right, chaps, I'm going to set the Crookes camera in front of you, Eve.' He stopped what he was doing and noticed that his niece wasn't looking happy at all. 'What on earth's the matter?'

Eve sighed again. 'I'm sorry, Uncle, it's just, you know . . . this feels so embarrassing.'

Uncle Rufus began to erect a camera tripod in front of Eve's cubicle, a small smile playing around the corners of his mouth.

Boris raised his head to his mistress and whined.

'See, even Boris can detect my embarrassment.'

Uncle Rufus bowed his head so Eve couldn't see his reaction, and busied himself. He snapped an odd-looking machine onto the tripod. It was obviously a camera, but it looked very old fashioned. Its black concertina body narrowed towards the front, where a main lens sat, around which many other, differently sized optical lenses protruded. It rather reminded Clovis of a Swiss army knife. At the back of the camera was positioned a rectangular perspex slimline box and on top of that, a little copper spout could just be seen jutting out from its corner.

Uncle Rufus was rather proud of his new invention. He had painstakingly put together an amazing little machine that was capable of photographing spirits. Not just ordinary pictures, but close- ups, showing all their details. Most images of ghosts that had been photographed were either very faint and wispy or they were just plain fraudulent. This camera was different, the first of its kind. It could take a ghost's picture that was so clear, there could be no disputing its authenticity. If there was a ghost in a room, the camera could capture it. Having a well-defined picture of a ghost was a step forward in being able to understand more about them and give clues as to who they were when they were alive. Uncle Rufus could look at the image and see if there were any strange features, scars or jewellery of any kind that might help detect who that spirit once was. It was proving very useful in cases where a ghost was causing trouble and didn't want to reveal itself. As he, and now his apprentices, had discovered, not all spirits and ghosts wanted to give too much information away about themselves. So, the Crookes camera, named after one of the professor's favourite scientists — William Crookes — was a little stroke of genius, even if he said so himself.

'Now, Eve,' said Uncle Rufus, 'remember we paranormal investigators have to throw ourselves into every situation possible — even if it means sitting on a toilet.' He placed his small, wire-rimmed spectacles on top of his curly mop of hair and squinted one eye through the lens of the camera.

Clovis was still trying not to laugh at Eve, and Boris didn't help matters, as he was now in the throes of a deep sleep and had let off the most ear-splitting fart. That was just too far for Clovis, who, seeing Eve sitting there and Boris adding the sound effects, exploded with laughter.

'Well, I suppose this is the right place to do it, Boris,' laughed Uncle Rufus.

Eve couldn't help it; how could she not laugh? Boris always

managed to lighten her mood. He was the funniest dog she'd ever known. She giggled and rubbed his ears affectionately, realising she was being silly and childish. Who cared what anyone thought? They were here to practise their ghost-hunting skills. This was what Eve loved to do, and her uncle had been training her and her friends to be the best in their field.

They had been inducted into a secret organisation called the SPI, the Society of Paranormal Investigations. The society's headquarters were top secret, and its entrance was hidden in the bowels of London's underground system. It was a mysterious place where ordinary people and ghosts worked together to monitor the country for wayward spirits. One of the many jobs of the SPI was to protect an alternate plane of existence called the Veil: the place where spirits first go to when they die. They are met there by their loved ones or guides before they ascend upwards onto the Otherside.

Every week, Uncle Rufus had been taking Eve and her two best friends to various haunted locations around the country. He wanted them to get as much experience as possible before Inspector Rutherford sent them out solo on an investigation.

Last weekend they had all spent two nights in an old, haunted manor house. Tom had managed to communicate with the ghost of a little girl who was still being chased by her murderer. Eve, Clovis and Tom had been able to successfully send her off to rest in peace. It was so satisfying to help reunite a trapped soul with a loved one. So far, even with a few bumps along the way, Clovis, Tom and Eve were doing well with their training. Mind you, they all knew that they had the best teacher in Eve's Uncle Rufus, the professor.

Eve looked at her uncle with affection. After losing both her parents in a tragic accident when she was small, her mum's brother Rufus had taken Eve in. He had lost his wife, Eve's aunt, in the same accident. An event that he still hadn't really come to terms with.

'That's better,' said Uncle Rufus. 'You have a lovely smile, Eve, just like your aunt.'

'Oh wow!' said Clovis suddenly. 'The temperature is dropping and it's falling quickly. Twelve, eleven, ten, nine, eight, seven, six!' Clovis's voice went higher the lower the temperature went.

'What's that *smell*?' asked Eve, her teeth chattering.

Everyone inhaled.

'Cigars,' said Uncle Rufus, recognising the pungent aroma.

Boris sprang to his feet, staring above Eve's head, the hackles on his back standing up straight like bristles on a brush.

'Here we go,' smiled Uncle Rufus. He looked through the camera lens once more and pulled a wire out of the back. This cable had a large button, and he hovered his thumb in readiness to take a picture.

Boris began to bark in quick succession, his gaze still fixed on a spot above Eve's head.

Suddenly loud rapping and tapping noises began to pound from within the walls, floor and ceiling. Eve could feel an icy blast of cold air on her neck. She knew that a spirit was close by. She just hoped it wasn't hostile. Clovis was now standing next to Uncle Rufus and the camera. The temperature gun shone a bright red beam of light across the cubicle and hit the wall behind Eve.

'Amazing! It's now minus twenty degrees. This is extraordinary, Professor,' said Clovis, wiping his fingers across the glass of his square, black-rimmed specs; they always steamed up when he became excited.

'Any second now,' whispered Uncle Rufus, his finger poised over the button. 'The camera will beep, and we'll have an image.'

'Well, I hope it beeps soon,' said Eve through gritted teeth, cos my bum feels like it's frozen to the seat!' She clenched her eyes shut tight and held her breath. The camera made a long beeping sound and Uncle Rufus pushed the button. Instantly the back of the camera emitted an enormous flash, followed by an explosion of white powder that shot out of the copper spout. The camera clicked, whizzed and whirred. Then, spewing out the front, just under the lens, was what looked to be a Polaroid picture.

Uncle Rufus grabbed the picture, slid his spectacles back over his eyes and smiled.

'It's OK, Eve, she looks friendly enough.' He briefly showed the image to Eve and Clovis. The camera had captured the ghostly image of an old woman standing behind Eve. She was wearing a white mob cap and an apron, whilst hanging from the corner of her mouth was a cigar.

'Looks Victorian,' said Clovis excitedly. He absolutely

loved the professor's new invention. So far it had worked really well.

The only downside was the spooky images dissolved from the polaroid film after thirty seconds, which was highly frustrating; but the professor was determined to find a solution and Clovis knew that he would work tirelessly to solve the technical problem.

Uncle Rufus put the picture into his pocket, then bent forward, placing his hands on his knees and concentrated on Eve. 'OK now, Eve, do the "welcoming", like I taught you.'

Clovis passed the tapping board to Eve.

She placed the little communication board onto her knees and slowly pushed her arm up above her.

'Hello, I'm Eve, I'm very pleased to meet you. Take my hand, you'll see I mean you no harm.' Eve gasped out loud as she began to feel the sensation of icy cold fingers entwining her own.

Boris had stopped barking and sat upright, his bottom wagging from left to right in excitement.

Eve continued to speak slowly and gently to the ghost of the mystery lady standing behind her. 'Can you tap out your name using this machine? Or if you prefer, you can talk into this timepiece on my wrist, it will capture your voice.'

The spirit obviously preferred the tapping board and began to spell out the word *Help!*

Eve pushed on. 'We need to know your name so that we *can* help you.'

Suddenly Eve's EVP watch pinged loudly, in unison with

her uncle's and Clovis's; a sign that a paranormal emergency had occurred. Everyone looked at their devices.

'Perfect timing,' whispered Eve sarcastically. The ghost must have sensed the immediate shift in energy. She understood her onlooker's interest had rather rudely dissipated. In frustration and anger, the ghost pulled the chain of the loo and the toilet suddenly flushed, causing Eve to scream and jump up off the seat. Immediately all the cubicle doors slammed with such a force that the large mirror behind the sinks cracked and fell into tiny pieces.

Fortunately, no one was hurt, but there was one hell of a mess.

'Well, our Victorian lady certainly doesn't like to be interrupted,' said Uncle Rufus, looking around at the destruction.

'She's got quite a temper,' said Eve, looking at all the glass on the floor.

Clovis looked down at his EVP watch. 'My message is from Tom: he says it's urgent.'

Eve checked hers. 'Mine too.'

'Well, I have a message from Detective Inspector Rutherford. She wants us to go to Euston Station.' Uncle Rufus looked puzzled. 'She says she will meet us there, and for us all to pack a bag.'

'I wonder what it's all about?' asked Clovis. Eve noticed the excitement in his voice. 'Do you think we're going to be sent on another mission?'

'I've no idea but whatever it is, I'm intrigued,' replied Uncle

Rufus. 'The sooner we tidy this place up, the sooner we can pack and get to the station.' They set about gathering all the equipment together, swept up the broken glass and made sure all was as they had found it. Uncle Rufus would explain to the landlord about the mirror — he reassured himself that his old friend would understand.

Just as they were leaving, Eve called out to the spirit of the Victorian lady: 'Whoever you are, sorry about the interruption. We'll come back and help you. I promise.'

As Eve closed the door of the ladies' loos behind her, she heard the toilets all flush together one last time.

CHAPTER 6

Peppermint Creams and a Demon

Eve, Clovis and Uncle Rufus had dashed home to pack their bags. Uncle Rufus had made the necessary arrangements with Clovis's mum, Claudette, to look after Mr Pig — his rather unruly and potty-mouthed parrot. Bizarrely, Claudette had taken a real shine to the bird and had been caught a few times trying to teach it some very upbeat life-affirming hymns. The last time she had tried to showcase their new singing partnership in Uncle Rufus's front room, it had turned into a melee of laughter. The beginning of the hymn had gone well, and Mr Pig had seemed to be enjoying himself until Claudette reached the chorus, singing 'Let the light shine on you'. At that point Mr Pig had begun to screech out loud several swear words. Claudette was not a woman to back down and had just sung louder, causing Mr Pig to swear louder — until the two of them were battling to be heard. Thank goodness Claudette had a great sense of humour.

'Now,' said Claudette, standing by Uncle Rufus's open doorway. She placed the bird onto her shoulder and popped a little nut into his beak. 'He and I are off to choir practice later,' she said proudly. 'He's under strict instructions to behave himself.' And she smiled and shook her head at the beady-eyed parrot.

Everyone said their goodbyes and the investigators jumped into a waiting taxi that whisked them off to the station. Once there, they hurried in through the main entrance. Boris, unaware of the urgency, took his own sweet time, waddling slowly behind his master.

'I love you, Boris, but I do happen to know that you are capable of moving a little faster.' Uncle Rufus tugged gently on the dog's lead; Boris responded with a burp.

Euston station was packed full of people rushing to and from train platforms. Huge crowds stood in the centre of the station's concourse staring up at an enormous screen that flashed with the arrivals and departures.

'Which platform did she say she'd meet us at again?' shouted Eve above the noise of the busy station.

'Ten,' replied Clovis. 'It's just up here. I think I can see her, well, her hat, anyway.'

Inspector Rutherford waved a gloved hand, the tassels on her velvet hat jostling about like leaves tumbling in a high wind.

'Yoo-hoo! Over here, Rufus, my good man. I'm here!' yelled the unconventional-looking older woman.

The inspector didn't resemble a typical police detective, she looked more like an eccentric grandma. Her clothes were very old-fashioned but incredibly vibrant. Most of the time she wore a brightly coloured hat and matching cloak. Today's ensemble was all lively tones of green.

Eve, Clovis and Tom liked and respected her enormously. She was their boss at the SPI.

'Rufus Pepper, I declare! By jingo, it's so good to see you. You're like a breath of fresh air, if that's at all possible in London.' Inspector Rutherford laughed and patted Uncle Rufus on the back with gusto.

'The feeling's mutual, Ruthers. Always a pleasure to see you.' Uncle Rufus was beaming, clearly excited at the possibility of a new case.

The inspector now turned her attention to her ghost-hunting students. 'Hello, my dears; my goodness! Now, I've got your tickets to Lancaster, and I've arranged for Tom to meet you there. Your accommodation is all sorted, it's in Pendle Hill, about sixteen miles from the station, so it won't take you long to drive there, Rufus.'

'But, Inspector, what's this all about?' asked Eve, looking concerned.

'Oh, my dear, don't worry, I'll explain everything on the train.' The inspector began to walk briskly in front of the small group, her cloak billowing. Looking over her shoulder, she shouted back, 'I'll travel with you until you have all the facts and then I will alight. I'm needed elsewhere, you see.' She turned back and marched on. 'Come on now, don't dally.'

The small group of ghost hunters and one British bulldog climbed onto the waiting train. After walking through several carriages, they eventually found one that was empty. Inspector Rutherford bustled into one of four seats around a table.

'Here will be fine,' she said, bouncing up and down in the

seat as she got herself comfortable. The others sat down and after they had all caught their breath, the inspector delighted her companions by pulling an enormous flask out from her carpet bag.

'Hot chocolate anyone?'

'Oh, perfect!' said Eve.

The inspector plunged into her bag once more, and brought out some paper cups and a square pink box.

'Peppermint cream?'

Clovis raised his eyebrows. 'I don't think I've ever had one before.'

'Aha, my dear boy, you haven't lived until you try one of my home-made peppermint creams.' The inspector opened the box and peeled back folds of fine pink tissue paper; she offered the decadent-looking chocolates to Clovis. He peered suspiciously inside.

'They're only chocolates, dear, they won't bite you.'

Clovis picked a chocolate out of the box and popped it into his mouth.

'Mm, it's delicious!' His eyes bulged in pure delight.

The inspector smiled and passed the box round to the others.

The train suddenly jolted forward, causing Boris to scuttle under the table.

'Now, you won't get to Lancaster station until late,' said the inspector, as she began to rummage around in her carpet bag once more. 'As I said, Tom will meet you at the station. Then, I've arranged for you to pick up Albert, and you're all booked into official accommodation.' Her head popped back up again, eye twitching and hat tassels jostling. In her hand she held a folder of paper, kept together by a rather large elastic band.

'Who's Albert?' asked Clovis.

'You'll see,' replied Uncle Rufus mysteriously. 'I assume this train is taking us to a case?' He twisted the lid off the flask and began to pour steaming liquid into the cups.

'Indeed, my friend, it *is* a case, and I'm afraid it's a rather frightful one.'

The train began to pick up a steady speed as it pulled away from London and into the darkness of the countryside. Inspector Rutherford placed the file on the table and snapped off the rubber band. She paused, reached for her cup and took a sip. 'Lovely,' she sighed. 'Right, now then, down to work.' She looked around to make sure the carriage was still empty. Satisfied that it was, she opened the file and there, typed in bold black letters on the first page, were two words:

PENDLE HILL

'Is that a place?' asked Eve, looking intently at the words.

'It most certainly is, my dear. It's a place of beauty and sadly much tragedy. And this investigation is centred around it. It's certainly a baffling case and, dare I say it, a frightening one.' She looked intently at the two young faces staring at her. 'But I know that you can handle it.' She leaned her head closer towards her companions, the tassels on her hat jumping and swaying about in rhythm to the train's hypnotic motion.

'About a week ago,' she said quietly, 'we received a report

42

of a young boy who had been admitted to the local hospital. The boy and his parents had just moved into their new home in the Pendle Hill area. There had been a violent storm on their first night, and the next morning the little lad had found an old artifact in the garden. In the early hours of the following morning his mother found him and discovered he wasn't himself; in fact he was, and I quote —' the inspector read from the notes — '*possessed*.'

'After his mother and father managed to restrain him, they witnessed the apparition of an old woman inside their cottage. They were terrified and made their escape by smashing a window, as the doors were locked from the outside.'

'What's happened to the boy?' whispered Uncle Rufus.

'I'm afraid he's still in hospital and in a very bad way,' said Inspector Rutherford.

Eve and Clovis looked at each other quickly, their excitement and trepidation obvious.

'So, you want us to find out who the old woman is?' asked Uncle Rufus. He was intrigued by what the inspector had divulged to them so far and had begun making notes in his trusty pocketbook.

'Yes, but there's more.' The inspector leaned forward again. 'A day or so later, three similar cases were reported, all within the Pendle area. And all four victims are in the same hospital with the same kind of injuries.' The inspector paused, thoughtful for a moment, and then began to drum her leather-clad fingers on the table. 'I've arranged for you to visit all the victims and find out what you can.'

Uncle Rufus pulled the case file over. He cleaned his glasses with a pristine handkerchief and popped them back on. He read in a hushed tone: 'Jamie Drake, male, aged seven; Judge Bromley, male, aged fifty; PC Rachel Nowell, female, aged twenty-five, and a market stall holder, David Law, aged forty-two. And you think these people are connected in some way?'

'I certainly do,' replied the inspector. Her face was stern, almost angry. 'I know it seems strange, Rufus, but their injuries are all very similar, apart from the lad, although he does have the same burn mark as the other victims. And his father, he describes experiencing the same sensation as the others when he was trying to save his son.'

'And what was that?' asked Eve, propping her elbows on the table and lacing her fingers together.

Inspector Rutherford lowered her voice to a whisper. 'Strangulation. I have a horrible feeling about this one.' No one missed the look of fear on the inspector's face. If *she* had a horrible feeling, then they were all in for a terrifying adventure.

Inspector Rutherford continued to whisper, 'Then as you know, earlier, we had a call from Tom. Apparently, he witnessed a spirit jumping to her death from Lancaster Castle.'

'Oh my God, is he OK? He told us there was something urgent going on, but nothing more than that,' said Eve, looking wide-eyed and fearful.

'He's absolutely fine,' assured the inspector, patting Eve's hand across the table. 'But apparently he had a very interesting

44

communication with the apparition. This spirit has sent a warning which ties in with some of the things the other witnesses encountered.

'He said that a young lady also saw the falling woman, and she may need a little help and advice. According to Tom, she was quite shaken up. We've already had a call from her mother, she's quite worried about her. I said you would go and pay her a visit.'

'Poor thing,' said Uncle Rufus. 'Seeing a ghost for the first time is scary enough, but witnessing someone fall to their death and discovering it isn't real could really mess with one's mind.' He zipped up his coat, finding that the temperature in the carriage had definitely got cooler.

Clovis had been quiet all this time, listening closely to the conversation. The place called Pendle Hill had been troubling him. He knew that something bad had happened there, he'd written an essay about it at school once, for Halloween. 'Witches!' The word shot out of his mouth.

'Shush, Clovis,' whispered the inspector quickly, looking about nervously.

'Sorry,' he whispered back, slightly embarrassed. Then, taking a huge breath, he began to reel off facts in his characteristic way: 'Pendle Hill in Lancashire, that was the site of the famous witch trials of sixteen-twelve, when about a dozen people were accused of witchcraft. Most of them were tried at Lancaster Castle and found guilty.' Clovis's eyes were shut tight as he recited the information. 'The case was strange because a young girl was used as the main witness in the case, and she gave evidence against her own family and friends, accusing them all of witchcraft.'

'Impressive as always, young man,' said the inspector, chuckling.

'It's like having a walking Wikipedia with us,' laughed Uncle Rufus, smiling proudly at Clovis.

'I shall leave the case file with you, Rufus,' said Inspector Rutherford, tapping the top of the file with her gloved hand. 'I suggest you all take the time to read and digest the information. And you'll need to fill Tom in when you meet up. I want you to get to the bottom of whatever is plaguing these poor people. I suspect it has something to do with witchcraft — so you must take extra care at every turn. Of course, I have the Witchcraft department at the SPI on the case too. No doubt they will be contacting you as soon as they have gained more information. But for now, I want you to find out who the ghost of this woman is that Tom saw, who the old woman in Malkins Cottage was, and most importantly, whether all these cases are connected. Let me know your every step and the SPI will be on hand if required. I'll be leaving you at the next stop, I'm needed on other urgent SPI business in Cornwall.'

'Oh, I love Cornwall, whereabouts?' enquired Uncle Rufus.

'Bodmin,' came the curt response. Just by looking at the inspector's face, they could tell that she didn't want to talk any further on the matter. She brought her cup of hot chocolate to her lips and took a long sip; the others watched as she exhaled out. Wisps of her breath were spiralling slowly out of her mouth. It was definitely getting very cold on the train.

As they continued on their long journey, Clovis and Eve went on their phones, while the inspector and Uncle Rufus talked quietly and seriously about SPI matters. But after a time, Clovis pointed out how cold their carriage had now become.

'Are you thinking what I'm thinking?' asked Eve, worried. 'Look!' she said, pointing at the large window. Little ice particles had begun to form on the inside of the glass. They all watched, open-mouthed, as the ice grew like tentacles, trying to find something to make contact with.

Suddenly the sliding doors of their carriage whooshed open and a uniformed man walked down the aisle with a machine. 'Tickets, please.'

The inspector took out the tickets and passed them to the conductor.

He kept his head down, didn't say a word and didn't look up, not once. He passed the tickets through his machine and handed them back one by one. The inspector sniffed and immediately made a disgusted face.

Eve, Clovis and Uncle Rufus soon realised what her complaint was as the smell reached their nostrils. Trying not to be obvious about the stench that seemed to have followed the conductor into the carriage, everyone covered their noses.

'That's not Boris,' whispered Eve, checking under the table to see if Boris was all right. He was was sitting up, hackles raised, and a low growl rumbled in his belly, his eyes locked onto the conductor.

'It smells like sulphur,' murmured Clovis, his hand covering his mouth and nose.

'It smells of death,' uttered Uncle Rufus, grimacing from the stench.

'My good man,' said the inspector to the conductor. 'Can you explain to me why it's suddenly very cold in here?'

The conductor simply shrugged his shoulders and left the way he had come, taking the terrible stench with him.

As soon as he'd left, the carriage began to feel warmer, everyone's breath could no longer be seen hanging in the air and the awful smell had totally disappeared.

'The ice on the windows, it's dissolving,' said Clovis. 'That was so weird.'

'I don't think we are alone, my friends.' The inspector gave a knowing look to her companions. 'I think our charismatic train conductor was not as he seemed. What do you think, Rufus?'

Uncle Rufus nodded in agreement.

'A ghost? Really? On a train?' Eve looked nervously around her.

The inspector already had her phone out and was tapping out a number.

'Yes, I need assistance at Coventry station, it's a level two apparition, malevolent undertones. Extraction needed and hurry . . . yes . . . just one, as far as I can tell. It's on the train from London arriving in twenty-five minutes. Disguised as a train conductor.' The inspector ended the call and put her phone and belongings back into the carpet bag.

'Is that it?' asked Eve.

'Yes, yes, no need for us to get involved. We've got bigger cases to deal with. The guardians will apprehend him.'

Eve and Clovis stared at each other, fascinated.

Twenty-five minutes later, the train slowed as it pulled into Coventry station, jolting and bucking like an obstinate horse that didn't want to obey its rider's commands.

'I'll leave the peppermint creams for you,' Inspector Rutherford said, smiling. 'Now then,' her tone serious once again. 'Be on your guard, do everything the professor tells you. I'll be keeping a close eye on you all and I'll be sending reinforcements, as I think you'll be needing them.' Uncle Rufus stood up and walked with the inspector to the doors, where their whispered conversation didn't go unnoticed by Clovis and Eve.

Once on the platform, the inspector waved and shouted, 'Goodbye . . . good luck.'

Eve and Clovis watched through the window as the detective inspector welcomed two smartly dressed businessmen, both wearing dark suits, bowler hats and carrying briefcases and umbrellas.

'Look, Uncle, isn't that Percival?' cried Eve, recognising the ghost from SPI headquarters.

'Yeah, it is!' whispered Clovis excitedly. 'He doesn't look like a ghost now, though. That's incredible.'

'Yes, you're right, that is indeed Percival,' said the professor, 'and by the looks of it . . .' Uncle Rufus squinted his eyes and pushed his face closer to the train window '. . . Mmm . . . I've not met the other fellow, must be new. I'll never forget your faces when you first met Percival in the underground station.' Uncle Rufus's eyes twinkled with amusement at the recollection.

'I don't think any of us will forget that moment, Uncle.'

'You'll find that the guardians can be summoned when the SPI needs them.' Uncle Rufus seemed satisfied that the inspector had made that call.

Clovis, Eve and Uncle Rufus watched on in amazement as the train conductor was gently guided away from the platform. To anyone looking on, they would have thought nothing out of the ordinary was happening. Eve noticed a couple of people staring but realised they were smirking at the guardians' attire. She supposed bowler hats were not normally seen these days. But Clovis, Eve and Uncle Rufus knew only too well what these two smartly dressed men really were.

Inspector Rutherford turned, smiled and waved one last time as their train left the platform.

CHAPTER 7

A Strange Hotel and
Mr Churchill Speaks

Uncle Rufus rested his head against the seat and spent much of the rest of the train journey asleep.

Eve and Clovis happily chatted about school, friends, family and Christmas. For the first time Uncle Rufus had invited both Clovis and Tom's famlies over for Christmas day.

Everyone was excited, especially as Claudette had volunteered to do the cooking.

'It's going to be a feast!' cried Eve, smacking her lips together.

'My mum's really going for it this year. She's practically living in the kitchen. I tell you, the smells coming out of there are just . . . amazing.' Clovis closed his eyes and licked his lips, imagining all the delicious tastes. 'Just wait.'

The tannoy system crackled into life as the train began to slow. 'Ladies and gentlemen, we are now approaching Lancaster.'

'Thank God!' groaned Eve, 'I thought we were never going to get here. Come on, Uncle Rufus, wake up!'

They all bundled their possessions away, and Boris snorted and farted loudly as he stretched and yawned like a cat.

'Quick get off the train,' sniggered Clovis, not wanting to smell one of Boris's deathly farts.

'Right, chaps, keep your eyes out for Tom, he should be on the platform with his parents,' said Uncle Rufus, zipping up his coat and winding his long patchwork scarf around his neck. The train gave one final screech of brakes and Eve and Clovis jumped off and instantly began looking for Tom.

'Can you see him?' asked Eve, standing on tiptoe and craning her neck over the heads of weary commuters to see if her friend was there.

'There he is!' exclaimed Clovis. At the other end of the platform, Tom and his parents, Dan and Ange, were also looking out. Tom suddenly spied his friends and burst into a run, a huge smile spreading across his face. He had really loved spending time with his parents, but there was only so much army talk Tom could stand from his dad.

The three friends hugged and beamed at each other; they had only been apart for a few days, but it was long enough.

'We've missed you,' said Eve, squeezing Tom's arm.

'Have you had a good time? What was it like meeting your dad's old mates?' asked Clovis.

'It was fun, actually, they kept telling me stories of what my dad was like, you know, in Iraq. I got to see where he trained, and they even let me have a go on an assault course.'

'Did you finish it?' asked Eve.

'Course I did,' shrugged Tom.

'Bet you didn't,' teased Clovis, knowing full well that his competitive friend would have nearly killed himself in the process to complete something like that.

Tom rolled his eyes. 'I'll show you the video later. Dad filmed me.'

Tom's parents wandered over. His mum reached out and patted down a stray clump of Tom's hair and he immediately moved his head away.

'At ease, son,' laughed his dad, sensing Tom's embarrassment at the affectionate display.

His mum didn't care though and hugged Tom to her. 'We'll see you in a couple of days; do everything the professor tells you.'

'Don't worry,' said Uncle Rufus. 'As I said, they're helping me out with my study on quantum physics and ancient stones.' Tom's parents looked at Uncle Rufus for a split second in total confusion and then laughed.

'Each to their own, eh, Professor?'

'Indeed, indeed,' nodded Uncle Rufus.

After all the goodbyes, Tom's parents went to get their train back to London and the others followed Uncle Rufus out of the station to a small carpark. There they watched curiously as Uncle Rufus strolled up to an old orange VW van. He stuck his hand under the wheel arch on the driver's side and pulled out a set of keys.

'This . . .' he said proudly, gesticulating at the van, '. . . is Albert.'

'You mean, this is yours?' asked Eve, astounded at yet another one of her uncle's surprises.

'It most certainly is,' he laughed. Uncle Rufus unlocked the van and threw his bag onto the passenger seat. Boris waddled up to one of the wheels, promptly lifted his back leg and peed on the tyre.

'Well, Boris has marked his territory,' laughed Clovis, before following Tom and Eve as they walked slowly around the van. Tom pointed at the reg plate. *SC13 NCE 2* 'Wow! Another vehicle of the professor's,' said Tom. 'I think I like the look of this one more than the Mini. It's cooler, for a start.'

The windows were all blacked out, presumably to keep nosy parkers from looking inside.

'Come on, in you get,' shouted Uncle Rufus from the driver's seat.

As they all clambered inside, Uncle Rufus was delighted by their reactions.

'Wow!' said Tom.

'This is incredible,' whispered Clovis.

'You kept this quiet, Unc!' said Eve.

The inside of the van was kitted out with screens and computers. There was a console with various knobs, buttons and dials. Clovis was so excited he felt almost dizzy. His two friends laughed at his reaction and Eve had to take his steamed-up glasses off for him and give them a rub.

Uncle Rufus had swivelled around in the driver's seat. 'I know I've not mentioned Albert to you before. All across the world, the SPI have many of these vehicles, and most have equipment inside, just in case we have to investigate in remote places. So we can still have access to the outside world. We can also sit in here and monitor the paranormal activity that goes on in some of these locations. I think, Clovis, you will especially love the equipment. These computers are like nothing you will have ever seen or used before. They allow you to take whatever is on the screen and manipulate the image or data in such a way that you can bring it out of the screen and project it into a room. Look, I'll show you.' Uncle Rufus moved over to a chair that looked like a racing car's seat, and it had castors so it could be moved across the wooden floor easily, from one screen to another.

He leaned forward, tapped on the screen and brought up a picture of a pizza. Then, touching the image with his thumb and forefinger, he made a pinching motion, then slowly moved his arm out into the centre of the van. Widening his fingers, the pizza suddenly appeared in front of the three friends. Uncle Rufus spun the image around, moving it in different directions so every angle could be seen. He tapped next to the pizza and all the information on how to make it slowly scrolled down.

'Incredible, isn't it?' said Uncle Rufus.

Clovis's eyes were agog. Tom was shaking his head in disbelief and Eve's mouth had flapped open.

'Inspector Rutherford thought we might need Albert, as a couple of the locations on this case could prove to be rather remote. The only problem is, Albert and I have a love-hate relationship. He seems to know that I have trouble driving him and he doesn't make it any easier. I sometimes think the van is laughing at me.' Uncle Rufus scratched his head, shrugged his shoulders and said, 'Come on, let's get going. Everyone belt up and let's hope Albert behaves. It's about a twenty minute drive into Pendle Hill and our hotel.'

Tom crossed his eyes and wiggled his fingers towards Eve's face. 'Ooh, Pendle Hill, *mwah ha ha ha.*' He tried his best to cackle like a witch.

Eve smacked her friend's hands away, rolled her eyes and breathed, 'Idiot.' Then laughed at Tom's ridiculous face-pulling. 'That's an improvement,' she said.

'I take it you know about the case, and that we could be dealing with witchcraft?' asked Clovis, looking serious.

'Yeah, Inspector Rutherford briefed me on the phone.' Tom's demeanour changed suddenly, remembering the ghost of the falling woman from the castle. 'I just hope that we can help.'

Uncle Rufus sat back down in the driver's seat and, just before he turned the key in the ignition, he closed his eyes and mumbled some incomprehensible words. Was he praying? He turned the key and suddenly, much to everyone's relief, the engine started with a cough, a bang and a plume of black smoke.

'Let's go!' shouted Uncle Rufus happily over the din of the engine.

Albert chugged away from the station and onto the streets of Lancaster. The van was filled with excited chatter as the friends talked about their recent ghostly encounters. Eve and Clovis told Tom all about their investigation at The Bow Bells

Pub and how they had managed to capture the image of the ghost that haunted the toilets.

'You should've seen Eve's face when she was sitting on the loo; it was brilliant.' Clovis began to laugh but soon stopped as Eve gave him one of her looks.

Tom explained to his fascinated friends how he had witnessed the ghost of the falling woman. He told them how awful and upsetting her ghost had been to look at, and of the warning she had given him.

Uncle Rufus and Boris had both taken the opportunity to share a packet of crisps, most of which ended up on the floor rather than in Boris's slobbering mouth.

'Has anyone ever told you, Boris, not to eat with your mouth open?' Boris cocked his head to one side, as if understanding what his master was saying. Uncle Rufus fed Boris another large crisp. 'No, I thought not!'

Clovis, Tom and Eve were beginning to get tired. Eve closed her eyes and leaned her head wearily on Tom's shoulder, but suddenly opened them again when she felt the van slow down to a bumbling crawl.

Uncle Rufus could be heard muttering to himself, and it soon became apparent that he was talking to the van.

'Now you listen here . . . *Albert*,' he said as he tried to get the vehicle to go down a gear. The noise was excruciating: cogs and wheels groaned, clunked and lurched, fighting Uncle Rufus as if the van or Albert didn't want to slow down.

'I told you it had a mind of its own,' shouted Uncle Rufus over his shoulder. The noise was deafening.

'Why's he called Albert?' asked Clovis.

'After Einstein, of course,' said Uncle Rufus. 'And *he* certainly had a mind of his own.'

Uncle Rufus navigated Albert carefully over snow-filled potholes and craters into what looked like some sort of driveway. It was long and wide and tall poplar trees lined the roads on either side. The van's headlights bounced around, illuminating the uneven road and a few startled rabbits. Up ahead Eve, Clovis and Tom could just make out a large building; the closer they got, the clearer it became. Uncle Rufus followed the driveway around a stone fountain sitting in the middle of the drive. A sign swung in a gentle breeze over the main doorway: *THE SAFE HAVEN*. It creaked as the wind nudged it back and forth.

'This looks a bit posh, Uncle,' said Eve, climbing out of the van. 'Is this where we're staying?'

The professor nodded.

'I'm starving,' said Clovis as he unfolded his long legs.

'When are you not?' said Eve mockingly.

'It might be too late to eat now,' said Uncle Rufus, getting out of Albert and brushing the remainder of the crisps from his coat onto the snowy ground.

'I like the name of the place,' said Tom. 'Look!' he pointed to the sign. 'Isn't that the same symbol as the —' he lowered his voice to a whisper — 'SPI?'

Everyone looked up and saw the image on the wooden sign. A snake wrapped around itself in a figure of eight, eating its own tail. It was small but just visible in the left-hand bottom corner.

'Yes, this hotel is part of the SPI. We'll be well looked-after here,' said Uncle Rufus. He grabbed his bag and clipped the lead onto Boris. 'Come on,' he said. 'Let's check in quickly, then straight to bed.'

Everyone followed Uncle Rufus up the stone steps and in through the main front door. They found themselves standing in a very old fashioned-looking square hallway. Dark wooden panelling lined the walls, strange old lamps flickered away, giving out a low level of comfort. A huge flight of stairs faced them and, on the left wall, dozens of pictures of men, women and children gazed down from their framed worlds.

The large wooden reception desk was the main piece of furniture in the room. On the wall behind it was a picture of a king. Clovis knew who it was straight away: George VI. Next to it was a clock, its pendulum swinging from side to side, its ticking a soothing sound.

Beside the clock was a glass cabinet filled with keys, presumably for the rooms.

Tom nudged Clovis and nodded towards the old-fashioned telephone that took pride of place on top of the desk. It was a black Bakelite phone, the likes of which Tom had only ever seen in one of his mum's black-and-white movies.

Suddenly a door opposite the reception area opened and out walked a very glamorous woman.

'Oh, Professor! I'm so glad you're here.' The woman wore

a pristine white blouse with pearl buttons. Her skirt was long and tapered, the material clinging to her hourglass figure. Her hair was curled in the most unique way: it was as if she had left two huge rollers in on either side of her head. The back was pulled up and reminded Tom of a curved sausage. She had a pretty face, pale and smooth. Her eyes twinkled, and her brilliant red lips went to kiss Uncle Rufus.

'Hello, Gerry,' said Uncle Rufus. His smile said it all. He really liked this woman, and it was obvious that he had known her for a long time. Uncle Rufus stepped back from their embrace.

'You always look fabulous,' he said.

'And you always look like you have the weight of the world on your shoulders.'

Gerry brought her attention to the three friends who were watching the exchange with interest.

'This beautiful young woman must be Eve. She's just as pretty as you described, Professor, and presumably as inquisitive.'

Eve blushed and smiled.

Gerry turned next to Tom and Clovis. 'We've heard all about Clovis, the brains, if I may.' She took Clovis's hand and shook it. 'Tom, I hear you are a sportsman. Just like my Stan in his youth.'

Gerry then dropped to her knees. 'And of course, who could forget the gorgeous Boris? Oh, how I've missed you, my little bear.' Boris wiggled his chubby bottom and barked once in acknowledgement.

'Well, now,' Gerry said standing up. 'I know it's very late and you're probably exhausted from your long journey, but the fire is still going and my husband, Stan, has made some sandwiches and tea for you all.'

'Oh, Gerry, that would be wonderful as we *are* a little hungry, especially Clovis,' said Uncle Rufus, rolling his eyes at him.

'Clovis is always hungry,' laughed Eve.

They all followed Gerry into the front room. It was a pleasant enough space but, rather like the reception hall, seemed very old-fashioned. Books and old newspapers lined the walls, and huge thick cream curtains, pulled closed, gave the room a cosy vibe. At the far end, a dining table was covered with plates of sandwiches and cake. A large brown teapot sat in the centre surrounded by dainty teacups and saucers.

An old-fashioned radio was positioned next to a big armchair close to the crackling fire. A matching armchair mirrored it and an incredibly plump-looking sofa ran along the middle of the room. Another clock ticked and tocked from the mantelpiece. On either side of it sat two white porcelain dogs, staring nonchalantly at the occupants of the softly lit room.

'I'll leave you for a moment to relax.' Gerry smiled at everyone and closed the door quietly behind her.

'This isn't an ordinary hotel,' said Clovis, ramming a sandwich into his mouth.

'I like it,' said Eve. 'But, Uncle, you've obviously been here before. I've never heard you mention this place, though.'

Uncle Rufus looked a little uncomfortable. 'It's a place I've used many times before. I've stayed here when I've had to come and investigate cases in this part of the country. I've known Gerry and Stan for a long time.' He bit into a sandwich and gave Boris one, too, which was gratefully received and instantly bolted down.

'What's in this sandwich?' asked Tom. 'It's nice, but I don't think I've ever had it before.' He chewed the food, trying to pinpoint what exactly he was eating.

'I think that one is shrimp paste,' laughed Uncle Rufus.

'Even the food is old fashioned,' said Clovis under his breath.

Tom walked over to the radio and turned one of the dials to the on position. 'This reminds me of the radio that we found in that secret World War Two bunker, do you remember?'

'How can we ever forget that! Hearing that German voice coming through the speaker was petrifying,' said Eve.

Uncle Rufus sank down into one of the armchairs. Balancing his china cup and saucer on the arm, he sighed deeply. Boris lay down next to his master's feet, enjoying the heat from the fire.

After taking its time to warm up, the radio sprang into life and made everyone jump as the sounds of some old-fashioned music crackled through the room.

'Oh lovely, a bit of Glenn Miller to relax to,' sighed Uncle Rufus, and his foot began to tap away to the melody of the big band sound.

'We're going to have to introduce you to some of our music, Uncle,' said Eve. 'This is truly ancient.'

'Don't diss Mr Miller,' said Clovis. 'He was a genius.'

'Well said,' agreed Uncle Rufus.

Eve and Tom rolled their eyes in unison. Just as Tom was about to reach for another sandwich, the door opened to reveal a rather portly looking gentleman. He was quite small, wore high-waisted smart grey trousers, a white shirt and tie and a pair of black braces. His hair was cut short, greased to within an inch of its life and parted severely over to one side.

Uncle Rufus shot up. 'Stan!' he cried happily. 'Everyone, this is Stan.'

'Professor, my old pal, it's lovely to see you, as always. When Inspector Rutherford told us you were coming, I told Gerry that we mustn't delay, let's air the beds and make lots of sandwiches.'

Clovis, Eve and Tom warmed instantly to this jovial man.

'Now, I hope you don't mind, but I must listen to the late night broadcast.' He waddled over to the radio and began to turn the dial. The machine churned out a variety of different voices and music as the gauge swept across different radio stations.

Clovis noticed that none of the stations seemed to sound familiar and all the music was either classical or jazz.

'Right, Stan, we'll leave you in peace. Come on, everyone,' said Uncle Rufus. 'Let's get to bed. We'll go over the case in the morning.' Uncle Rufus began herding everyone towards the door. Eve noticed his odd behaviour but put it down to the fact that they were all tired.

'Goodnight, Stan,' they all chorused, making their way out of the room. Uncle Rufus closed the door hastily and began to trot up the stairs.

'Come on, quickly,' he said, smiling through gritted teeth.

'Uncle, whatever has got into you? We're coming,' said Eve, surprised at his peculiar behaviour.

Suddenly a voice could be heard coming from the radio. Stan had obviously turned up the volume. Everyone stood still on the stairs as a man's voice cut through the scratchy sound of the crackly static.

'Now, this is not the end. It is not even the beginning of the end. But it is, perhaps, the end of the beginning. Henceforth, Hitler's Nazis will meet equally well-armed, and perhaps better-armed troops.'

'That's Winston Churchill,' said Clovis, looking very confused.

'It must be a recording Stan's listening to,' said Tom.

'Come on, you lot, to bed,' said Uncle Rufus. 'I'm too tired. I'll explain in the morning.'

Clovis, Eve and Tom had decided to share one room. They lay in their single beds ready for sleep to come and take them, but there were just so many questions running through their heads.

'This hotel is really lovely, but there's something I can't quite put my finger on,' whispered Clovis.

'Yeah, I know what you mean,' said Eve. 'Uncle Rufus was odd, wasn't he? It's as if he didn't want us to hear what was being said on the radio.' She turned onto her side and gazed sleepily at the old-fashioned curtains shutting out the night sky.

Tom yawned. 'I've got a feeling that this place is not what it seems.' He didn't know what it was, but hopefully the professor would explain everything in the morning.

Eve always slept with the curtains open; she loved to see the night sky. Back at home she would often lie awake, just staring up at the stars and marvelling at the wonder of it all. Hopefully it was a clear night tonight. She got out of her warm bed and tiptoed over to the window. Ever so carefully, trying not to disturb Tom or Clovis, she gently pulled back the curtains.

'What are you doing?' mumbled Clovis, nearly asleep.

'You know I like to see the sky. Do you mind?' Eve asked.

Clovis sighed deeply and then whispered that no, he didn't mind.

'Like we ever have a choice,' whispered Tom sleepily.

Eve pulled the curtains back fully, only to reveal not a starlit sky but a view with nothing but criss-cross white tape all over the glass. She took a step back, totally confused.

'Hey, guys,' she whispered. 'Look at this.' But there was no reply. Both Clovis and Tom were now fast asleep.

Eve got back into bed and stared at the strange window. She'd only seen this before in movies or programmes about the war. What was going on? She tried to figure out the mysterious hotel, but soon drifted off into a very deep and dreamless sleep.

CHAPTER 8

Old Friends and Powdered Eggs

The next morning Clovis, Eve and Tom dressed and bundled their belongings into their rucksacks. They made their way downstairs, past the rows of painted faces staring at them from within their picture frames.

The table in the front room was set for breakfast. A loaf of bread had already been cut into slices and it sat with a small pat of butter and a pot of jam. A stream of steaming golden tea was being poured into a pretty china cup by a very tired-looking Uncle Rufus. He waved Eve, Tom and Clovis into the room. Boris lay under the table, patiently waiting for any stray crumbs to fall.

A plate of something that resembled the leftovers of a cooked breakfast sat in front of Uncle Rufus. He sipped his tea politely, and the young ghost hunters saw that he wasn't alone. Sitting opposite him was a man, with his body turned sideways so he could read the enormous paper that he held open. His back was turned to the three friends. The stranger, whoever he was, had dark, shoulder-length hair and wore a white shirt with rolled-up sleeves, revealing some very familiar-looking tattoos. Suddenly he snapped the paper shut and turned around, grinning, revealing two rows of pearly white teeth.

'Good morning, my friends.'

'Anwaar!' Eve, Clovis and Tom all leaped forward to welcome the striking-looking gentleman.

Anwaar Saygh was a sight to behold. He was originally from Syria but had spent many years travelling the world hunting, capturing and destroying demons. He was a handsome man in his mid-thirties. He had huge dark eyes, brown skin and an infectious smile that could win over the coldest of people. His tattooed face was highly unusual and caused people to stare wherever he went. Strange symbols in black ink were positioned under each eye. His arms were covered in weird and wonderful inked figures and shapes. Each tattoo had been branded into his skin as a talisman of protection, given to him by the ethereal beings from the Otherside.

Anwaar had been a friend of Uncle Rufus's for many years, and between the two of them, they had investigated haunted locations around the world. But an encounter with the ghost of Jack the Ripper had torn their friendship apart for a while. Anwaar had fled in fear and confusion, leaving Uncle Rufus to defend himself. Anwaar, ashamed by his actions, had gone to live a nomadic lifestyle deep in the Iranian desert, learning the ancient ways from an old and wise master. These ways were to change Anwaar's life for ever: he had learned how to expel demonic entities and evil spirits. Anwaar Saygh had become a demonologist, a demon hunter with extraordinary skills. Eventually he had agreed to come back and rejoin the SPI.

He had helped Clovis, Tom and Eve to finally send Jack the Ripper's soul to the deepest darkest depths of the Abyss in a previous investigation, a place no living person would ever want to end up.

Seeing Anwaar reading a newspaper in this strange hotel was a wonderful surprise.

'When did you get here?' asked Clovis.

'I arrived only a few hours ago,' said Anwaar, his accent strong and enchanting. He was clearly delighted at seeing his young friends again. The demon hunter shook Clovis and Tom's hands. Then, making Eve's elfin face turn bright crimson, Anwaar picked up her hand, bent forward and kissed the back of it.

'I'm so pleased to be back with you all,' he said.

'Now, sit down, everyone,' said Uncle Rufus, dabbing the corners of his mouth with a napkin. 'The food is not quite what you're used to, but it's lovely, nonetheless.'

Suddenly the door opened to reveal Stan and Gerry, carrying various plates of breakfast.

'Good morning!' chirped Gerry, beaming happily. She looked just as glamorous as she had the night before, not a hair out of place, her clothes exactly the same, and her ruby red lipstick was still perfectly applied.

Stan waddled behind her, he too wore the same clothes as last night, the braces and Brylcreem ever-present.

'I hope you all slept well?' said Stan, placing a plate of food in front of Eve.

Gerry put plates in front of the boys. 'There you are, dears,' she said sweetly. 'Tuck in, and don't forget to eat the crusts, or you won't grow up to be big and strong.'

Eve guffawed but controlled herself after receiving one of her uncle's looks over the top of his glasses.

Tom and Clovis looked down at the food and then at each other. They had never seen a breakfast quite like it. The scrambled eggs looked strange, a funny off-white colour, and as Tom tried to lift some onto his fork, the odd substance wobbled like jelly. Next to it was what they thought was some sort of meat. The boys nudged each other, not sure what to make of the food at all.

Gerry repositioned the jam pot. 'I'm so pleased there wasn't an air raid last night. We didn't fancy tripping down to the Anderson shelter, did we, Stan? I think we would've all frozen to death, wouldn't we?' She directed this last question to Eve, who just looked totally bewildered, but nodded in agreement anyway.

'I'm sorry, Gerry, but what do you mean?' asked Clovis. What on earth was Gerry talking about?

The looks between Uncle Rufus and Anwaar didn't go unnoticed.

Gerry put one hand on her shapely hip and said: 'The war, silly! Honestly, Professor, have you got everyone in on one of your jokes? Anyway, enjoy your food.'

Stan leaned over Eve's shoulder and whispered in her ear, 'The eggs are powdered, but they don't taste too bad if you wash them down with the tea.' He then nodded at everyone in the room, smiled happily and followed Gerry out through the door like an eager puppy.

'Right,' said Eve, putting her cutlery down onto her plate: the powdered eggs could wait. 'What's going on, Uncle?'

Uncle Rufus looked cagily at Anwaar, who glanced away quickly, rustling his paper, suddenly very interested in the news of the day.

'I think I know what this place is,' said Tom, surprising everyone. Uncle Rufus looked up and Anwaar coughed.

'What do you think it is?' asked Uncle Rufus, pouring himself another cup of tea.

'They're not real, are they?' Tom whispered.

'Who aren't real?' asked Eve. She looked between Tom and her uncle.

'Gerry and Stan,' Tom whispered again, realising that what he was saying was crazy, but he also knew that he was correct. His head was bent low, leaning over his breakfast plate, careful not to make eye contact with anyone.

'Are you saying that they're *ghosts*?' asked Clovis. He was clearly thrilled at this possible development, and he leaned further over the table.

Uncle Rufus shuffled in his chair and brought his hands to rest on the back of his head.

'Clever lad, but not quite,' he said, smiling.

'Oh, my God!' said Eve, pushing her chair back and standing up. She was clearly frustrated now. 'I don't understand. If they're not ghosts, what *are* they? I mean . . .' she stammered.

'They're so real, so solid, so *lifelike*.' Eve was gripping the back of the chair, her knuckles turning white.

Sensing his niece's anxiety, Uncle Rufus walked over to her and took her hands in his.

'This place, Eve, my love, truly is a safe haven. There are many of them around the world. Gerry and Stan, this whole building, is what's called a time slip. You and the rest of us are now in . . .' Uncle Rufus looked down at his feet, took a breath, then brought his head back up. '. . . nineteen forty-two.'

Eve's mouth dropped open in astonishment. Clovis actually yelped with excitement and Tom just grinned. All the while Anwaar tapped his foot, still transfixed with the paper.

Uncle Rufus carried on: 'This hotel used to be here all those years ago, but it was demolished in the seventies. Gerry and Stan were the owners when it was first built and still are today. But what we see and experience now, here in this front room, your bedrooms, the whole building, is what it was like during World War Two.'

'This is mind-blowing, Professor,' whispered Clovis, his face an absolute picture of joy. He had heard of time slips, even read into a couple of cases, but thought them just fantastical stories made up for entertainment purposes. But now, seeing, feeling and even eating in a place that had brought them back in time, was just amazing.

'But the building, the food, the drink. How can it all be real?' Eve was slowly turning around on the spot, marvelling at the pictures on the wall, the fire sizzling in the grate, the clock ticking away. 'It's just too bizarre to understand.'

Uncle Rufus placed his hands on her shoulders and pushed her gently back down into her seat.

'Isn't it marvellous?' said Anwaar, smiling broadly, his kind eyes dancing with the amusement of it all. 'This place —' he folded his newspaper away — 'is protected. Nothing can enter here unless with a member of the SPI. As the professor said, there are many of these places around the globe. From the outside world looking in, there is nothing here, just space, a field, a waste ground. These places are run by energies who have chosen to help and protect the investigators of the SPI. They all believe that our organisation has some association with the government of their time. These people, like Gerry and Stan, are a living memory, being played out for us to interact with. Their real spirits, their souls, have long departed and are now living happily on the Otherside, but what we can see, hear and feel now in this moment is a reenactment, if you will, their life force being emitted in front of our very eyes.'

Anwaar looked round at the three confused faces, and turned to Uncle Rufus for help.

'Think of it as if you were watching a movie and the people in it can interact with you. Talk to you, laugh with you, eat and drink with you.' Uncle Rufus said all this in a whisper, aware that Stan and Gerry could come into the room at any moment.

'Oh, like . . . a . . . a . . . VR game?' asked Clovis, who was just so shocked, he had begun to stammer.

'Yes, I suppose so,' answered Uncle Rufus. 'It's mind-boggling, isn't it?' He smiled warmly at his three young students. 'Even now, I still don't understand all the complexities of it and yet it works.'

'What do you mean, *works*?' asked Eve.

'Well, as you know when you're dealing with negative and angry spirits, the last thing you want is for them to follow you home. And we know only too well what that is like, don't we? So sometimes you have to come to a place like this.'

'So, Gerry and Stan, they're still living through the war?' said Eve.

Uncle Rufus had moved to stand in front of the fire, warming the backs of his legs. 'Well, their memories are. During the war, Gerry and Stan would have behaved in the way that you are seeing them today, but remember, like I said, their real souls are long gone and living on the Otherside. The Safe Haven is one of my favourite protected places to stay in, mainly because of Stan and Gerry. Some of the other places . . .' Uncle Rufus pulled a disgruntled face at Anwaar. '. . . the owners aren't as welcoming.'

Anwaar smiled and nodded at his friend, a silent acknowledgment of past adventures gone by.

Uncle Rufus continued, 'One of the founding fathers of the SPI discovered these places and found a way to harness and use them as a way to protect paranormal investigators.'

'So do Gerry and Stan know who we are and what we do?' asked Tom.

'They think that the SPI is a secret organisation working

to help the war effort. Remember they are not spirits; they are memories, so they wouldn't understand anything that goes on outside of these four walls. For them, it's still nineteen forty-two.'

'And we'd like to keep it that way,' said Anwaar. Uncle Rufus nodded in agreement.

Anwaar made everyone jump as he suddenly slapped a brown folder onto the table. Everyone recognised it as the same file Inspector Rutherford had given them on the train. Anwaar snapped off the elastic band and opened it to the first page.

'Now,' he said softly. 'The Pendle Hill case, shall we begin?'

They spent the next few hours poring over all the details of the case. Uncle Rufus and Anwaar were very concerned about certain aspects of the paranormal activity, particularly the physical harm that had seemingly been inflicted on all the victims.

Everyone stared in horror at the photographs of the horrific burn marks seared into each of the victims' skin.

'All the markings are very similar,' said Uncle Rufus, as he slowly moved a magnifying glass over each image. 'What do you think, Anwaar?'

Anwaar didn't need a magnifying glass. 'I know what they are,' he said with authority, and a hint of dread.

Clovis also had an inkling about what the marks could mean, but he bit his tongue and waited to hear what Anwaar had to say.

Anwaar looked deep in thought, his dark eyes fixed on the

horrific images in the file. Then he spoke very quietly: 'The marks are an ancient symbol that witches were alleged to have on their bodies. They are believed to have been the bite marks of the devil, and they were placed on a witch as a sign that she was truly a slave to Satan.'

'Gosh! Are you all right?' Uncle Rufus asked him.

'Yes, sorry, I'm just remembering a case I worked on two years ago that involved witchcraft. It wasn't pleasant, not pleasant at all.'

Clovis closed his eyes and tried to remember more of the information he had learned about witchcraft a while back. 'The witch's mark, I've read about those,' he began. 'They were something that the courts in the seventeenth century would search an accused witch for. They would strip the person and look for a mole or wart, which was thought to be a third nipple that the devil would suckle upon. A birthmark, indeed, *any* mark, was deemed a curse for the victim. But a witch's mark that was blue in colour and shaped like a skull was the final deciding factor in the accused's case.' Clovis came up for air, realising that everyone was smiling at him.

'So, I think we can definitely say that all these burns are the witch's mark then,' said Eve, happy with the progress they were making.

'Don't be too pleased with our findings,' warned Anwaar. He looked very troubled. 'I don't like the fact that all but one victim endured strangulation,' he said. 'The little boy seems to have been possessed by an entity, but according to his mother and father, he didn't experience the strangulation, thank goodness. Unfortunately, it was the boy's father who suffered this terrible manifestation.' Anwaar shook his head. 'A terrible thing to have happened to a young family.'

'It certainly is,' said Uncle Rufus. 'They are also the only people to have encountered a ghost during their experience, whereas the others did not.'

'Yeah,' said Tom, reading more information in the file. 'Although it says here that the judge *did* witness objects moving in his office.'

'And what about you, Tom?' asked Uncle Rufus. 'Can you tell us about your encounter with the falling woman?'

Tom scrunched his eyes tight shut and brought the image of the ghost of the falling woman back into his mind's eye. There she was, fragile and grey, her face full of agony and longing. He heard her voice and quickly repeated her words. 'She said . . . "They are coming . . . she's so angry and so are the others . . . they are rising."' Tom bit his lip and took a breath. '"They are rising to get their revenge."' Tom opened his eyes, relieved to get the awful image of the ghost out of his head and to be in the comfort of the room with his friends. 'I also remember lots of voices shouting different words,' Tom added quickly.

'Like what?' asked Eve. She was leaning forward over the table, eager eyes glued on her friend.

'Words like . . . *witch, guilty* and *hang them all.*'

'And did she tell you her name, this ghost at the castle?' asked Uncle Rufus.

'It was Jennet . . . Jennet Device.'

76

Clovis jumped. 'I know that name from somewhere!' he said.

He went to get his laptop out of his rucksack, but Uncle Rufus smiled and said, 'Unfortunately that won't work here.' Clovis nodded knowingly at the professor, remembering that he and his friends were locked in the year 1942. Tapping the side of his head, as if willing his mind to give him the information, Clovis said, 'I believe that this Jennet Device definitely had something to do with the Pendle witch trial. I'm sure of it.' Clovis looked frustrated, almost angry with himself for not recalling it straight away.

'It will come to you,' said Tom, putting a reassuring hand on his friend's shoulder.

'So, the inspector was right, it sounds like we're dealing with witches then?' asked Eve, looking to her uncle and Anwaar for confirmation. They both sighed and nodded.

Uncle Rufus closed the file. 'I suggest we pay a visit to the hospital and see what the victims can tell us. Inspector Rutherford has messaged me to tell me that the hospital is expecting us.'

'Good,' said Anwaar. 'I don't need to tell you all that this is going to be a dangerous case and that you must do exactly as the professor and I tell you.' Anwaar directed the last part of his sentence to Tom, who on a previous adventure had taken matters into his own hands and caused no end of worry. Tom nodded; he would never do anything like that again. He had been forgiven by everyone but that didn't mean to say that they had forgotten it.

Gathering their belongings, Tom, Clovis, Eve, Anwaar and a reluctant Boris followed Uncle Rufus into the reception hall where Gerry and Stan were waiting for them.

'You all off, then?' asked Gerry cheerfully.

'Yes, off to fight the enemy,' said Uncle Rufus, winking slyly at Eve.

'If you come back tonight,' said Stan, 'make sure you close the blackout curtains across the door after you. Last night you forgot, Professor, and I thought we might get a fine. We don't want the ARP warden coming round. He's a miserable old git.'

Eve nudged Clovis and Tom, who were staring at the couple.

'Are they solid to touch?' whispered Clovis to Tom.

'Er, *hum*!' said Uncle Rufus, loudly trying to cover up Clovis and Tom's conversation. 'We'll definitely be back later, but don't wait up.' He smiled warmly at Gerry and Stan.

Clovis and Tom were continuing to unsubtly eye Stan and Gerry, totally in awe at standing so close to two life-sized memories. Uncle Rufus took both boys by the arm and quickly led them out of the house. The fresh air was cold and crisp, and Eve zipped her leather jacket up and stuffed her hands into her pockets; not one for sensible clothing, she had forgotten to pack her gloves. She squinted as she looked upon the bright, fresh blanket of snow that had fallen in the night, making everywhere look bright and clean.

Once inside Albert, they bucked slowly all the way up the

long driveway. From there, Albert coughed once, the horn beeped by itself, and then things settled down after Uncle Rufus had given the van a good talking to. Albert smoothly turned left and joined the main road and, to Clovis, Eve and Tom's relief, the twenty-first century.

CHAPTER 9

Possessions and Blue Skulls

'I hate hospitals,' said Eve as they all walked up the long corridor towards the men's ward.

Tom and Clovis both knew why. The last time she had visited one had been to see her aunt Jess just before she died.

To Eve, the smell, the sounds, the whole atmosphere, made her sick to her stomach; it brought back too many painful memories. Goodness knows how her uncle was feeling. She turned round to check on him and was relieved to see that he was deep in conversation with Anwaar, their two heads close together, whispering conspiratorially again as they walked along.

Everyone gathered around the main reception desk. A young nurse asked, 'Can I help?'

'Yes,' replied Uncle Rufus. He straightened his tie and smiled politely. 'We're here to see Judge Bromley and Mr Law.'

'Ah, yes,' said the nurse. 'They're both in private rooms on either side of the ward. Mr Bromley is just through that door behind you, and Mr Law is in the room at the end.'

They went to Judge Bromley's room first. They looked

through the long rectangular glass panel in the door and saw a rather ill-looking gentleman asleep in a bed, attached to machines which blinked and bleeped. Sitting in an uncomfortable-looking chair beside him was a thin, smartly dressed woman. She sat motionless with her back ramrod straight, her legs crossed at the ankles, her small wrinkled hands placed neatly in her lap. She looked up as the door opened slowly. Tissue in hand, she wiped her nose, patted her coiffed hair and stood up.

'Professor Pepper?' she asked gently.

'Hello there, yes, that's me,' said Uncle Rufus, walking over to the lady and shaking her hand. 'Mrs Bromley, so glad we could come. As the inspector explained, we're here to hopefully help and find out what's happened to your husband.'

'Well, here he is.' She sniffed, gesturing towards the sleeping man. 'He hasn't woken, murmured a word or moved since he got here. I just don't know what to think.' Mrs Bromley sat back down and blew her nose quietly.

Suddenly, the judge's eyes burst open. The eyeballs were an opaque pearl colour. He stared straight up at the ceiling, then began to moan and retch, before shouting in a voice that sounded like something from a horror film: 'Damn you, damn you all!' Eve, Tom and Clovis jumped in fright. Uncle Rufus immediately rushed to Mrs Bromley, who had begun to cry.

Anwaar went over to the bed, pulled the sheet down to the judge's waist and watched as the blue burn mark began to burn brightly and pulsate under the hospital gown.

'Who are you?' whispered Anwaar, close to the judge's ear.

The judge immediately swung his head to face Anwaar, then roared in a low, hellish voice, 'I am Chattox!'

The door abruptly swung open and in charged a doctor and nurse. 'Sorry, can you clear the room, please,' said the nurse. He immediately went over to the judge, pressed some buttons on the machines whilst the doctor pushed a needle into his arm. The judge's eyes shut, his body went limp, and he fell back into a deep sleep.

Everyone was shocked at what they had just witnessed. Out in the corridor, Tom, Clovis and Eve agreed in hushed tones that they had to be brave, it was part of their job now. Uncle Rufus asked: 'Are you all OK? Do you want to carry on? I completely understand if you don't. It's a frightening business . . . possession.'

Tom, Clovis and Eve all shook their heads and told Uncle Rufus that they were scared, but they were happy to continue and try to help these people.

'All right, then,' said Uncle Rufus, smiling.

They went into Dave Law's room and again were greeted by family members. As soon as they came close to the bed, the same thing happened. Dave Law shouted out, and this time when Anwaar asked who he was, he screamed: 'My name is Alizon, Alizon Device.' The blue marks fizzed and bubbled, causing the family members much distress. They immediately called the doctors and the ghost hunters left.

Tom, Uncle Rufus, Clovis, Eve and Anwaar walked quickly to the women's ward and on the way, discussed how so far each of the patients did indeed seem possessed. But what was the connection? Why *these* people? And why had they woken up when the ghost hunters walked into their rooms?

Maybe Rachel, the police officer, would give them another clue.

They entered her private room. This one was a little bigger than the others and an elderly man had his back to them, staring out of the window.

'I've been waiting for you,' said the man, turning round. 'The inspector's a friend of mine; we're old colleagues and she has promised me only the best. I'm Rachel's grandfather, Ernest Nowell.' He held out his hand to Uncle Rufus.

'Ernest,' said Uncle Rufus, 'I promise you we're going to do everything in our power to get Rachel better.'

Eve, Tom and Clovis stood with their backs against the wall, in anticipation for the comatose policewoman to cry out.

Anwaar walked over to the bed and took Rachel's hand. He stroked it and waited, but nothing happened. Rachel just breathed slowly, in and out. In and out.

Just as Anwaar was about to move away, Rachel's body began to arch upwards. Her back bent in a perfect curve, her head pushed down, embedded in the pillow, and her heels dug firmly into the mattress. A high-pitched scream came from deep inside her. A noise no one in the room would ever forget. Rachel's arms shot upwards, as if a huge electrical surge had bolted through her.

'What's happening?' shouted Ernest, rushing over to his granddaughter's bedside.

'Stand back, Mr Nowell!' commanded Anwaar.

Just as quickly as Rachel's unnerving movements had started, they stopped. Her body slowly relaxed back onto the bed. A quiet filled the room.

Slowly, Rachel began to sit up. Her eyes shot open, marble white, no pupils visible at all. It was a terrifying spectacle. She moved like a robot, facing the wall. Her mouth began to move, stretching and sawing from side to side, then the most awful noise escaped her lips.

'We are coming,' she growled. 'We will have our revenge. You know nothing and will never stop us.'

'Oh, my God!' whispered Ernest Nowell. 'That's not Rachel,' he murmured, staring in horror at the horrific sight before him.

Anwaar sidled up to the other side of the bed and put out a hand to look at the pulsating blue scar, visible now through her nightgown. Suddenly Rachel swivelled her head to look at him. She gurgled and spat in his face. Then, in a quick, violent motion, she lunged, growling like a demented wild animal. He moved quickly to one side and grabbed with both his arms, encircling her upper body in a bear hug. He began to chant something in the young woman's ear. At first it seemed his words were having no effect as she continued to screech and grunt, struggling to free herself. 'I am James, James Device,' she screeched. The body of PC Nowell tried one last time to free itself from Anwaar's grip, rearing up like a bird trying desperately to take flight, all the while biting and scratching. But Anwaar held fast and whispered more unrecognisable words into the young woman's ear. Whatever he said had the desired effect. PC Nowell's body at last began to relax, her eyes closed and she slumped back down onto the bed, once again beginning to breathe evenly and peacefully.

'Will someone tell me what's going on?' cried Ernest, who now was visibly shaking.

'Here, Mr Nowell, please sit down,' said Eve, who was also shaken. 'I'll get you some water.' Eve sat Ernest down in the plastic chair and began to pour him a beaker of water from a jug on the side table.

'Mr Nowell,' said Uncle Rufus. 'What we are dealing with here is possession. I'm afraid your granddaughter is a victim of some kind of . . . it seems witchcraft.'

Ernest Nowell was a logical man and had never believed in anything he couldn't see, hear or feel. But his brain couldn't deny what he had just seen, and he knew with all his heart that his Rachel was not the creature he had just witnessed. He also respected his old friend Inspector Rutherford, and if she said to trust these people, then that was what he must do.

'What can I do?' he asked meekly.

'For the moment,' replied Anwaar, 'just be here for her. She will be all right; it may take a little time, but we will get to the bottom of what this is, and get Rachel better.'

'So, whatever that thing inside Rachel is, will it come out again?' Ernest got up from his chair and moved to the foot of the bed, staring intently.

'She will sleep deeply now and for a long while. I've calmed the spirit inside her,' said Anwaar. 'Hopefully it will give us enough time to clear up this case.'

'In the meantime, Ernest, you must try to keep calm,' said Uncle Rufus. He placed his hand on the old man's shoulder. He felt so sorry for him. He wanted to do more but right now, he couldn't.

'We'll leave you now, Mr Nowell,' whispered Anwaar, 'but you must let us know if anything changes.'

'That I will,' said Mr Nowell, clearing his throat. He sat quietly by Rachel's bedside and held her limp hand whilst tears slid down his tired old face.

Everyone walked out, talking quietly to each other about the judge, Mr Law and the police officer, wondering how they could all possibly be connected.

Uncle Rufus was very concerned. This case was proving to be more than he had bargained for. His stomach was strong but that last scene in Rachel's room had been harrowing to watch, and he wondered whether it was too much for the young investigators.

Clovis, Eve and Tom all said that they were fine. 'That's what it's all about, isn't it, Uncle — I mean, hopefully we can help these poor people?'

'Indeed,' replied Uncle Rufus, smiling proudly at his niece and her two friends.

After a long walk down several corridors, they arrived at the children's ward, ready to visit the last victim.

A nurse greeted them pleasantly: 'Can I help you?'

'Yes,' said Uncle Rufus. 'We've come to see Jamie Drake.'

The nurse's face changed instantly. Her brow furrowed; lips tightened into a thin hard line. All was not well, it seemed.

'Ah, yes, well, I'm afraid he's not awake. Perhaps if you come back tomorrow?' It was clear that they were not welcome.

'Professor Pepper?' Everyone turned to see a tall, well-built man who looked like he hadn't slept in days. He stood in the doorway at the far end of the reception area.

'Yes?' answered Uncle Rufus, walking towards him.

'I'm Steve . . . Steve Drake . . . Jamie's dad.' He stuck his hand out for Uncle Rufus to shake. He looked dishevelled and exhausted. His clothes were crumpled, his face creased, grey, drained of colour. His salt-and-pepper hair was tangled, messy and unwashed.

'Thank God you've come!' said Steve. 'Me and my wife Molly have been waiting for you. Inspector Rutherford told us you'd be coming today.'

Steve pumped Uncle Rufus's hand and eyed the others, waiting for an introduction.

Taking his cue, Uncle Rufus gestured with one hand. 'This is Eve, Clovis and Tom, they are all part of my team, as is Mr Anwaar Saygh.'

Everyone nodded to Steve in turn. Eve smiled politely, and felt instantly sorry for him: he looked totally broken, lost and confused.

'Jamie's through here,' he said, pointing down the corridor.

'Er . . . Mr Drake?' shouted the nurse. 'They can't stay too long,' she warned.

'I know,' he replied in a defeated tone.

Anwaar was the last to pass the nurse. He gave her his best smile, eyes sparkling, white teeth shining. The result was almost comical. The poor young woman practically melted into her chair. Anwaar had that effect on most people.

'Have a most blessed day,' he whispered, his smooth voice purred at the nurse as he walked past.

Steve led Uncle Rufus and the others into a small room. A bank of monitors was stationed on either side of the bed, while tubes flowed down from drips into the small arm of Jamie Drake.

Everyone stood at the foot of the bed. The young boy lay on his back, his hair had been brushed off his face, and his skin was a terrible colour: pale, almost blue. A small thin vein could be seen throbbing in his neck.

His eyes were closed, and his puny arms were splayed out on either side of his lifeless body.

'He was on a ventilator,' said a woman in a chair by the bed. Her eyes were red and swollen. 'He can breathe on his own now,' she whispered. She picked up Jamie's small limp hand and stroked it gently.

Uncle Rufus spoke kindly. 'Hello, Molly,' he said. 'I know Inspector Rutherford has explained everything to you: what we do and how we can help, but to fully understand what has happened to Jamie, we need to ask you a couple of questions. Is that OK?'

Molly and Steve just nodded. They seemed confused, scared and exhausted.

'Can I ask,' began Uncle Rufus, 'about the item that Jamie unearthed?'

'The bottle?' sniffed Molly, wiping her nose with a tissue.

'Yes, where is it now?'

'It's back at the cottage, last time I saw it, it was on the floor in the kitchen,' said Steve. 'Weird-looking thing, it had stuff inside of it, some kind of liquid, and lots of little figures attached to the outside. We think, when Jamie opened it, he must have breathed in the fumes from the liquid inside.'

'And the ghost that you saw?' pressed Uncle Rufus.

Steve sucked in some air and ran a hand through his unruly hair. 'It was bloody terrifying, I can tell you. We both saw it. It was a dark shape at first, and the room . . . God, it went so cold, then the shape changed into this thing . . . a hideous old woman. It was like a nightmare coming towards us. I didn't believe in ghosts until this, and I tell you, if anyone says I'm making it up, I'll bloody thump 'em.'

Uncle Rufus smiled and said, 'Well, we believe you. We've seen more than our fair share of ghosts and know one hundred per cent that they are real. It's just sometimes the bad ones love to get attention by doing the most terrifying things. Try not to worry, we're here.' He motioned to the others. 'And along with Inspector Rutherford, we will do everything we can to help and find out what's happened to you and your young man.' Uncle Rufus then looked to Anwaar, who stepped around the side of the bed and stood close to Molly.

'Molly, if I may?' He spoke so softly that Eve, Tom and Clovis had to strain their ears to hear what he was saying. 'I need to see the burn mark.'

Molly gave a nod, and Anwaar carefully and slowly turned the bedsheet down. Everyone had seen the pictures of all the victims' burns in the case file and had witnessed a glimmer of them through the other patients' hospital gowns, but when Tom, Eve and Clovis saw Jamie's blue, puckered skin with their own eyes, it was a shock.

Uncle Rufus leaned over Anwaar's shoulder and looked in horror at the blue mark in the centre of Jamie's stomach.

Eve moved closer to the foot of the bed to get a better look at what they now understood to be a witch's mark. But who had put it there and why?

Suddenly, the quietness in the room exploded into a whirlwind of horrendous sounds. Jamie's body came to life. His exposed torso and stomach arched upwards, while his spindly white arms remained splayed outwards to his sides. They shook with energy, like they had been plugged into an electrical socket. All the machines around the bed began to bleep and ring loudly. The cacophony of ear-splitting noises filled the small room. Something was wrong, very wrong with the little boy.

'Jamie!' screeched Molly. 'Steve, get a doctor, quick!' Steve ran out of the room, calling for help.

Jamie's eyes abruptly flicked open: the eyeballs did not look human, they reminded Clovis of two white stone marbles rolling uncontrollably around in a couple of red raw eye sockets.

His little mouth stretched open, and a most terrible sound was emitted: an unholy, unnatural noise, guttural, like an animal snorting and grunting. It was deep, venomous and evil, nothing like the voice of a child. It was something not of this world: wicked, malevolent and most foul.

'You will never stop us, we will have our time, we will have our revenge,' the voice crowed. Jamie writhed and kicked, tossing his head from side to side, spittle beginning to form around the edges of his mouth. Molly screamed as Jamie spat at her, big bubbles of phlegm spraying over her shocked face.

Jamie, or whoever it was, began to laugh, the most heinous noise. Eve put her hands over her ears and scrunched her eyes shut. Clovis watched in amazement. Here it was again. Another possession. He had seen this kind of thing in documentaries but to see it so many times in one day was frightening, and yet exhilarating at the same time. His scientific brain was trying to fathom what was happening here. More research was needed when they all eventually got back to Whitechapel. He couldn't wait. His attention went to Tom, who wasn't watching the young boy at all. He was standing motionless, his eyes tightly closed. Clovis knew then that his friend was having one of his visions.

Anwaar stepped forward and quickly laid his hands on Jamie's shoulders and began to whisper some foreign words into the boy's ear. No one could hear what was being said, but yet again, it seemed to be having a calming effect on the boy.

'Look!' whispered Eve. She pointed to the burn mark on Jamie's stomach. 'It's reacting the same as the others.' The symbol had begun to pulsate, a blue light throbbed in and out all around the mark.

Uncle Rufus was concerned now for Tom. 'Can you hear me, Tom?'

Tom instantly opened his tear-filled eyes. The vision that

he had just seen had really upset him. But he quickly pulled himself together and whispered to Uncle Rufus, 'I'm OK, Professor.'

Suddenly Steve rushed into the room with two doctors and a nurse, who shouted for everyone to 'Get out!'

Anwaar turned to them calmly and said, 'Let me carry on, otherwise he will not last the night.'

The doctors didn't listen and tried to push Anwaar out of the way, but they couldn't move him. He was determined to stay and finish what he had started.

Molly screamed, 'Leave him. Let him help my baby.' She had become hysterical. Steve rushed to her side to try to comfort her.

The doctors, totally baffled at the scene unfolding in front of them, stood back and watched in horror as Jamie flailed, bucked and spat in the bed.

'Who are you?' Anwaar spoke quietly but with authority at the body, which was twisted in the bed.

'I'm Elizabeth, Elizabeth Device!' spat back the voice. It began to laugh again, deep, fiendish chuckles rumbling through the room. 'I curse you; I hex you. I curse you all!'

The room was silent as they watched the middle-eastern man with the unusual tattoos hold Jamie's head in place and whisper more incomprehensible words. He then took out of his waistcoat a tiny bottle of powder. Eve held her breath as she watched Anwaar blow a purplish coloured substance into his ear.

To everyone's relief, Jamie stopped moving and his body suddenly went limp.

'He will sleep now,' Anwaar said to no one in particular. 'But she,' he continued, 'Elizabeth, is not finished.'

The doctors looked at Anwaar in amazement, then jumped into action. One of them turned to Anwaar and said, 'If you've harmed this boy in any way, I shall be informing the police.'

'I don't think that will be necessary,' said Uncle Rufus. He gathered Clovis, Eve and Tom and walked them out into the corridor.

Anwaar spoke quietly to Molly and Steve and then followed the others. 'It's much worse than I thought,' he said, shaking his head.

'Yes, I agree,' said Uncle Rufus. 'We need to get to the source to find out exactly what is going on.' He stopped short when he noticed that Tom still looked very troubled. 'Tom? Are you all right? You saw something earlier, didn't you?'

'Yes, I'm fine,' he replied. 'I was getting some very strange images and emotions in my head, and they wouldn't go away.'

'What did you see?' asked Clovis.

'It was unclear at first but then all I could see was a rope. It was being placed over my head, and I saw a little girl, she was smiling and pointing at me.'

Uncle Rufus put his arm around Tom's shoulders and squeezed him. 'Are you sure you're all right, young man?'

'Yeah, don't worry, Professor, I'm OK,' smiled Tom, feeling a little better already.

'Good,' said Uncle Rufus. 'Try to remember the details, they may be important later.'

Steve and Molly walked out of Jamie's room and approached the small group. 'What just happened in there, Professor?'

Molly had her head down, crying.

'Well, it's clear that Jamie has been possessed by a negative entity.' Uncle Rufus looked about, aware that what he was saying sounded very odd indeed.

'Will he be all right now?' sniffed Molly, looking hopeful. Her hands shook as she pushed back a strand of hair that had escaped from her ponytail.

'All will be well,' reassured Anwaar. 'I've managed to push the entity back for now, but it won't stay subdued for long.'

'No,' said Uncle Rufus. 'I think we have to go to your cottage. We must find the bottle that Jamie discovered and go from there. It seems to me that all this strange, frightening behaviour and activity started as soon as Jamie unearthed that artefact. It must have some meaning.'

'All right,' said Steve. He dug into his jeans pocket and pulled out a set of keys. 'You'll need these to get in. Hopefully the door will open for you. It wouldn't for us, so I had to smash the window to get us all out.'

'Thank you,' said Uncle Rufus, putting the keys in his coat pocket. 'I have your number; I'll call you and let you know how we are getting on.'

'Jamie will sleep for a good twenty-four hours now,' said Anwaar. 'He will pull through.' He placed his hand on Steve's arm, smiling warmly.

As they walked out of the hospital, Clovis asked, 'Anwaar, why didn't you give the same powder to the others?'

'A good question,' replied Anwaar. 'The other possessions are strong but not as dangerous or as powerful as the boy's. For some reason the spirit of Elizabeth is much greater than the others. Hopefully when we find the bottle, I can discover more.'

Everyone was pleased to be out of the hospital and breathed in lungfuls of the cold December air. As they got closer to Albert, they could see a very excited face bobbing up and down. Boris was beside himself with joy at his friends' return.

Once they were all inside the van, Clovis set the sat nav to Steve and Molly's address and they set off in the direction of Malkins Cottage.

CHAPTER 10

A Haunted House and a Bottle of Fear

Uncle Rufus slowed Albert down as he steered over large potholes and uneven humps in the small country road.

'Where *is* this house? Talk about the middle of nowhere,' moaned Eve.

'The place where no one can hear you scream,' said Tom, putting on a ridiculous American accent.

'Not funny, Tom,' said Eve. She rolled her eyes and stared out of the window; this place had to be close, surely, she thought.

'It's got to be coming up soon,' sighed Uncle Rufus, crunching Albert's gears as he slowly manoeuvred the van round a massive hole in the road.

Anwaar smiled at his friend, sensing his frustration. He was also amused at the professor's handling of Albert. Mutterings, splutterings and deep concentration were etched all over Uncle Rufus's face as he tried to handle the large vehicle. Anwaar burst out laughing as he watched his friend accidently press the horn. A long, high-pitched *parp* bugled out, making the professor jump with fright.

'My friend, you and this machine are not as one,' chuckled Anwaar.

'He hates me,' replied Uncle Rufus, grimacing once more as he tried to change the gears.

'Is that it?' shouted Tom suddenly. He pointed to a small house off to the right of the road. Another smaller dirt track led up to the single-storey white cottage.

Uncle Rufus slammed on the brakes, and everyone lurched forward.

Crunching the van's gears into reverse, Uncle Rufus looked over his shoulder and slowly backed Albert up.

'Well spotted, Tom,' said Anwaar.

'That looks to me like it could very well be the place.' Uncle Rufus turned off the engine and jumped out. 'Come on then,' he said cheerfully. 'I'm certainly not going to attempt taking Albert up the drive. We'll have to walk. It's not far.'

Everyone followed Uncle Rufus towards the house but Eve lagged behind. As soon as she'd seen the cottage, she'd known there was something bad about it. She didn't know what it was, it was just a feeling. As she walked closer to the building, she tried to understand why the Drakes had chosen to live here. The house and garden were pretty enough, but it felt so isolated. She shivered as she walked on: it was as if the cottage were watching her. The windows were dark, reminding her of mean little eyes slyly judging them all. The trees surrounding the place were bare, the branches swaying in the breeze reminding Eve of long sinewy arms and clawed hands outstretched, readying themselves to grab and squeeze them all to death. Although in the middle of the countryside, Eve suddenly felt claustrophobic and edgy. If the Drakes' story was anything to go by, then really, they should be running in the opposite direction from this cottage, not about to go inside and investigate it. But if they could help Jamie and the other victims get better, then it had to be worth it. Eve shrugged off the negative thoughts and jogged to catch up with the others.

The group of ghost hunters stood at the front door. A new, shiny plaque, which had obviously just been screwed onto the wall, read in bold letters: *Malkins Cottage*.

'Right, then,' said Uncle Rufus. 'This is it.' He took the house keys from his pocket and unlocked the door. It swung open with an ominous creak. No one moved. Although the inside of the house looked pleasant enough, there was something stopping them from crossing the threshold. The echoes of Jamie's possessed demonic voice rang in all their ears. What were they about to step into? Tom gulped, Eve grabbed Clovis's sleeve, and Anwaar whispered something under his breath.

Uncle Rufus was the first to step inside, the sound of crunching from underfoot breaking the silence. Broken glass from the window was strewn all over the floor.

'Right,' said Uncle Rufus. 'Clovis, Tom, you take Boris and go and get the equipment from the van, meanwhile we'll clean up the glass.'

Whilst the three went quickly back up the drive to Albert, the others set about trying to find a dustpan and brush.

'Wow! It's cold in here,' exclaimed Eve, pulling the collar of her biker jacket around her ears.

'I'd say it's colder inside than outside,' said Anwaar, shivering. This was his first British winter since he had come back from Iran. He remembered how he used to pine for ice and snow when the sun blistered down on him in the scorching southern desert. But now he was here, all he craved was the sun to come out and heat up his freezing body.

'You all right?' Uncle Rufus asked him.

'Of course, just a little chilly,' he replied, cupping his hands together and blowing into them.

Clovis and Tom came back and joined the others in sweeping and picking up broken glass. Boris seemed happy enough sitting outside.

It wasn't long before the floor and surfaces were clear and safe, and Boris was allowed to enter.

'It must have been really scary, not being able to get out,' said Tom, wrapping the last of the glass in some old newspaper.

'Yeah, we know what it's like when doors won't open,' said Eve, reminding them of the times they too had experienced this frightening phenomenon — once in Eve's house, and then in the underground Nazi war rooms during their first investigation. It had been terrifying knowing that a spirit could deliberately lock them in.

'Put the bags on the countertop, please, boys,' commanded Uncle Rufus.

As soon as they'd done so, a loud bang thundered through the building.

'Nobody move,' instructed Uncle Rufus. He stood completely still, arms stretched out either side of his body.

'It could have been a draught,' whispered Clovis, always trying to be logical. 'I mean, this window is broken, so that could explain the bang, maybe a breeze shut a door?'

Eve leaned closer to her uncle, hoping that Clovis was right.

'Let's get the equipment out and begin our investigation,' said Uncle Rufus, satisfied that Clovis had made the right call.

Anwaar moved next to Tom, who was very quiet and nervously chewing his thumbnail.

'Can you sense anything?' Anwaar asked him quietly.

'Only that there's something wrong with this house. A darkness, it's evil, almost.'

Anwaar patted Tom's shoulder and said, 'If you get anything, anything at all, you must tell us straight away.'

'I will,' said Tom. 'I do think there's something cloaking itself, like it doesn't want to talk. You know, like it's hiding deep in the shadows, watching us. I don't like it, Anwaar.' Tom shook his head and went back to chewing on his thumb.

'It will be all right,' said Anwaar, smiling kindly at his young friend.

Everyone else brought out the ghost-hunting equipment: electromagnetic field meters, temperature guns, infrared cameras, tripods, the communication board, and the newest invention: the Crookes camera.

'Right,' said Uncle Rufus, busying himself with cables and leads, 'turn the electronic voice phenomena watches on, and clip the Go-Pro cameras onto your coats. Switch them to record now.'

Anwaar preferred his own practices when he was investigating the paranormal, he didn't feel the need for Uncle Rufus's devices — although he respected them and was always intrigued when his friend had developed a new invention. Anwaar smiled at his genius of a friend, but he preferred to work in his own way.

Whilst the others prepared, Anwaar walked slowly around the small cottage, breathing in the atmosphere as he looked in all the rooms. Boris snuffled behind him, burping and farting as he went. The house had two bedrooms, the first belonging to Molly and Steve, then further down was Jamie's room. Next to that was the bathroom at the end of the hallway. Coming back on the opposite side was the lounge, and then the kitchen. Now that Anwaar had seen the layout of the building and that one of the doors was closed, he had to agree with Clovis: perhaps the loud bang had indeed been a draught caused by the breeze coming through the broken window. It wasn't a large house, so it seemed plausible. Anwaar also realised that Tom was right: he too could sense something was here, but it wasn't going to give itself up so easily. He took a deep breath and joined the others in the kitchen, where he privately hoped for the best.

'Anything?' asked Eve, looking uncomfortable.

'No, nothing yet,' said Anwaar, shaking his head.

Eve was relieved. Of course a part of her was excited too, but after seeing Jamie in the hospital and hearing that voice, she was a bit spooked.

'Shall we set up the cameras in the rooms and the EMF meters, Professor?' asked Clovis, keen to get going.

'Yes, thank you, Clovis. You three crack on with that, whilst I get the Crookes camera ready.'

'Keep your eyes open for the glass bottle,' said Anwaar, helping Uncle Rufus unwind the cable to the Crookes camera. 'Steve described it as weird-looking, with little white figures attached to it, so it shouldn't be hard to recognise.'

'Yes,' agreed Uncle Rufus. 'He said the last time they saw it was in the kitchen, but I've had a look and I can't see it.'

Eve, Tom and Clovis took some equipment and began to set it up in all the rooms. They came to Jamie's room last. Posters of superheroes and famous footballers filled the walls. Shelves opposite the single bed were lined up with small painted figures, cars and planes. And there, sitting at the back, was a strange-looking glass bottle.

'Is this it?' asked Eve. She stared hard at the object. It was really unusual and reminded her of something her uncle might bring home from one of his far-away expeditions.

The glass bottle was a peculiar shape. It was the same height as a can of Coke, but it had two blown-out curved parts, one halfway down and the other at the bottom. The glass was dark blue, and a dirty cord had been wound around its neck; hanging off the cord were tiny white human figures. A black seal had once been on the top but now the remains of it hung wilted and cracked down one side. Inside the glass, a spiral of something long and plaited floated in a dark liquid. Eve put her face closer to the bottom of the bottle and also noticed little fragments of what looked like breadcrumbs.

'What's all that inside it?' she asked, not sure she wanted to hear the answer.

'Not sure, but it looks creepy as hell,' said Tom. He stared at it, then tentatively reached his hands out to take it, but as soon as his fingers touched the blue glass, he snatched them away as if he'd been blasted with an electric shock. A feeling so awful and dark had rushed through his entire body. His head began to pound, his hands started to shake, and his skin felt as if it were on fire.

'What's wrong, Tom?' asked Eve, concerned. Getting no response, she intuitively reached up for the bottle herself and instantly Tom snapped, 'No, Eve!'

Startled, she snatched her hands away. 'What the hell, Tom? You scared me.'

'What is it?' asked Clovis. He knew his friend was picking up on something. 'Go on, Tom, what is it? Can you see something?' he asked gently.

'Something's not right about it. I dunno what it is, but it . . . it . . .' Tom shivered. 'It's evil.'

'It's just a bottle, Tom,' said Clovis, trying to soothe his friend. 'An inanimate object cannot possibly be evil, surely?'

'Well, after what Tom's just said,' pouted Eve, 'there's no way I'm touching that thing. We all know anything's possible. We've seen stuff with our own eyes that most people would never even imagine. C'mon, Clovis, you've got to agree with me.'

'Don't get me wrong, I agree with you both, but I'm not scared of a little bottle. It doesn't look evil to me. C'mon, I'll take it to the professor,' said Clovis. He carefully picked up the glass vessel and brought it down from the shelf at arm's length.

'Put it down,' commanded Uncle Rufus.

Boris, Anwaar and Uncle Rufus were standing in the doorway. Boris made everyone jump as he began to bark; it was clear he was agitated by something. Everyone followed the dog's stare and realised he was looking directly at the bottle.

As Clovis carefully placed the object back on the shelf, Tom and Eve began to step slowly back towards the door. No one said anything, the only noise to be heard was the incessant deep bark from Boris.

Uncle Rufus and Anwaar walked cautiously towards the bottle. Anwaar tilted his head to one side and stared intently at it. Uncle Rufus grabbed his stills camera and began to take photos.

The young ghost hunters watched the backs of the two men, as Anwaar began to utter some incomprehensible words.

'What's he saying?' murmured Tom.

'I think it's Arabic, but I'm not quite sure,' whispered Clovis, frustrated at not being able to understand.

Uncle Rufus put his camera away and then brought out his EMF meter and began to wave it slowly all around the glass container. Instantly the little machine's lights began to flash, and the static screeching noise it emitted was at its highest, indicating to everyone that a strange and supernatural force was definitely present.

Boris was still looking at the bottle; his fur had risen into sharp bristles, and he growled deeply over and over again.

'It's all right, Boris,' cooed Eve, trying to comfort him. She kneeled by his side and began to stroke the dog's small ears.

Anwaar turned to them: 'No one must touch this bottle.'

'Why? And why are Boris and the EMF going crazy?' said Eve, not at all liking what she was seeing. Anwaar and her uncle didn't have to worry, there was no way she was going to go anywhere near that thing again.

'It's a witch's bottle,' replied Uncle Rufus, putting the EMF meter back into his pocket.

'Oh, I've heard of those,' said Clovis, his voice giving away his enthusiasm. Eve and Tom looked at each other, not surprised at all that their friend knew about such things.

Clovis pushed his glasses back up the bridge of his nose, a habit he usually did before an informative monologue.

Tom whispered cheekily in his ear, 'Is this the short version?' Clovis just rolled his eyes in reply, sighed and began to explain.

'Objects like these were quite commonplace in the seventeenth century. Most people used them to protect themselves from a witch's curse or spell. The bottles were usually made from clay; sometimes jugs or urns were used. Inside these bottles, a victim, someone who believed they were under threat from a witch, would put some of their own hair, a piece of their clothing, teeth and metal nails, and then . . .

wait for it . . .' Clovis grinned, his handsome face crinkling in amusement.

'Then . . . what?' asked Eve, shaking her head in frustration.

'. . . They would wee in it,' concluded Clovis, with a satisfied grin.

'Urgh, that's gross!' said Eve.

'But why?' asked Tom.

'Apparently,' continued Clovis, 'it was believed that the essence of that person would then be sealed in the bottle, normally by wax, and buried deep beneath the ground. Some of these bottles were found stuffed up chimneys in old houses, as the victims believed that any metal placed inside the bottle would heat the ingredients up, making the antidote to the witch's curse more effective. They believed that by undergoing this practice, a witch would never be able to curse or inflict any harm.'

'Well done, Clovis,' smiled Uncle Rufus proudly. 'That is exactly what we have here. The real genuine article. How absolutely fascinating.'

'But I'm afraid, Professor,' said Anwaar, still staring at the artefact, 'that this is no ordinary witch's bottle, no . . . not ordinary at all.' He turned to look at everyone, his tattooed face creased with worry. 'In fact, I would say, my friends, that this witch's bottle is the work of some very powerful dark magic. This bottle was created for something completely different, and I believe that this particular one once housed the souls that are now possessing our victims, and some of their negative energy is still present in and around it. And I also know that this bottle has been moved recently — and not by any mortal.'

At that announcement, everyone took a step back, including Boris. Anwaar was staring at the bottle with his head now tilted to the other side. 'This witch's bottle was made with hate and revenge. I think we need to speak to the Witchcraft department at the SPI, Professor, to confirm my suspicions. I suspect this witch's bottle was made to bind souls together, and if I'm right, I sense five souls were all placed inside this artefact. Something terrible is at play here. I can feel the residual energy coming off it.' Anwaar closed his eyes and sucked in some air. 'Yes, definitely five souls, and their energies that once were light, are now very dark.'

Anwaar opened his eyes. He brought his voice down to a low whisper. 'I fear that Jamie has released all the energies of those souls and they have entered our victims' bodies.' He unzipped his coat and pulled a small blue crystal from inside his waistcoat. Tom, Eve and Clovis watched in amazement as he placed the curious blue stone on top of the bottle. The little round stone began to shake and vibrate, and slowly started to melt, folding itself over the mouth of the bottle and forming a seal.

'There,' said Anwaar, satisfied. 'It's closed for now.'

Tom suddenly burst out, 'Only *four* spirits are possessing bodies!' Everyone looked at him as he stood, visibly shaking.

His eyes were clenched tight as he described the feelings rushing around in his head.

'The fifth soul is free,' he breathed. 'Its energy is so *strong*.

I can feel its rage. It's controlling the others and it's here! It's so close.' He shouted out the words and suddenly his lips twisted into a thin spiteful line. He frowned and clenched his teeth.

Sensing that Tom was getting too close to the source of negative energy, Anwaar grabbed him by his shoulders and spoke quietly to him. 'Tom, I want you to listen to me. It's Anwaar, take a deep breath and open your eyes.'

Recognising the familiar voice, Tom did as Anwaar instructed. He took a huge gulp of air and slowly opened his eyes.

'Look at me,' instructed Anwaar, staring intently at him. 'What did you see?'

Tom blinked and whispered fearfully, 'It was terrible: a darkness, a black mist. I felt it would squeeze the life out of me.'

CHAPTER 11

A Knife and a Hanged Boy

Just as Anwaar managed to bring Tom round, something came flying into the bedroom. Whatever it was made an almighty clatter, bringing all of Jamie's toy cars and figures on the shelf smashing onto the floor.

Eve screamed and instantly clutched at the nearest thing to her, which much to her embarrassment, happened to be Anwaar.

Clovis and Tom had cried out in shock and grabbed each other too, and Boris had begun to bark excitedly. Uncle Rufus just turned slowly around to see what had made all the commotion. The noise had been so loud that nobody had heard the EMF meters screeching.

'What the hell was that?' gasped Eve, looking wildly about the room.

'I've no idea,' replied Uncle Rufus. 'Are you all right?'

Everyone confirmed that they were, including Anwaar, who had taken his coat off and rolled the bottle up inside it. He carefully placed the thick wad of material under his arm to protect it.

'This is not good,' said Tom. He had begun to shake again.

Not because of the cold, but because he had seen something rather disturbing. 'Look!' he whispered, pointing to something glinting on the carpet in the corner of the room. 'It wasn't there before, I know that for certain.' He bent down to look more closely at the object.

Uncle Rufus picked up the huge carving knife and held it to the light, turning it over carefully in the palm of his hand.

Eve recoiled at the sight of it. 'Oh . . . my . . . God!' she whispered, visibly shaken by the realisation that it had been thrown at them.

'Are we sure that wasn't there before?' asked Clovis.

Eve and Tom gave him a disparaging look.

'I'm just checking,' he said, looking a little hurt.

'Quite right too, Clovis,' said Uncle Rufus. 'I think I'll take this outside and any other sharp implements I can find.' He held the knife by the handle between his finger and thumb as if the knife itself were contaminated by some terrible disease. He walked carefully with the blade facing downwards, but as soon as he reached the doorway, an awful noise exploded all around them. Uncle Rufus stopped dead in his tracks for a second.

'That was a woman's laugh,' said Eve, still staying close to Anwaar.

'It most certainly was,' replied Anwaar, 'and it wasn't a pleasant one.'

'Everyone,' hissed Uncle Rufus, who was now halfway down the hallway, facing the kitchen doorway. 'I think you're going to want to see this.' And he waved them over.

'Temperature's dropping,' said Clovis, the little machine had beeped to let him know how many degrees it had fallen. Then the EMF meters began to squawk. A sign that a ghost or something paranormal was with them.

Clovis, Tom, Eve and Anwaar walked up behind Uncle Rufus to see what was causing the machines to fluctuate.

And there at the other end of the hallway, standing in the doorway of the kitchen, was a ghost. A full-bodied apparition.

'Can we all see it?' whispered Uncle Rufus excitedly.

Eve and Tom nodded. Clovis was having trouble because as soon as he confirmed that he could, his glasses began to steam up with excitement. He took them off quickly, wiped them on the front of his coat and placed them hastily back onto the bridge of his nose. There she was, in all her glory. A wonderful, ghostly manifestation.

Anwaar placed his hand on Uncle Rufus's shoulder and whispered into his ear. 'My gut tells me she is responsible for the flying knife.'

Uncle Rufus nodded in agreement.

The ghost was standing side on, and it was clear that she was from a time long past. Her clothes were ragged and torn.

Tom suddenly blurted out, 'It's Demdike.' The name had shot into his head, but in a voice that was scratchy and menacing. It hissed again: *'Old . . . Dem . . . dike.'*

'Well done, Tom,' said Uncle Rufus, his gaze fixed on the ghostly sight. 'Can you get anything else?' he asked.

'Nothing, it's like . . . all I can hear is static.' Tom had scrunched his eyes shut in concentration. 'It's like she's blocking me. She's not happy with us being here, that much I can tell.'

'No kidding,' said Eve sarcastically under her breath. She bent down and stroked Boris's thick, sturdy body. The little dog had pushed his head in between their legs, needing to get a better look at the energy that was floating in the hallway. Suddenly on stalk mode, he had locked onto the ghost and was ready to attack. Sensing Boris's mood, Eve put her fingers through his collar.

'Old Demdike,' said Clovis, thinking hard. 'She was definitely one of the Pendle witches. If I remember rightly, although all the other Pendle witches denied being witches or dealing in witchcraft, Old Demdike admitted that she *was* a witch. This must be her!' he cried, staring intently at the apparition in front of him. 'This is Old Demdike, the true witch.'

'Brilliant, Clovis,' said Uncle Rufus. 'Well remembered.' Slowly Uncle Rufus took his rucksack off his back and delved inside to get the Crookes camera. He didn't have time to get the tripod up, so held the camera in position, trying to keep as still as possible. He slid his glasses onto the top of his head, squinted through one eye and brought one of the many lenses down in front of the eyepiece.

'Come on,' he murmured to the ghost. 'Turn around.'

Still, the ghost didn't move, although her old, tattered skirt and coat fluttered slightly in an ethereal breeze.

'Shall I call her name?' asked Tom nervously.

'Please do,' whispered back Uncle Rufus, his thumb ready to press the button on the camera's cable.

'Be careful and speak softly,' warned Anwaar.

But Boris ruined the moment by escaping Eve's tight grip. He pelted down the hallway, snarling and barking at the spirit.

'Boris!' shouted Eve.

The ghost yanked its head around and, in that moment, the young ghost hunters gasped. She was old, her face wrinkled, teeth rotten. Her hair was tied up on top of her head, like a scraggy, grey bird's nest. Tom cringed as he noticed the warts covering her face. But it was her eyes that were the scariest: dark holes, a soul riddled with loathing and revenge.

'She's not a pretty sight, is she?' mused Uncle Rufus, who winced as he continued to look through the lens.

'Boris, come here,' said Eve through gritted teeth.

Boris did no such thing. He stood in front of the apparition, in attack mode, fur on end, continually barking.

Suddenly the apparition of the woman moved. She turned her whole body to face Boris and then slowly brought her hand up. A long crooked forefinger pointed straight at him, and then smiling wickedly, she whispered some strange-sounding words.

'Frey . . . a . . . la . . . groog . . . shy . . . visage.' As the last word was hissed, the old crone pushed her ridged, taloned finger in between Boris's eyes. Instantly a flash of intense dark green light fizzed and flashed around his head. Straight away the brave bulldog whined and tried to run back to the others, but kept banging and crashing into the walls. Eve dashed forward and grabbed him.

The ghostly old hag floated up the hallway towards them all, her black-eyed gaze locked onto the group. She flung her arms into the air and rushed forwards. And her strangulated vile voice screeched: 'Leave!'

Uncle Rufus heard the beep, a sign that the camera could get the shot and he pressed the button. A huge plume of white powder projected into the air from the little copper spout. The camera then signalled that the picture was being developed.

Everyone had ducked down close to the floor. They waited for the powder to settle before looking to see if the ghost had disappeared. As the final specks of fine powder fell to the ground, it was clear the apparition had dissipated, although the horrific sound of her cackle still echoed around the house. Slowly but surely, the horrendous noise began to fade.

'Has she gone?' breathed Eve.

'I think so,' said Uncle Rufus, standing up and brushing the powder off his clothes. 'The machines aren't fluctuating any more, and the temperature is returning to normal.'

'Bloody hell,' said Tom, his voice shaking.

'Look at Boris!' said Eve, cuddling the poor dog, who was shaking in terror. She waved her hand in front of his face, but he didn't react.

'Let me take a look,' said Anwaar. He kneeled on the floor and cupped the bulldog's face gently in his hands. 'She's blinded him,' he said quietly.

'She's done what?' said Uncle Rufus, sounding panicked. He joined Eve and Anwaar on the floor and looked at his dog's eyes carefully.

'Good God, you're right, Anwaar. Can you do something?' asked Uncle Rufus, now visibly upset.

'Yes, don't worry, Professor.' Anwaar stood up, opened his coat and unbuttoned his waistcoat to reveal many little pockets holding lots of different vials and crystals. 'This one should do the trick,' he smiled. 'Now, all we have to do is get him to drink the mixture.'

'What about pouring it onto one of his treats?' suggested Eve.

'Good idea,' said Anwaar.

Eve took a treat out of her coat pocket and passed it to Anwaar.

Everyone watched as he dropped a pink-looking liquid on top of the biscuit before placing it gently under Boris's nose so he could smell it. Instantly he opened his big mouth and gobbled it down whole.

'There, he'll be able to see almost immediately,' said Anwaar satisfied.

'Have you got a cure for everything in that waistcoat?' asked Tom.

'It's my life's work,' replied Anwaar, buttoning it back up.

'Do you think the ghost was after the bottle?' asked Tom.

'I'm not sure,' said Anwaar. He held the witch's bottle close; he knew that the SPI would want to analyse all its elements. He had known of witch's bottles before, but not one that could bind souls and keep them entrapped inside for eternity. This bottle was different.

'Look, the photo's developed,' said Clovis, pulling the piece of celluloid out of the front of the camera and handing it to Uncle Rufus.

'Isn't she a pretty picture?' said Tom mockingly.

Everyone leaned in to have a look at the image the Crookes camera had caught.

'Clovis, before her image disappears,' said Uncle Rufus, 'take a picture of it on your phone. There might be something we've missed that the Crookes camera has caught, perhaps something to verify her identity.' Clovis did just that, but when he went to take the shot on the phone, it revealed nothing but blackness.

'Argh,' said Clovis in frustration. 'I'm afraid the image won't transfer onto modern tech, Professor.'

'Something else to work on, I suppose,' said Uncle Rufus in frustration. 'Right, I think we've encountered enough paranormal activity for one day, it's time to get out of here.'

They all packed the ghost-hunting equipment up, and Anwaar placed the bottle, still safely rolled up in his coat, inside one of the kit bags. Everyone began to make their way towards the cottage door.

Suddenly the front door slammed shut in front of them.

Old Demdike's ghostly voice rumbled eerily around the building once more.

There are eleven but only five will rise,
Those who condemned us, shall be our prize,
On the night of the blood moon, where children make their
*   play,*
We shall bind together, and the world you know will pay.'

'Stand still!' barked Uncle Rufus. 'No one move a muscle.'

'She's close,' whispered Anwaar, looking around him. 'Too close.'

Suddenly Tom dropped to his knees. His own fingers were grappled around his throat. Gurgling, coughing and choking, he desperately tried to breathe.

Anwaar instantly went into action and grabbed him, carrying him through the broken window, laying him on the snow-covered grass outside. The others quickly followed.

Tom was still gasping for air, his eyes bulging, hands clawing at his neck, as if he were trying to get something off. Eve and Clovis watched on helplessly while their friend struggled.

Anwaar opened his waistcoat again and pulled out another small vial of liquid. With Uncle Rufus's help, he tipped Tom's head back and poured the clear fluid into his mouth. He took out a long, white, pointed crystal. Eve and Clovis had seen Anwaar use this strange and magical stone before during a previous investigation.

Anwaar drew the tip of the crystal around Tom's throat. Then Uncle Rufus and Anwaar tilted Tom's body forward so he could move the crystal around the back of Tom's neck. Around and around he went with the strange implement.

Eve and Clovis watched in amazement as Anwaar whispered some mystical words, whilst the crystal began to emit a beautiful white light. A thick string of silver thread pulsed and crept all around Tom's neck and then the strange substance disappeared into Tom's skin.

When Anwaar stopped whispering the foreign words, Tom's body relaxed and he took a deep, long-awaited breath.

Tom opened his eyes to see everyone standing over him anxiously. Anwaar was putting something back into his waistcoat.

'Are you all right?' asked Uncle Rufus, looking very worried. 'You gave us quite a fright, young man.'

'I think so. All I could see was a rope being put over my neck and then I felt the floor give way, like something was kicked from under me. I couldn't breathe, I knew I was dying and yet all I could see was a little girl smiling at me. She was watching me hang!'

CHAPTER 12

The Discovery of Witches and Some Old Maps

The van pulled up in front of The Safe Haven hotel, and all its occupants got out quickly, relieved to be away from Malkins Cottage and its terrifying ghostly inhabitant.

Gerry and Stan were there to greet them. As soon as they saw Tom, they both knew instantly that something bad had happened.

'Get caught in that last air raid, did we? Bit of a bad one, that,' said Stan, shaking his head in sympathy.

'I'll put the kettle on, a dose of hot sweet tea will soon get some colour back in those cheeks,' said Gerry, trying to lighten the mood.

'Fire's going good in the front room,' added Stan. 'Why don't you all go in there and relax a bit and we'll bring you through something to eat. Gerry's managed to do one of her sponges. That will put a spring back in your step, young Tom, eh?'

'I need it,' croaked Tom, smiling weakly and rubbing at his neck.

Uncle Rufus went into the front room and slumped down

into the comfy armchair. Eve, Tom and Clovis made for the inviting sofa and Anwaar warmed himself in front of the blazing fire.

Boris, pleased to be back in the cosy house, yawned, smacked his chops and flopped down at Uncle Rufus's feet.

'Are you sure she can't follow us back here?' asked Eve, nervously looking at Tom.

'No, my dear, certainly not,' assured Uncle Rufus. 'As I said, this place is totally protected from any negative spirits. These time slip locations are truly magnificent, a complete bubble of safety.' Uncle Rufus placed his head back and closed his eyes for a moment. Eve noticed his foot tapping and she knew he was thinking. She wondered what about. She had a sneaking suspicion that he was concocting a plan.

Anwaar also seemed to know what Uncle Rufus was doing.

'So, my friend, what's the plan?'

Uncle Rufus's eyes shot open, and he suddenly jumped up and began to walk around the room with renewed vigour: Head down, hands behind his back, round and round the dining table. Eve and the others knew they were in for a long brainstorming session.

'Right, chaps,' said Uncle Rufus eventually, still walking around the table. 'We need to get all the information we have gathered so far and try to get to the bottom of this appalling phenomenon.'

Just then Gerry and Stan entered the room with a tray of tea, sandwiches and sponge cake.

Instantly Clovis, Tom, Eve and Boris got up and followed the food and drink to the table.

'Gerry, Stan? I know you have many books in your library, but would you happen to have any on the witches of Pendle?'

'Ooh, let me think,' said Gerry, pausing briefly from pouring the tea. Her bright red lips pursed as she thought, then something seemed to spark in her mind as she put the teapot down and smiled. 'Stan? Aren't there some books and stuff about those witches on the top shelf?'

'Aye,' confirmed Stan. 'That's right, one of your colleagues brought them here a while back. If my memory serves me right, we have quite a few, including the transcript of the trial itself. Nasty business, that,' he said.

'That's wonderful, would you mind if we had a look at them?' asked Uncle Rufus.

'Of course, we'll go and get them for you now,' said Gerry, patting the curls on her head.

Uncle Rufus looked very excited. Gerry and Stan bustled out of the room, chattering quietly between themselves as to the precise whereabouts of the books.

Clovis mumbled something incomprehensible as he was chewing, crumbs fell from his lips, which he tried in vain to catch with his hands. He was starving as usual, and had managed to stick two sandwiches into his mouth at the same time.

'What did you say, Clovis?' asked Eve, picking up a cup of tea.

'He said,' laughed Tom, 'that he's remembering more about

the Pendle witches.' It always amazed Eve how Tom could understand Clovis when he spoke with his mouth full.

'*There's* a surprise,' grinned Eve. 'It's lucky they've got some Pendle witch books here,' she added.

'Not luck at all. Every Safe Haven hotel has its own fabulously-stocked library,' said Uncle Rufus proudly.

'Is that because there's no Wi-Fi here?' asked Tom.

'Precisely,' answered Anwaar.

'And I know you three won't agree with me,' said Uncle Rufus, 'but I love the feel of books, the smell of them, the sound when the pages are turned. I much prefer getting information that way than from the internet, although I do recognise that cyberspace definitely has its uses when I'm researching something. For now, though, let's just enjoy doing it the old-fashioned way.' The teenagers rolled their eyes but smiled. Uncle Rufus pulled a chair out at the table and sat down. 'Besides, it's far more comfortable in here than in Albert. More tea?'

Everyone tucked in and even though the food was a little tasteless, it was greatly appreciated, especially by Clovis, who couldn't get enough of the Spam and powdered egg sandwiches.

Tom had seemingly recovered from his terrifying ordeal. He did sound a little hoarse, but everyone was relieved to see that he was smiling as he stuffed his face with the unusual but much-needed food.

'So, this is the sort of food that was available during the war with rationing?' said Eve, nibbling on a Spam sandwich.

'Indeed,' said Uncle Rufus.

The door slowly opened to reveal Stan's bulk walking backwards into the room. In his arms was a pile of books stacked precariously. He wobbled in, followed by Gerry, who carried lots of rolls of paper.

Anwaar shot forwards and helped Stan while Eve quickly made space on the table. One by one Stan unloaded the books and Gerry dropped the rolls, which turned out to be lots of old-looking maps onto the tabletop.

'Every house in the Pendle area will have a few books on these lasses. There's loads there, plus we found some old maps of the Pendle Forest area. Will that do?'

'My dearest Stan, this is first rate! Absolute top notch,' said Uncle Rufus, patting Stan on the back.

'Rightio,' said Stan, wiping a little perspiration off his brow.

'We'll leave you to it then,' said Gerry, giving the coals in the fireplace a stoke before shutting the door.

Everyone immediately began to look at the books.

'*The Discovery of Witches* by Thomas Potts,' said Tom, flicking through a very old volume.

'This looks a bit serious,' said Eve. '*Malleus Maleficarum, the Hammer of Witches*.' She turned the old copy over in her hands.

'Look at this one,' said Clovis. 'It's by King James the First, *Daemonologie*. What's that about?'

'Some of these books are about witches,' said Uncle Rufus, 'and more importantly how to find one. You must remember, in the sixteen hundreds the country was terrified of witches and their magic, especially King James, who wrote a book on the subject, the very one you have there. It describes the many ways of finding a witch. Courtrooms around the country used this as a guide to capturing, putting on trial and executing many men and women, most of whom were innocent. This one,' he said, picking up a thin book, '*The Wonderful Discovery of Witches in the County of Lancaster*, looks like an account of the sixteen-twelve Pendle witch trials.'

'Look at these maps, they're amazing,' said Clovis, chomping on another sandwich. 'The date at the top here says sixteen-twelve, and this looks to be the city of Lancaster.'

'So were the witches of Pendle real witches?' asked Eve, her eyes wide with fascination. She was very intrigued by the whole witch thing, but admittedly very scared. Having seen the ghost of one today and witnessing what that ghost was capable of made Eve tremble just thinking of it. She looked over at Anwaar and thought how lucky they were to have him with them. If he hadn't been there earlier when Boris was blinded or when poor Tom was attacked, what would they have done? Tom could have died!

'Most people at the time believed the Pendle witches to be real, yes, but today we know that most of them were innocent,' said Uncle Rufus, sipping at his tea.

'It says here,' said Tom, who'd plonked himself next to Uncle Rufus, 'that eight women and two men were found guilty of witchcraft and hanged.' Tom went quiet, engrossed, as he continued to read.

Clovis pulled up a chair opposite Uncle Rufus and began to read out loud from another book, *Pendle and its Witches*.

'On the twentieth of August, sixteen-twelve, in the courts at Lancaster Castle, eight women and two men were found guilty of witchcraft after a two day trial and hanged. One woman, Elizabeth Southernes, also known as Old Demdike, admitted to the prosecuter that she was indeed a witch and, at the age of eighty, died in her prison cell before coming to trial.'

'Oh my God!' shouted Eve. 'That's the ghost, the ghost of the old woman in the cottage.'

Anwaar sat down next to Uncle Rufus and said quietly, 'So, it's really true, my friend. Just as I feared. It's witchcraft we're dealing with, and I fear at its darkest.'

Everyone's heads jolted up. Anwar's statement was a little worrying, to say the least.

'Right,' said Uncle Rufus. 'We will only understand what's really going on here when we have all the facts laid out in front of us. So, let's begin: what have we got with regards to the Drake family, what information do we have so far?'

'Well,' said Eve, 'we know that Jamie changed when he found the bottle.'

'The bottle,' said Anwaar, 'is safe in the van. I have taken a picture of it and sent it to the SPI. They will come back with more information for us, hopefully later.'

'Why is the bottle so important?' asked Clovis, leaning forward in his chair.

'When you found the bottle,' said Anwaar, 'the seal was broken. That means that Jamie had opened it, and unbeknown to him, the poor boy released dark spirits into our plane of existence. As far as the souls are concerned, I don't think they need the bottle again, but that's not to say *we* might not need it. The bottle was created to contain souls until the time was right for them to be released.'

'But why?' asked Tom, looking a little lost.

'My guess,' said Uncle Rufus, 'is that the strongest soul, Old Demdike, is responsible for making the bottle. I'm thinking, and tell me if I'm going off-track here, Anwaar, that she knew, *foresaw* what was about to happen to them all. She was a true witch, yes, so in her mind she wanted to protect her family and friends. Knowing what she did, she planned and schemed to get revenge, on all the people who were responsible for her demise. Imagine being alone in a dark prison cell, knowing what was about to happen to them all. She must have been so enraged and terrified. But she went to her death knowing that one day she and four of her companions would rise up and take their vengeance.'

'Who are these souls then?' asked Eve, fascinated.

'Spirits of some of the other hanged witches, of course,' said Clovis.

'Well, we know that one of them, Old Demdike, is haunting Malkins Cottage,' said Anwaar. 'But I firmly believe that four of them have possessed our victims in the hospital. If I'm right, we are not just dealing with the dark forces of witchcraft, but we are witnessing full-blown possession.'

'So, do you think that the ghost we saw today, Old Demdike, do you think that she's definitely the catalyst?' asked Clovis.

'I'm sure of it,' said Tom suddenly. 'She's incredibly strong and powerful. I could feel her anger bubbling inside of me. I tried so hard to push her energy away, but I'm afraid I'm not strong enough yet to deal with an energy like hers, and that was when I felt something around my neck.' Tom's hands shook at the memory of the ghostly strangulation he had experienced. He placed his cup down on the table and sighed. 'I never want to go through that again.'

Anwaar placed a hand over his and patted it. 'You won't,' he said confidently.

'I wonder if she wanted you to feel what the Pendle witches went through during their death?' said Eve thoughtfully. 'I mean, was she making you go through a hanging?'

'Good thinking, Eve,' said Uncle Rufus, 'and yes, I believe you could be right. Anwaar, would you agree?'

'I think so,' replied Anwaar, standing up and drawing too close to the fire. How his trousers hadn't gone up in flames was a miracle.

'OK, so we have our starting point. The witch called Old Demdike, the one in Malkins Cottage, she seems to be the instigator.'

'Hey, everyone, look at this.' Clovis had rolled out one of the oldest-looking maps and had placed a teacup at one end of the paper and a saucer on the other to hold it in place. Clovis pointed to the centre with his forefinger. 'This shows the location of a place called Malkins Tower, which allegedly was where Old Demdike and her family lived. The old cottage isn't there any more, but if I'm right, look at *this* map.' Clovis then took a similar map and placed it over the top, the date at the top of the paper said *1972.*

'Will you look at that!' said Uncle Rufus happily.

Everyone stared: the Drakes' cottage was shown to overlay the faint image of the original Malkins Tower cottage.

'Well, that answers my main question,' said Eve, looking satisfied.

'Which was?' asked Clovis.

'Well, why there? Why was the bottle discovered in the garden of that old house? It's been bugging me. But now we know it's because Demdike's house used to be in that exact spot.'

'Inspector Rutherford told me that the house had been empty since the nineteen-seventies, apparently no one has been able to live there. Everyone always said they felt uncomfortable inside it. Now we know why,' said Uncle Rufus. 'It seems Old Demdike's energy was waiting for someone to find the bottle and it just so happened to be an innocent little boy who she could influence into discovering it.'

'But to what end? Is revenge the only reason?' said Anwaar, as much to himself as to his friends.

'Tom, what was the ghost's name at the castle again? It was Jennet something, wasn't it?' asked Uncle Rufus, flicking through his notebook.

Tom closed his eyes, the ghost's face flashed before him, and he heard her once more whisper her name. 'Jennet . . . Jennet Device,' said Tom quietly.

'Here she is,' said Clovis, and he began to read out loud

from one of the books again. 'I knew it! First in the dock was an eighty-year-old woman known locally as Chattox or Ann Whittle. She was accused of the murder of Robert Nutter. Then Elizabeth Device stood trial, accused of three counts of murder using witchcraft. Elizabeth's nine-year-old daughter, Jennet, was brought into the court, placed on a bench and asked if she thought her mother, Elizabeth Device, sister, Alizon Device, brother, James Device and grandmother Old Demdike were witches. She said that they were and then was asked to describe some of the acts that her family had all taken part in on a Sabbath in Malkin Tower. Young Jennet described how her family and some friends had all summoned spirits and made poppet dolls together. During this meeting of the supposed witches, they had allegedly conspired to blow up Lancaster Castle. Jennet also spoke of all the witches mounting ponies and flying off, disappearing into the night sky. She even told the court of how her mother had a familiar, a spirit of a large brown dog called Ball. According to this, Elizabeth, Jennet's mother, was so furious at her daughter, she screamed at the court to take the nine-year-old outside.'

'Is there a list of names there, of the people who were hanged?' asked Uncle Rufus.

'Yes, just a sec,' said Clovis, quickly thumbing through the book. 'Ah, here it is . . . Ann Whittle, or Chattox, Elizabeth Device, James Device, Ann Redfearne, Alice Nutter, Isabel Roby, Katherine Hewitt, John Bullcock, Jane Bullcock, Alizon Device and of course we now know Old Demdike died in prison.'

'We heard some of those names in the hospital,' said Eve.

'You're right,' said Uncle Rufus.

'Alizon Device, that was one,' whispered Tom. 'Her voice came from Mr Law.'

'And Chattox, was inside Judge Bromley,' added Clovis.

'And James Device is possessing Rachel Nowell,' said Eve quietly, remembering the horrific image of the white eyes and convulsing young police officer. 'And who was the other one?' she asked. 'The one in poor little Jamie?'

'Elizabeth Device,' murmured Tom. He realised he didn't like any of them speaking the names out loud.

'Yes, that's right,' nodded Uncle Rufus. 'That's old Demdike's daughter, Jennet's mother.' Uncle Rufus gave a long sigh and continued, 'Poor Jamie, Elizabeth's soul was strong, very angry and far too determined for a little boy to handle.'

'So it seems that Old Demdike is the only soul who isn't possessing a living body,' said Clovis. He held another sandwich close to his mouth, one bit of egg wobbled in time to his excited statement.

'She's the puppet master,' said Anwaar, after a long pause.

'That makes sense to me,' said Uncle Rufus. 'So, there we are, we've identified five of the witches, including Old Demdike.' Uncle Rufus's head was now buried in his notebook as he scribbled down what looked like some kind of flow chart. 'Also, that number fits in with the rhyme that Jamie kept singing, what was it again, Clovis?'

Clovis instantly spoke the words of the little boy's haunting rhyme.

'Witches in the garden,
Witches in the tree,
Turn around, turn around, one, two three.
Look inside the bottle,
You will see,
Five witches in the garden,
Will come to you and me.'

'Five witches,' whispered Eve.

'One thing that is puzzling me though . . . is . . .' said Clovis, his brow furrowed, his black-framed glasses sliding down his nose. 'It looks like Chattox is the only soul from the bottle who wasn't related to Old Demdike. That's strange, isn't it?'

'Good point,' replied Anwaar. 'I'm sure the SPI will be able to help with that question.'

'Yes, a very good point, young man,' said Uncle Rufus, putting a large question mark next to Chattox's name.

'I just can't believe that all those people were hanged for being witches,' said Eve. 'It just seems so ridiculous now, and hearing all those names makes me feel so sad.'

'You're right, Eve,' said Anwaar. 'In those days, especially if you were poor and a little different, you raised suspicion. Even if you tried to help a sick man with perhaps a potion you had made with herbs and plants, then that was a sign that you were a witch. Sadly, so many men, women and children were executed for innocent acts.' Anwaar's voice suddenly changed from one of sadness and sympathy to one of dread. 'But there were those who were *not* so innocent and I'm afraid that Old Demdike was one of them.'

'So who do you think she wants revenge on?' asked Eve.

Uncle Rufus looked to Eve, Clovis and Tom and then to Anwaar. Suddenly his face exploded in exhilaration as if a big light had gone on in his brain. He smacked the table with his hand, making the cups rattle in their saucers. 'Revenge on the people who accused them,' said Uncle Rufus. 'What were the names of the people in hospital?' Uncle Rufus clicked his fingers. He was excited. They were getting somewhere.

Clovis flicked through his notebook and spoke out the names slowly. 'There's Judge Bromley, PC Rachel Nowell, David Law and of course, Jamie Drake. Do you think that's relevant, Professor?

'Maybe . . . maybe,' mused Uncle Rufus, and he tapped the end of his well-chewed pencil on his teeth, a habit he was prone to when deep in thought. 'Right, now, Tom, Eve — look through that book,' he said, pointing to the book *The Discovery of Witches,* 'and see if there are any names that might match with our victims'. There has to be a reason why Old Demdike has made the souls of the witches possess those particular people.' Uncle Rufus was keyed up, and paced back and forth between the table and the fire. Boris watched from his prostrate position in front of the hearth, his eyes half closed as they followed his master around the room.

Eve and Tom were both hunched over the book at the table, using their fingers to go down the lines, looking for any names that might connect them to the victims.

'What about this, Unc?' said Eve. 'Here's one of the judges at the trial, Sir Edward Bromley.'

'And,' said Tom, chiming in excitedly, 'here, look, there's a Roger Nowell, he was the local magistrate.'

'Anything about anyone with a name like David Law?' asked Anwaar. He too was now excited and joined Tom and Eve at the book.

'Er . . . Oh my God! Yes . . .' cried Eve. 'It says here that in sixteen-twelve, a pedlar called John Law was walking along a country lane when a young girl called Alizon Device stopped him and asked if he had any pins.'

'Alizon Device,' said Clovis, 'isn't that Jennet Device's sister, Old Demdike's granddaughter, yes? One of the people hanged?''

'Yes,' said Uncle Rufus, 'we are getting there. Carry on, Eve.'

Eve cleared her throat and continued to read: 'As witchcraft was prevalent in those times, he refused her and told her to go away. The pedlar suspected that the young girl might well be a witch and want the pins to use in some sort of spell. Alizon shouted out a curse in anger and instantly John Law fell to the ground, paralysed, and found he couldn't talk. Later, when he was better and found his voice, John Law forgave the young girl after Alizon asked for his forgiveness at his bedside, but his son Abraham did not. John Law appeared in court and spoke out against Alizon. This fateful meeting on that country lane started the whole process of finding the witches of Pendle.' Eve closed the book and sat down.

'The pieces are fitting together nicely,' said Anwaar.

'It seems they are,' agreed Uncle Rufus. 'It looks to me like we have to rid this plane of Old Demdike and purge our four victims.'

'How do we do that?' asked Clovis.

'We need to capture the spirits of the five witches, or destroy them,' said Anwaar. He was thinking, his eyes closed, his head down.

'That sounds easy,' said Tom sarcastically.

'We're going to need help,' said Uncle Rufus. 'I'm thinking we should go and see the ghost of Jennet. She's obviously the little girl who gave evidence against them all. She seems to know a lot, so maybe she can help us. Maybe give us an insight into her grandmother, Old Demdike, and perhaps a few more clues to help capture her ghost.'

'So, we go to the castle?' asked Clovis, sounding keen to get going right away.

'I think so, don't you agree, Anwaar?' asked Uncle Rufus.

'Yes, I think that is the right thing to do,' he answered. But he still had his head down and his hand rubbed his chin. Eventually he said, 'You'll all be fine, I'm assured of that.'

'What do you mean, *you'll*?' asked Tom, sounding alarmed.

'I'm sorry to say this to you all, but I'm going to have to leave you.' Anwaar looked uncomfortable as he broke the news.

'What?!' chorused Eve, Clovis and Tom.

'Now, now,' cooed Uncle Rufus. 'It's quite all right, we can manage on our own.'

'But where are you going? And what if that thing happens to Tom again — you know, that thing around his neck?' asked Eve, sounding hurt.

'I'm needed urgently on another case,' said Anwaar. 'The inspector has called me back, but I will return, I promise.' Anwaar smiled weakly at his young friends. 'Tom, you will be fine, I've placed a protection spell around you all, you're safe for the next few days.'

Everyone looked relieved, especially Tom who never wanted to go through that terrifying experience again.

'We'll be fine,' said Uncle Rufus quietly. 'If we need help, we'll send out the signal.'

'Good,' nodded Anwaar, smiling. 'Remember, the SPI will be calling you with information about the witch's bottle and about Chattox. I've placed the bottle in a drawer in the van. I've made it safe, so if you do come into contact with it, it can't affect you.' Then Anwaar hugged his dear friend, Uncle Rufus, and whispered, 'Professor, I'm hoping that this powder will work for you.' Anwaar pressed a leather pouch into Uncle Rufus's chest and smiled, showing his gleaming white teeth. 'Place it inside the Crookes camera, this powder is very powerful and is used to capture the strongest of souls. I believe it will help trap all the souls you need and put this case to bed.' Anwaar winked at his friend and grinned mischievously. 'You'll see . . . as-salamu alaykum,' and he brought his hands together and bowed once. Then he turned to the others, smiled charmingly and said softly, 'Goodbye, my friends.' He picked up his coat and bag and, without a backwards glance, walked out of the room and shut the door quietly behind him.

'Well, that was a surprise,' said Eve sulkily.

'It was to you, but I suspected,' said Uncle Rufus, rather matter-of-factly. 'Inspector Rutherford called him earlier in the van on the way back from the cottage.'

'What's the other case?' asked Clovis, intrigued.

'Never you mind, young man,' laughed Uncle Rufus. 'Now, back to *our* case. Tomorrow, early evening, shall we go to the castle and see if we can make contact with your friend Jennet, Tom?'

CHAPTER 13

There's Something About Maisie

After a good night's sleep followed by an ample breakfast of bread and jam, Uncle Rufus gave the young ghost hunters a lesson in how to work the computers inside Albert. Clovis just couldn't get enough of the highly advanced technology. Eve took longer to get to grips with it and Tom watched happily, letting his two friends enjoy the new equipment. It wasn't long before they went in for some lunch, which apparently was pea soup but tasted like warm sea-water. Everyone was polite as Gerry and Stan fussed over them, promising more if they finished up their bowls.

As the light began to fade it was time to leave and set off for Lancaster Castle.

The Professor was right, thought Tom, if they were going to get to the bottom of this case and help all those poor victims, they had to talk to the ghost of Jennet.

'Are you sure you're all right to do this, Tom?' asked Clovis, concerned for his friend. The thought of Tom coming to any more harm was unthinkable.

Tom nodded and said, 'Yeah, I'm good. Don't worry, Clovis, I'm a lot tougher than you think.'

They all climbed aboard the van and talked constantly as Uncle Rufus had polite yet stern words with Albert. After much gear crunching, windscreen wipers swishing manically and the odd blast of the horn, Albert settled down and began to trundle along the dark country roads, heading towards the city of Lancaster.

As they drew into the town, it was nice to see the bright Christmas lights of the shops, bars and restaurants illuminating the busy streets.

Boris was enjoying the ride immensely, back to his normal happy self. He sat in the front passenger seat, head held high, his hind legs pushed through his front paws. He was staring straight ahead, out of the windscreen, looking like a king who meant business.

Uncle Rufus laughed at his travel companion and stroked the top of his head affectionally. Boris looked to his master and snorted.

Suddenly Uncle Rufus's phone rang. He tapped to answer it and a familiar voice erupted around the inside of Albert on loudspeaker.

'Ah, Professor, it's Ruthers here, can you hear me?'

Everyone stopped chattering and leaned forward in their seats.

'Hello, Ruthers, yes, we can hear you,' shouted Uncle Rufus. He crunched the gears, called Albert a few names under his breath, then added, 'You're on speakerphone, we're in Albert and heading towards the castle.'

'Oh, marvellous,' cried the inspector. 'Now, listen, everyone, we've had another call from a Mrs Shaw, she's the mother of Maisie, the young lady you met at the castle, Tom. According to her mother she's been behaving very strangely. I've said you'll go over, seeing as you're in the area. I think it's shock, but you never know. See what's what, and report back, Rufus, dear boy.'

'Rightio,' said Uncle Rufus.

'I'm sending you the address now, and be careful tonight, everyone. I've arranged for the curator to let you inside the castle. Let me know how it all goes and any developments.'

The line went dead, and Uncle Rufus's phone pinged an alert to let him know that his satellite navigation was taking them on a new route.

Albert headed back up the main road, passing late-night shoppers, carol singers and a bored-looking Ho-Ho-Ho-ing Santa, who had obviously had enough and given up for the day.

They were soon passing the castle on the left and at the top of the road they turned right into a small street of Victorian terraced cottages.

Uncle Rufus parked Albert and everyone got out, apart from Boris, who jumped into the back and took the opportunity to have a nap. Clovis, Eve and Tom followed Uncle Rufus across the street and up to the front door of number twenty-three.

'Right, Tom,' said Uncle Rufus, 'when we see Maisie, you say hello first. She'll remember you from the castle.'

Uncle Rufus rang the doorbell, which blasted out a robotic chime that seemed to last a little too long. The batteries were running down and the tune that originally would have sounded upbeat and welcoming now belted out a noise that was reminiscent of a drunken organ player.

'How extraordinary,' said Uncle Rufus, his head cocked to one side. 'Beethoven, I think.'

Clovis, Tom and Eve all nudged each other as they noticed the closed curtains being pulled open for a second or two and then dropped back into place. Someone was peeking to see who was at the door.

Suddenly it jerked open, and a rather buxom, older lady stood smiling at them all.

'Hello, Mrs Shaw, I'm . . .' said Uncle Rufus, sticking his hand out for the lady to take.

'. . . Professor Pepper,' barked the lady. 'Come in, come in, all of you. I'm Maisie's mum, Jackie Shaw.' She backed up a little to let everyone inside. 'Sorry about the mess, but as I said to your lady inspector —' Jackie Shaw lowered her voice and whispered — 'she's just not been herself since, you know, that weird thing she saw up at the castle.' She then raised her voice as if talking to a very young child, 'Isn't that right, Maisie love. I've just said, you're not feeling yourself, are you?'

Maisie was sitting on the sofa, rocking back and forth, fidgeting with her hands, her greasy hair falling about her pale face. She turned her head slowly to see that they had company, and smiled shyly.

'Hi,' said Tom gently. 'Remember me? We met at the castle.' He studied the young woman and to his horror realised that he hardly recognised her.

Her face was pasty, blue bags of skin hung under her red

swollen bloodshot eyes, a clear sign that she hadn't slept at all. Her hair was matted, one long strand stuck to her cheek.

'Yes,' whispered Maisie. 'I remember you; you were kind to me and gave me that card.'

Uncle Rufus moved towards Maisie and touched her shoulder. 'Maisie.' He spoke gently to her, like she was a nervous animal. 'Are you OK? Your mum has contacted us because she thinks we can help. I'm Professor Pepper and this is Eve, Clovis and of course, you remember, Tom.' Uncle Rufus gestured to each of the three friends and they smiled back in return.

'Well,' butted in Mrs Shaw. 'As you can clearly see, she's not all right, is she? I mean, just look at her.'

Maisie leaned back on the sofa and began to rock again. It was clear to everyone that Maisie was suffering some kind of distress. Had seeing the ghost of the falling woman caused this? Uncle Rufus doubted it.

'How long has she been like this?' asked Clovis.

'Like I said to the inspector,' replied Mrs Shaw, 'it was after she came back from Christmas shopping. She said she'd seen summat awful up at the castle, some woman falling to the ground. Since then, she hasn't slept a wink and hasn't touched any food.' Mrs Shaw lowered her voice even further and continued, leaning closer to Uncle Rufus, 'It's like she's not here, like she's someone else! Poor baby Alex is right fed-up, I can tell you. He's really unsettled as well, like he doesn't recognise her. What do you think is up with her, Professor? Do I need to take her to the hospital?'

'Well, I'm sure it won't come to that,' answered Uncle Rufus gently.

Eve, Clovis and Tom had perched together on a large black leatherette chair in the corner of the room, Tom and Clovis on each arm and Eve in the middle, balanced on the edge of the cushion.

'I'll put the kettle on,' whispered Mrs Shaw as she left the front room.

Nobody said anything, and they didn't take their eyes off Maisie, who was still rocking on the sofa. Eve was just about to ask how she was feeling when Maisie's voice croaked.

'It's this voice,' she said, so quietly that they had to lean forward to hear what she was saying.

'Right, I see,' said Uncle Rufus, nodding his head. 'What kind of voice is it?' he asked carefully.

'It's a woman's voice,' whispered Maisie, her face still hidden by her unwashed hair. Suddenly she whipped her head up and stared hard at Uncle Rufus, then shouted in despair, 'She's always yelling at me, telling me to do things I don't want to do.'

'What sort of things?' Eve asked.

Maisie brought her hands up to her ears and covered them as if she were trying to block out some loud obtrusive noise. 'Horrible things, she wants me to hurt people.' Maisie began to cry, great racking sobs. Her mum came rushing into the room, slopping tea all over the floor. Putting the mugs down on the side table, she went to her daughter.

'There, love, calm down, sweetheart, it's all right . . .

I'm here, your mum's here.' Jackie stroked Maisie's head and shushed her.

'Maisie?' asked Tom. 'Can you talk to us, tell us who is shouting at you? It will help you, you see, to make it stop.'

Uncle Rufus smiled and nodded at Tom, a sign for him to carry on talking.

'This woman, I don't think it's the woman we saw falling at the castle, is it?' said Tom. He had moved from the armchair to sit on the other side of Maisie now. He put his hand out and placed it over the top of Maisie's cold one.

Maisie sniffed and snivelled. 'She says her name is Alice, and that she wants her revenge. She's very angry all the time. She says that we share the same soul, but how can that be?' Maisie shifted uneasily on the sofa. Her head rolled back; her eyes shut. 'I keep having this terrible nightmare,' she whispered. 'It's always the same. I'm standing on the back of a cart. My feet are dirty, and my clothes are very old-fashioned. Then I feel a rope around my neck and I fall. I can't breathe.' Maisie began to scream, her eyes open and staring out in front of her. Eve thought it was as if she were seeing something that they couldn't. Maisie began to cry again, and her mum held her tight and continued to soothe her.

A thought had struck Clovis, though, when Maisie had mentioned sharing the same soul.

'Professor?' he whispered. 'Can I talk to you?'

'Of course,' replied Uncle Rufus, getting up and following Clovis into the narrow hallway.

Eve, Tom and Mrs Shaw sat in an awkward silence as

they listened to the hushed whisperings between Uncle Rufus and Clovis, while Maisie rocked and whimpered on the sofa.

In the hall, Clovis spoke as quietly as he could. He knew that what he was about to suggest might sound really crazy to Maisie and her mum, and he didn't want to alarm them.

'Could Maisie have lived before?' he asked, trying to keep the excitement out of his voice. 'Another life, perhaps involving the castle? I've done some research on past lives and some of the things Maisie is saying match with other cases I've read about.'

Uncle Rufus stroked his chin. 'An interesting idea, my boy! Yes, that could explain the woman's voice in her head. I find the subject of reincarnation fascinating, but I've never been involved in a case where the past life is influencing the present one. If your theory is correct, Clovis, it would be a first for me. Come on,' said Uncle Rufus excitedly, nudging Clovis in the ribs. 'Let's see.'

Uncle Rufus and Clovis came back into the room and Uncle Rufus gently probed further. 'Mrs Shaw? Has Maisie ever shown any apprehension towards the castle before now? Perhaps even as a child?'

'Well, yes, she has, actually. She's always hated it, haven't you, pet?'

Maisie nodded in reply.

'She could never look at the castle and if she did, she always felt sick. I just put it down to nerves, or something.'

'I think,' said Uncle Rufus, 'that Maisie definitely has a

connection to the castle, but what that connection is, we don't know yet — but we'll find out, I promise you.'

'It would be good if we could get a surname for this Alice?' said Clovis. He had his phone out and was looking at a website that listed some of the people who had been imprisoned or executed at the castle.

'Nutter!' screeched Maisie. Her head snapped back. She stared this time at Clovis. 'It's Nutter,' she sputtered. 'I hate her, she's always wailing, moaning. She says she wants revenge.' Maisie was moaning now, her voice getting louder and louder as she became more agitated.

'Can I speak to this Alice?' asked Tom gently.

'No!' hissed Maisie. 'She only talks to me. To me, to *meeeee*.' Maisie was now standing on the sofa and pummelling her chest.

Tom took Maisie's arms and pulled her back down to a sitting position. He closed his eyes and felt a familiar buzzing sensation inside his head. Instantly he saw a woman in his mind's eye. She was crying and pleading. 'Help me, help my soul, I'm not a witch. I never was, wrong place, wrong time. Help me.' Then Tom witnessed the woman's face turn from one of pity to one of pure hate. 'I will take my revenge on anyone who tries to stop us. We will all have our retribution. Maisie and I are one with the others, we will seek our vengeance.'

Tom took a breath. 'So you're Alice, Alice Nutter?'

'Yes!' hissed Maisie, then collapsed in her mum's arms.

'She's here, Alice Nutter, on that list of names we found,' cried Clovis, getting excited. 'Alice Nutter was one of the

145

accused Pendle witches. It says here that she was most likely innocent and just happened to be at Malkin Tower at the gathering on the Sabbath. Jennet Device pointed her out to the court and that sealed Alice's fate.'

'Make it stop, please,' moaned Maisie from beneath her mum's embrace.

'*Could* this be reincarnation?' whispered Clovis, looking at Maisie in wonder.

'I think you might be right, Clovis,' sighed Uncle Rufus. He crouched down in front of Maisie and gently took both her hands. Maisie's face was hidden by her tousled hair, but sniffing could be heard. She seemed to have calmed down a bit.

'It's all right, Maisie,' he soothed. 'My friends and I are here to help you.'

Suddenly Maisie snarled and sprang up like an angry cat. Uncle Rufus jumped out of the way. 'Get out,' she shouted, 'all of you, we don't need your help. We will do it in our own way.'

Clovis, Eve and Tom all stood close together, wide-eyed and bewildered. What was happening to this poor woman?

Suddenly she locked her gaze straight onto Eve and stood within an inch of her face. Eve moved closer to Clovis for protection.

'You, girl, can help us.' A low whispered voice came from Maisie's mouth. She shoved her index finger into Eve's chest. 'You must join us and fight for our revenge.' Maisie paused, looking Eve up and down slowly and then asked, her head cocked to one side: 'Will you?'

Eve was frightened but replied simply in a strong voice, 'No, I'm sorry, I can't help you.'

Maisie's face turned to thunder; her eyes blazed with fury. Uncle Rufus stepped over quickly, catching her hands before she could do any damage and brought Maisie back to the sofa once more. He pulled her down onto the seat and motioned for Jackie to keep a hold of her.

Suddenly Eve felt something trickle down onto her lip. She wiped away whatever it was, and to her surprise and horror realised that her nose was bleeding.

'Eve!' cried Uncle Rufus, dashing over and looking into her face. 'Here, take my handkerchief.'

Eve wiped her nose and held the handkerchief in place.

'I'm OK, just a little blood, that's all.'

Maisie had begun to rock again as if nursing a poorly stomach.

Uncle Rufus went back to the sofa, got down on his haunches and looked up at the young woman. 'Maisie?' She didn't respond in any way. 'I'm sorry, Mrs Shaw, but we're going to have to go now. Eve isn't feeling too well.'

'But what about Maisie, what's wrong with her? You said something about reincarnation? Don't tell me there's nothing you can do for her, like that useless doctor?'

Uncle Rufus took her hands in his and said, 'Jackie, it's clear to me that an energy, perhaps linked with a past life, is trying to control Maisie's mind and body, to make her do things she wouldn't normally do. We have visited other people in the area who have similar symptoms, but Maisie's seem to be a slightly different case. I think maybe Maisie was a woman called Alice Nutter in a past life, a woman who was wrongly accused of being a witch. And for some reason she is acting out through your daughter. Why now? We don't know for sure, or for what reason. But we will come back, and we will help, I promise you.'

'But what do I do with her in the meantime?' whispered Jackie, looking nervously over her shoulder.

'She needs sleep,' whispered Uncle Rufus. 'This will calm her down and help you. Here . . .' Uncle Rufus brought out of his rucksack a small bottle and handed it to Jackie. 'It's a natural sleeping tonic, made from lavender and chamomile. I will get a specialist in reincarnation and hypnotherapy to call you and help. They will be from the SPI and they will be here as soon as possible. She *will* be all right, Mrs Shaw, I'm certain.'

Jackie sighed and wiped a tear away from her cheek. Just then, a baby could be heard crying from upstairs.

'Best go and get baby Alex up,' she said, smiling weakly. 'He's due his feed. Then I'll get Maisie to bed. Thank you, Professor.'

Everyone said their goodbyes politely and left the room. Eve was the last out and unbeknown to her, the bloodied handkerchief that she'd used to wipe her nose fell from her pocket and onto the floor.

CHAPTER 14

A Castle and a Prison

It was nine o'clock in the evening and everyone was huddled inside Albert. They ate their pizzas and drank hot chocolate laced with cream and chunks of fudge that Uncle Rufus had treated them to from a nearby takeaway.

Albert was parked within the grounds of Lancaster Castle, the heater that Uncle Rufus had adapted for the van was plugged in and giving everyone a toasty warm feeling. Right now, all Eve wanted to do was curl up and go to sleep in their little camper, not confront a ghost.

'I think it's a good idea, before we go inside the castle, to take stock of all the information we've gathered so far,' said Uncle Rufus, wiping his mouth with a napkin.

'Right,' said Clovis, taking his notebook out. 'We're hopefully about to contact the ghost of Jennet Device, who by your description, Tom, doesn't sound like a nine-year-old girl.'

'No, definitely not. She said she had ended her life as she couldn't take the torment of her mother any more,' said Tom. He looked sad as he said this, he wasn't really relishing the thought of seeing Jennet's ghost again, but he told himself it looked as though Jennet was essential to them understanding what was happening to the modern-day victims.

'So,' said Eve, 'if we're going off the notes given at the trial, that means Jennet's mum is Elizabeth Device?'

'Yes, that's right,' said Uncle Rufus.

'And Old Demdike?' she asked. 'She's Jennet's grandmother?'

Everyone nodded and took bites out of their pizzas.

'And Demdike's the one calling all the other dead witches together?' asked Eve. She was nodding as if trying to sort out the story so far in her head.

'But to do what?' asked Clovis, looking at his friends.

'Well, we know they want revenge against people they consider responsible for convicting them,' said Uncle Rufus.

'Do you think the victims in the hospital could die?' asked Tom, looking very worried.

'Let's not think of that,' said Uncle Rufus. He was aware that the scenes Tom, Eve and Clovis had witnessed recently must have been very harrowing for them all. 'Let's think positively, all right? Those people are being cared for by brilliant nurses and doctors. We'll find a way to help them, I'm sure. But hopefully Jennet's ghost will be able to point us in the right direction. Incidentally, Clovis, can you look up Jennet Device on the computer and see if there are any records of her after her family were killed? If you can't find anything, I can always message the SPI.'

Clovis set to work, facing the large screen and tapping away.

'Ever since we heard about Jennet,' said Tom, looking over Clovis's shoulder, 'and how she was used in the trial, I've wondered what happened to her. You know, where did she go, who looked after her?'

Clovis swiped through various pages and stopped suddenly on the site that he was looking for.

'It says here . . .' Clovis leaned further forward and brought the information out of the screen by moving his arm, into the middle of the van so everyone could see what he had found. The reflection of the images shone onto his black-rimmed glasses, making his face look slightly blue. 'Oh my God! You won't believe this.' Clovis made himself comfortable by removing his jacket, all the while never taking his eyes off the information. 'It says here that in a strange twist, more than twenty years after Jennet accused *her* family and neighbours of witchcraft, she *herself* was accused of the same crime. In sixteen-thirty-three, a young lad named Edmund Robinson accused Jennet, who was probably in her early thirties at this point, and sixteen others of witchcraft.

'They were found guilty, but the court needed physical evidence. During this time Edmund admitted to making up stories as he had heard all about the Pendle witches.

'Jennet was acquitted, but sadly had to stay in prison as she couldn't afford to pay her debt for her time spent in Lancaster Castle.' Clovis finished reading and looked up at his friends, who were all following intently.

'So, what happened after that? Did she die in prison?' asked Eve impatiently.

'It says here that the last prison record they have of Jennet is in sixteen-thirty-six,' said Clovis. He shrugged his shoulders, swiped the data from the centre of the van, bringing it back onto the computer screen.

'Poor woman,' cried Eve. She shivered and shook her head in disbelief.

'The irony is incredible,' said Uncle Rufus. 'So, here's a nine-year-old girl, she is used as the main witness in a trial and accuses her grandmother, her mother, her older sister and brother plus seven more people of witchcraft. They're all hanged, apart from her grandmother, Old Demdike, who we know died before the trial. And then years later, Jennet is accused of the same crime!'

'And now, the poor soul is haunting the castle as a tortured lost ghost,' added Tom.

'I really want to find out what happened to her, and hopefully help her,' said Eve. She put her biker jacket on and then pulled a black beanie hat over her short blonde pixie haircut.

The others took Eve's lead and began to get ready.

'Well, hopefully, my dear,' said Uncle Rufus, opening Albert's door, 'we will be able to talk to her in a few moments. Right, make sure we've all got our bags with the right equipment. The caretaker has left the door open for us.'

Everyone climbed out of Albert and walked towards the impressive gatehouse of the castle.

'Wow! Look, it has a real medieval portcullis,' exclaimed Clovis. His head was bent back, looking high up to the top of the archway.

Uncle Rufus was just as excited as Clovis. Eve nudged Tom

as they watched Clovis and Uncle Rufus ooh and ah over stones and ancient slabs of brickwork.

'This castle dates back to the Roman times,' said Uncle Rufus, putting his spectacles on to look closely at a cornerstone, 'and is now owned by the Duke of Lancaster, who just happens to be . . .'

'The King!' shouted Clovis, grinning happily.

'You two are a nightmare together,' laughed Eve.

Boris added more to the merriment as he cocked his short stubby leg over one of the stones and peed.

'Boris! You have no manners,' said Uncle Rufus, shooing Boris in through the archway.

Their laughter and chatter soon ebbed away though as they walked through the darkness into an open area, a concourse of sorts, where many different buildings, doors and barred windows looked down upon them all.

It was really cold now, blasts of freezing air whipping round them. Eve shivered and blew onto her hands, giving herself a second or two of welcome heat. Uncle Rufus tightened his long patchwork scarf around his neck. Tom pulled his West Ham beanie snugly down onto his head and Clovis zipped his very sensible ski jacket up to his chin.

'Right,' said Uncle Rufus, 'let's synchronise our EVP watches, and turn our night-vision cameras on.'

Everyone did as instructed and followed Uncle Rufus further inside the castle walls. 'Once inside, we'll choose a room as a base.'

He turned back and with his powerful torch began looking in some of the barred windows as they walked past.

'Where did you first make contact with Jennet?' he asked.

'In a courtroom. It wasn't far from the main gate, but it looks so different in the dark.' Tom paused and bit on his thumbnail. 'I'm sorry, Professor, I can't remember exactly where the courtroom is.'

'Don't worry, we'll find it,' said Uncle Rufus kindly. He moved the torch over all the buildings, hoping that Tom would be able to remember which door to go through.

'There!' shouted Tom with relief as Uncle Rufus's light passed over a large door opposite them.

'Right, come on then, let's see if she's still there,' said Uncle Rufus, walking quickly across the concourse.

'You'd think I'd be getting braver, wouldn't you?' said Eve to her friends.

'You are, we all are,' said Clovis kindly.

'Well, I'm really nervous. I don't like this place. Just thinking about what went on here makes me go cold.' Eve threaded her arm through Clovis's for comfort and endeavoured to match his steps.

'This is going to be great,' said Clovis. He was excited and couldn't wait to get inside the castle. A place with so much history made his mouth water. Of course he was a little nervous too about seeing Jennet's ghost but that was his job now. He was a ghost hunter. Clovis stepped forward with renewed vigour, leaving poor Eve practically skipping to keep step with him.

Uncle Rufus pushed the large door open and swung his

torch around. They had arrived inside a grand reception hall. Peering down from on high were many huge paintings of lords, ladies, judges, kings and queens.

Tom looked around and pointed, leading the way. As he moved towards the court room, he felt his stomach flip over.

'This is where I first saw her,' he said in a quiet voice. He was mentally preparing himself for what was to come. He hoped the others would see her too.

They all walked into the court room and instantly stopped dead in their tracks. Clovis whistled in awe.

The room was impressive and imposing, with its dark wooden benches. Towards the back was the dock where the accused would have had to stand to be questioned and stared at. From there, if found guilty of a crime, whether it be stealing a sheep or murder, they would have been sent down to the cells to await their fate.

Eve decided that she didn't like this place, not at all. Just the thought of all the innocent people who'd been sentenced here made her blood run cold.

'So, what sort of people were tried here?' she asked, staring up at the judge's bench.

Clovis pushed his glasses up to the bridge of his nose and spoke quietly. 'Lancaster Castle was the largest place for trials and executions outside of London. Two hundred people were executed after being tried here. This place has been a prison since the twelfth century. It has hanged people for as little as stealing a rabbit or transported them to Australia for stealing a sheep. It was a pretty barbaric place all those years ago.'

'Not everyone was so innocent. There were murderers and real villains jailed in here too,' said Uncle Rufus, who was taking various pieces of equipment out of his rucksack.

'Well, let's hope their ghosts aren't here with us now,' said Tom, looking anxiously around.

'This is where we'll set up the night-vision cameras and we'll use it as our base. If this is where you saw Jennet's ghost, Tom, then hopefully she'll come back to the same place. We can put two of the night-vision cameras on tripods on either side of the judge's bench looking out across the room.'

Uncle Rufus pointed to where he wanted the cameras positioned and the ghost hunters got to work setting things up and recording the temperature.

Boris had stayed close to Uncle Rufus. He snuffled along, nose close to the ground, taking in all the unfamiliar smells of the grand court room.

They all moved into the centre of the court room and one by one began to call out for the ghost of Jennet Device. After about ten minutes, they thought perhaps she wasn't going to show, but they were wrong.

Suddenly, footsteps could be heard walking above them: loud, purposeful and heavy.

'No one else is here,' said Uncle Rufus, looking up at the ceiling.

'It's Jennet,' said Tom. His eyes were closed again. 'She's calling to us, she wants us to go up to the roof.'

CHAPTER 15

The Girl on the Roof and a Silver Soldier

'Right,' said Uncle Rufus, 'let's go then. Leave one of the night-vision cameras here. I'll take the other one.'

Clovis led the team out of the court room and up the impressive staircase in the reception hall. Boris, as usual, brought up the rear, letting out little squeaks and parps from his large trembling bottom. When they all got to the top, they followed Clovis around the gallery.

The ancient floorboards creaked and groaned under their feet as they moved through the eerie darkness. They shifted their torches nervously around, lighting up stern faces in paintings and statues on plinths.

'Blimey,' said Tom, looking at the harsh face of an elderly gentleman. He stared down at Tom accusingly from within a picture frame. 'Imagine standing in that court and being told by someone like him that you were about to be hanged, or spend the rest of your days in prison.'

'This must have been a terrible place to be imprisoned,' said Clovis as he stopped to check which way to get to the roof.

Clovis had memorised the layout of the building. One of

his many talents was recalling images of drawings and maps, as well as memorising facts and figures. He closed his eyes briefly and the others waited patiently for him to remember the right way.

'Over here,' he said with purpose and strode down another long dark corridor.

'So, were the witches hanged here?' asked Eve, keeping close to the others.

'They were imprisoned in the castle and tried here, but hanged outside of the city, a location called Gallows Hill,' replied Clovis.

'God, it's an awful place,' said Eve. She hoped that Jennet's ghost would give them the information they needed so they could get the hell out.

'Whoa!' shouted Uncle Rufus, who was walking just behind Clovis and filming their journey on the night-vision camera.

'What!' shouted Eve, suddenly frightened.

'I think I've just caught a ghost walking through a wall.' Uncle Rufus crouched down and rewound the device. Everyone bent over to look at the screen. Uncle Rufus pressed play and there, walking quickly across the screen, was what looked like a man dressed in silver armour. The apparition was blurry but it was definitely there. It marched silently across the shot and then disappeared through the wall.

'Wow!' exclaimed Clovis. 'That looked like a soldier. What a catch, Professor!'

'It was so quick, I wasn't sure at first, but there it is on camera. It looks like a Roman soldier to me.' Uncle Rufus was delighted, but Eve looked about her uneasily; what else was lurking inside these walls?

Clovis typed quickly into his phone. 'According to the history of the castle, it stands on what was once a Roman Fort. Tom, can you sense anything?'

'No, nothing,' said Tom, shaking his head thankfully.

'It could have been a memory,' said Uncle Rufus. 'That would make sense, with it disappearing through a wall. Perhaps there used to be a door there.' Uncle Rufus was grinning from ear to ear. 'My first Roman soldier,' he sighed happily. 'How wonderful!'

Everyone walked along the corridors and landings, talking quietly about what they had just captured, when suddenly Clovis stopped in his tracks and whispered: 'Here they are.' He patted a handrail belonging to another set of stairs. 'These should lead us straight up to the roof.'

As if on cue, the sound of footsteps could be heard walking directly above them again.

'Can you hear that?' asked Uncle Rufus.

'It's as if someone is pacing back and forth,' whispered Eve nervously.

Tom suddenly began to feel his head buzzing. 'It's Jennet, she's waiting for us.' In Tom's mind he saw her as before, black cloak fluttering, her hair whipping about her withered grey face.

'I'll go first,' whispered Uncle Rufus. He shone his torch up the flight of narrow, stone steps and made his way towards the roof. At the top he found another door, pushed it open and to his relief discovered the rooftop of Lancaster Castle.

'Up here, chaps,' he shouted down. 'Make sure you give Boris a hand, please.'

Clovis was first up the stairs, closely followed by Tom and Eve, who together carried a rather confused-looking bulldog.

'If he makes one of his smells on my hand,' said Tom wincing, 'I'll never talk to him again.'

Fortunately for Tom, Boris behaved himself and eventually, with lots of huffing and puffing, everyone made it to the top.

This part of the roof was vast and it gave a fabulous view of the town. The clear night sky was awash with bright twinkling stars. The icy chill of the December weather enveloped its frosty fingers around them all. They stood in the centre of the empty roof, huddling together, a little nervously but mostly to keep warm. Uncle Rufus stamped his feet and rubbed his hands together, trying to ignite some heat. 'Anything yet, Tom?' he asked.

'I think so, my head feels light, and I do feel a bit queasy.' Tom rubbed his stomach and closed his eyes again, concentrating.

Suddenly, a thudding, knocking sound reverberated all around them.

'She's here,' whispered Tom. He opened his eyes and looked over his shoulder, unsure where on the huge roof she was about to appear.

They all stood still. Even Boris didn't move. His eyes had locked onto something, his hairs standing up. He whined. It was a pitiful sound, as if he were in pain. Eve dropped to her knees and stroked him.

'Listen, can you hear that?' whispered Eve. She squinted her eyes and followed Boris's intense gaze.

'Yeah,' said Clovis. 'I hear it, sounds like those footsteps again.' He pointed his camera towards the end of the roof directly in front of them and zoomed in. There, pacing back and forth, was a ghostly figure.

'I think,' he said, keeping his eye on the viewfinder, 'we've found Jennet.'

Jennet's ghost was obviously agitated. As everyone moved towards her, they could see that she was every bit as scary as Tom had described.

Her scraggy body was bent over slightly; the scrawny outline marched over to the edge of the roof and then back again. The black cloak billowed behind her and what was left of her long dark hair lashed across her skeletal face. It seemed she hadn't seen her onlookers at first, but as Tom spoke out nervously, she suddenly stopped pacing.

'Ahem,' he coughed politely. 'Jennet? It's me, Tom. Do you remember?'

Jennet turned her head to look at them all. Eve, shocked at her appearance, drew a sharp intake of breath.

The ghost smiled a horrible smile: teeth black and yellow, many missing. Her skin grey, her eyes just dark holes.

'I said I'd come back, didn't I?' continued Tom. 'And look —' he moved his hand up slowly and gestured to his companions — 'I've brought my friends. We're here to help you.'

Uncle Rufus pulled the Crookes camera out of his

rucksack. Jennet's head twisted over to look at what he was doing.

'What is that?' The words rattled inside Tom's head.

'It's all right, Jennet, it's just a device to take your image,' said Tom quietly.

'And that?' Jennet lifted her bony arm up and pointed a long thin finger at the small night-vision camera Clovis was holding.

'It's the same.'

'I don't like it, take them away!' Tom could tell that Jennet was becoming nervous about the strange contraptions.

'She doesn't like the cameras; she wants us to put them away,' said Tom quickly.

'Put the camera down, Clovis,' instructed Uncle Rufus. He too put the Crookes camera back into his bag and then turned his hands out to show Jennet that he no longer had it on him. Uncle Rufus was relieved that the tiny cameras they had fitted onto their coats were filming the whole thing though. They just wouldn't be able to get close-ups if the ghost were to move away.

Jennet walked towards them all. The cloak buffeted about in the air, and her body seemed to float, as if walking on a cloud. Her tortured image would come into focus for a second or two and sometimes seem quite solid, then, like an unfocused image on a screen, it faded, becoming transparent.

'What happened to you, Jennet?' asked Eve, suddenly feeling very sad for this woman.

Tom inhaled deeply and, taking Eve's hand for support, he

waited for a response to the question. He didn't have long to wait. Jennet was very keen to tell her story. Tom listened and relayed it back to his friends.

'I was so small, so frightened. I didn't have any friends, just my family. I was always hungry and cold. My family never really knew I was there. I would sit in the room and watch my granny make spells, concoct potions and tonics for the villagers. They never liked us; always thought we were witches. I never saw me mam do spells, not like granny. She was a witch, and she was nasty. She scared me, made me cry.

'One day, a man came to me and told me that if I were to tell him that all my family were witches, then he promised me they would all go up to Heaven — otherwise they would go to a dark dungeon and the Devil would come and take them away. He said that God would love me for ever and one day I would see my family again in Heaven. All I had to do was stand up in a big room and point out all the witches in my family. I did as the man said and I regret it to this day. My mam was very angry with me and screamed and shouted, but all I could think about was what the man had said. He looked after me for a bit though, when I'd done it. I was warm and given a new dress and I had some hot meat and potatoes to eat.'

Jennet suddenly stopped talking and Tom realised that she had begun to cry. Little pitiful sobs tumbled inside his mind. He opened his eyes to see that Jennet's ghost was indeed crying.

'Are you all right, Jennet?' asked Uncle Rufus, gently, not wanting to alarm the spirit.

Jennet's ghost looked up at Uncle Rufus and nodded that she was fine.

Her voice spoke softly into Tom's head again. Her old Lancastrian accent was strong, but Tom could just about understand what she was saying.

'What happened on the day of the hangings?' asked Uncle Rufus.

'I was so afraid, frightened that the man had lied to me. When I saw them standing on the back of the cart, my mother, my sister, my brother and the others, I was told to smile. He said to do it, to smile and point, even laugh; if I didn't, God would not come for them. So, I did what the man told me to do. I watched them all hang, and I smiled as they dropped. I didn't want to. He made me do it, he made me kill everyone. That night, back at the man's house, I was given one last meal, then I was pushed out of the house and left to my own devices.'

'Where did you go?' asked Clovis. He had read that Jennet had indeed watched her own family hang and that the man, presumably Roger Nowell, the local magistrate, was the person who had taken her in and cared for her during the trial. But what happened to her after her family's tragic demise?

'Where did I go? Well, where *could* I go? I wandered the streets,' she said quietly. 'No one wanted me, I was the child of witches, you see. People were frightened of me, afraid to be seen with me. But that first night, sleeping under a bridge, that was when she first came to me.'

164

'Who?' asked Tom quickly.

'Me mam, Elizabeth. Her voice inside my head began to taunt me, threatening to kill me, she was so angry. I realised I'd done a terrible thing. I thought I'd been doing good. But oh no, my mam told me, what a bad girl I'd been. She hates me now, always there in my mind, always screaming at me, telling me that she will get her revenge. Even when I was older, I couldn't go anywhere, do anything, without her being there in my head, telling me that I was useless. Luckily as I got bigger people didn't recognise me any more. The girl who hanged her family of witches was forgotten about. She'd disappeared. I changed my name and became a pedlar, selling what I could to buy bread. I became a wretch; I wished I'd hanged with my family. But me mam never let up, no, she carried on with her ranting and raving. Her screaming soon changed to laughter, when I was accused of witchcraft meself. Stupid lad, he made it all up, didn't he?' Jennet's voice began to get higher in pitch, her head shook in anger.

'Well, she loved it, didn't she, my mother? She laughed and screeched in my head and damned me. She said she would be waiting for me when the hangman had finished his job. But the hangman never did do his wicked deed. I were innocent, see, and they dropped the charges. But I couldn't leave, could I? I was imprisoned, I couldn't pay the prison debt and they left me to rot in that stinking hole. My mam pushed me, she did, she pushed me over the edge. One night, I managed to slip out with the help of my jailer. He were kind to me. Used to sneak me mutton and ale. I think he just felt sorry for me;

said he had a daughter the same age. And so I came up here. I wanted to end it all, so I did what my mam wanted me to do, and threw myself off this top 'ere. But I didn't get to Heaven, see. I've been here, going over and over the same old thing. Throwing myself off this damned castle roof, in the hopes that one day someone will come and help me. You see, it's the curse. Old Demdike, Granny, she cursed me. She must have known what I would do, that I would betray everyone. She was funny that way, you know, seeing the future and all. She said I was doomed to walk the earth plane for eternity. She said that to me after I spied on her, doing her binding spell with a bottle. She hit me and told me to leave, but I know what I saw. Granny took some of her own hair, hair from me mam, our Alizon and James, and off Chattox too. We all thought Granny hated her, but she said she was a strong one and would be useful. She added their flakes of skin and fingernails, her own pee and made a spell:

> *"There are eleven but only five will rise,*
> *They who condemned us, shall be our prize,*
> *On the night of the blood moon, where children make their*
>   *play,*
> *We shall bind together, and the world you know will pay."*

'She knew what was going to happen, she knew that Alizon's curse of the pedlar would be their downfall. She had seen it; she had foretold our demise. So, she began to plan — plan for her and her family's revenge. But she needed her daughter and her grandchildren to help and of course another powerful woman. Chattox. Although Granny never liked to admit it, she knew, we all knew, that that old woman had powers. I remember watching my Granny that night as she chanted and cast her spells. When she threw the blue bottle into the fire and said more strange words, I realised in that moment that she was calling up dark forces. She was an evil woman. I saw the smoke and fire come up and out into the room, I could see evil faces swirling all around her. I was scared and screamed, and that's when she discovered me, and hit me hard. I ran outside and hid in the cowshed, but I watched through the slats in the wood. She dug a hole under a tree and buried the bottle. The next day, the men came and took my family away, and I met Mr Nowell, the man.

'When they were all brought here to the castle, they put them in the dungeon down below and Granny died there. She never smelled fresh air again. She's with the Devil now. I know it.'

There was a long pause, the only sound that could be heard was the gentle breeze that blew over the top of the roof.

Uncle Rufus stepped forward very slowly and spoke quietly. 'Jennet, can you help us?' he asked. 'We believe that your granny and four other souls that were bound together in that bottle have been released and are hurting people, possessing them. One is a little boy. There are two men, and a young woman, who seem to be descendants of the people who accused your family of witchcraft.'

'Whaaat!' Jennet screamed and rushed towards everyone.

Boris leaped forwards and began to bark at the ghost, trying to protect his companions.

Jennet's ghost leaned down and put her head close to Boris's. Then with her bony fingers she placed them on her thin cracked lips and shushed the dog. Boris whimpered and shot back behind Eve's legs.

Jennet smiled weakly and looked closely at Tom.

'I will help you,' she whispered in his head. 'When the time is right, I will come. When you call me, I will be there. I must face them, rid myself of this curse, face my past and hopefully find my future.'

Tom nodded then relayed what the ghost had just said to the others.

'Is there anything we can do to help you, Jennet?' said Uncle Rufus.

Jennet blinked once and moved back. 'It's important for you to trap the souls. You must put them all back inside the bottle. That is the only way to stop their energies from rising again. There are four souls doing my granny's bidding. My granny is the most powerful one, it's her hatred that's swallowing her up whole and she's forcing the others to commit revenge and murder! Her spirit isn't at its most powerful yet. But I fear when the others join her, she will be unstoppable. You must find a way of trapping the four souls who have possessed those poor people. Five souls will rise on the night of the blood moon, and if they are not stopped, they will take revenge by killing the descendants of the ones who branded them as witches. This is their retribution for the torture, humiliation and death they suffered. You must go to the place where the hangings took place, capture the souls and save the descendants. If you don't, the power of the blood moon will give Demdike so much control, who knows what evil she will do. She has to be stopped.'

Clovis, Uncle Rufus and Eve watched as Jennet's ghost began to fade.

Her last words to Tom as she walked towards the edge of the castle roof were, 'I will help you, Tom. When you need me, I will come. If you succeed, I will finally be released from my curse.'

Jennet's ghost clambered up onto the top of the wall. She stood tall, the black cloak twisting and whipping about in the wind. She turned her head to look at the small group, who were watching her, threw her arms out to her sides and tipped forwards. Eve screamed and hid her face in Tom's chest as Jennet plummeted down to the ground.

'It's all right, Eve, it's just Jennet repeating what she's been doing for hundreds of years,' said Uncle Rufus. 'But if we get this right, we can save her, so she never has to go through that ever again. How we do that, right now, I don't know. But I promise, we will figure it out.' Eve looked up at her uncle and smiled weakly.

'I know we will, Unc, and sorry, everyone,' she said, sniffing and wiping the tears from her face. 'It's just a shock, you know.'

'It was horrific,' said Clovis, 'but I bet any minute now, we'll see her again and she'll do exactly the same thing.'

'Clovis is right,' said Uncle Rufus. 'We've just got to make sure that we do exactly what Jennet told us to do, and then we can help her poor soul.'

'C'mon,' said Tom, who by now was exhausted and bone cold. 'Let's keep positive,' he said, smiling at Eve. 'We'll get the job done, we always do, but right now, I could do with another hot chocolate and some sleep. Can we go now, Professor? I'm freezing.'

'Of course, I think we've done more than enough tonight. I will check when the next blood moon is, and more importantly how we can trap the witches' souls.'

Uncle Rufus led the others towards the door on the roof, but they began to hear the footsteps again, pacing back and forth.

'Let's hurry, I think we've all seen enough for one night,' said Uncle Rufus, ushering everyone through the door and down the stairs.

As they walked back down the long corridor towards the main staircase, Eve asked what a blood moon was, and of course Clovis was delighted to explain as they walked slowly back through the labyrinth of hallways and passages.

'Well, you see, during a full eclipse, the Earth's shadow fully covers the moon, causing a red hue. Many people believe it to be a bad omen, possibly signalling the end of the world. Other people, however, see it as a time to draw from its powerful energies to cast spells and awaken our subconscious. Many believe that this can be a time to investigate our darker sides and to possibly harness that energy. It happens about three times a year and is an incredible sight, if you're lucky enough to see it.'

'Oh, so, I guess it's no wonder then that Old Demdike and the others are planning to kill on the blood moon,' said Eve.

'Well, let's hope we can stop her before she goes too far,' said Tom, secretly fearing the worst.

Back at The Safe Haven, Eve, Clovis and Tom made their way sleepily upstairs to bed. But Uncle Rufus didn't retire with them. He sat by the fire, Boris snoring contentedly by his feet. His mind was buzzing. He began to plan a way in which he could save as many souls as possible. It wasn't going to be easy, no, not easy at all. Boris lifted his head, blinked his large brown eyes at his master, sighed and then let out a very loud, explosive fart.

The door opened and Stan popped his head around, his large pink face looking very worried indeed, 'By God, Professor, did you hear that bomb drop? Hitler's certainly trying his luck this evening.'

As the hours passed, Uncle Rufus didn't sleep. Eve woke in the night and on the way to the bathroom noticed, as she passed his door, the soft sound of old-fashioned big band music and his shadow passing back and forth across the light under his door.

She smiled to herself. She knew that he must be working on something, another invention, perhaps. She crept past the door, hoping he wouldn't hear her.

She was wrong, the door opened quickly and her uncle peered out.

'Why aren't you asleep?' he whispered, looking concerned.

'Why aren't you? What are you up to?' Eve asked, knowing full well.

'Well,' grinned Uncle Rufus, 'before Anwaar left, he gave me some strange-looking powder. He told me it was to be put in the Crookes camera and it would capture the witches' souls. I've just been calibrating the camera and making small adjustments so that when we use the camera it will do just that. Of course we won't know for sure if Anwaar's powder will definitely work but it's the best we've got. And if Anwaar says it will, then I trust him implicitly.' He leaned his head against the door frame and closed his eyes briefly. Tiredness suddenly enveloped him.

Eve could have hugged him in that moment. He was so hard-working, so dedicated to his profession. She just hoped that he was right and that the Crookes camera and the new powder would do the job.

'Well done, Unc. I love you.' Eve stepped forward and kissed his stubbly cheek.

Uncle Rufus seemed a little taken aback but smiled, and ran his fingers through his curly greying hair.

'I love you too. Now off you go, back to bed, young lady.'

CHAPTER 16

A Coven of Witches and an S.O.S. Switch

It was the middle of the night and Maisie Shaw woke up suddenly. She didn't know what had disturbed her. The low rumblings of her mum's snoring beside her brought her back to reality. She was home, with her mum and baby son Alex. But something was prodding away at the back of her head. It was the woman, Alice Nutter again. Maisie moaned and turned over onto her side, throwing a pillow over her head in an attempt to block the voice out. She could hear her own heartbeat racing, pumping through her body, her breath quickened as the familiar but sickening feeling lurched inside.

'*We must join them,*' the voice of Alice whispered in Maisie's head.

'No, Alice,' moaned Maisie, under the duvet. 'I don't want to do this.'

'Yes, you must, *we* must! Now is the time. We must join them and prepare for the rising. Maisie, you and I are one, we must go to them now. We are to help them.'

Maisie sat upright. Her mum groaned at the disturbance

and mumbled, 'Go back to sleep, Maisie, love.' She then rolled over and began to snore once more.

Maisie didn't move a muscle, she remained sitting in the same position for quite a while. She didn't blink, she just sat and stared. It was if she were waiting for something.

Suddenly baby Alex began to cry in the room next door. Maisie got up and made her way towards him.

'You OK to get him, love?' slurred her mum.

'Yes,' replied Maisie very matter-of-factly, closing the door quietly behind her. Then walking robotically, she went into the baby's room, picked him up and rocked him. Alex stopped crying and fell back to sleep once more in his mother's arms. Maisie placed him back in the cot and covered his little body with his warm blanket. She stared at the sleeping baby for a few seconds then picked up a small ragdoll that lay beside her son. She held it carefully in her hands, smiled wickedly, traced the outline of the doll's face with her fingers and then whispered, 'Naughty girl.'

Downstairs in the kitchen, Maisie opened a drawer and felt around for something, her fingers fished about and then to her satisfaction felt the soft material she'd been looking for. The handkerchief that Eve had used for her nosebleed. Maisie, and the influence inside her, knew the power that young girl had, even if she didn't know it yet herself. But at all costs they had been told that the girl Eve must either join them or be destroyed.

Maisie took a sharp knife and began to cut down the side of the ragdoll, its smiling, happy face never changing as the sharp steel sliced deep into its side. The blood-spotted handkerchief was then pushed inside the toy. Maisie brought the doll up to her mouth and began to whisper and chant. Her voice was different, it was dark and menacing, deep and foreboding. '*Abray . . . ye . . . doom . . . liko . . . visage . . . un . . . drem . . . otto.*'

Satisfied that her task was complete, Maisie put on her coat and boots then placed the doll carefully inside the pram. 'Shush, little one,' she cooed. She opened the front door quietly and then without a backward glance, Maisie Shaw pushed her pram into the dark freezing night.

All the streets of Lancaster were empty and deathly quiet. The moon was full, and its light bathed the hospital in a pearly iridescent glow. Everything was still. The only sound came from the huge oak trees that stood guard on either side of the building. The winter wind had picked up and was forcing these ancient sentinels to creak and groan; the lone sound was strangely haunting. The hospital was quite small, a modern building that had served the community well for a long time. But in all the years of caring for the sick and injured, the staff there had never come across patients like those admitted a few days before.

Each patient who had been brought in had caused confusion and intrigue amongst the staff: from the little boy Jamie to the eminent Judge Bromley. What was happening to them? Not one of the doctors could identify exactly what was wrong, and yet they all seemed to be suffering from the same symptoms. Experts had been sent for, but after examining each one of the comatose victims, they had all left scatching their heads in confusion. An undiagnosed virus, perhaps?

Seven-year-old Jamie Drake was in a private room off the children's ward. He lay completely still; wires and tubes surrounded his all-but-lifeless body. Machines beeped and rang out intermittently. Otherwise, Jamie's small room was quiet and calm.

Suddenly the overhead fluorescent light began to flicker on and off, making an irritating noise, like a fly that couldn't be swatted.

The boy lay still as the room went from light to dark, light to dark, until slowly, and ever-so-quietly, Jamie began to move. His eyes opened first, then, like a zombie, he sat up. Clutching at one arm, then the other, he pulled out the intravenous drips that had been placed there. Tiny rivers of blood trickled down his arms; he didn't flinch. He sat with his back straight, head still, his eyes staring ahead. Then, as if on autopilot, he pushed the bedsheets back and positioned himself on the edge of the bed. He began to hum quietly but the noise wasn't pleasant; it didn't sound like a child humming — it was deep, low and gravelly. He began to swing his small, pale legs backwards and forwards in time to the song. Suddenly, as if receiving an instruction, he jumped off the bed and stood completely still in his hospital gown, before marching out of the room and down the dimly lit empty corridor. The night nurse was sitting watching a comedy show on her computer screen; she giggled, preoccupied. She didn't hear or see anything as Jamie walked straight past her, the top of his head bouncing along level with her desk. Without a backward glance, Jamie Drake made his way out of the children's ward towards the main entrance of the hospital.

There, waiting for him were three other patients: PC Rachel Nowell, Judge Bromley and Dave Law. Without greeting each other, they immediately huddled together, like football players discussing their next move. What were they planning? Then Jamie made for the front door. His small body walked with purpose, he lifted his hand up and pressed a green button on the wall, and the door began to open automatically.

Suddenly a man in a security uniform walked into the reception area. As soon as he saw the group of patients standing together, he shouted, 'Hey, you shouldn't be here.'

PC Nowell turned her head slowly round. A look of rage exploded across her face and immediately she ran over to the guard. With no warning, she grabbed the shocked man by the throat and threw him as if he weighed no more than a doll, tossing him backwards and over the reception desk. His body landed with a heavy thud and a crash.

PC Nowell walked back to join the others as they made their way through the door.

A huge gust of wind blew down the street, and the oak trees' branches twisted and groaned in defiance. They were the only witnesses to a very peculiar sight. Three adults walked together, arms outstretched, holding each other's hands. They walked in a line in the middle of the empty street. Their bodies moved unnaturally, their hospital gowns fluttered and danced about as the wind circled around them. Trancelike they followed a little boy who skipped and sang with joy as he tripped down the hill. His demonic voice trilled as he went past the sleeping residents of Lancaster, all tucked up warm in their beds.

> *'Witches in the garden,*
> *Witches in the tree,*
> *Turn around, turn around, one, two, three.*
> *Look inside the bottle,*
> *You will see,*
> *Five witches in the garden,*
> *Will come to you and me.'*

The strange figures came to the end of the road. Nothing stirred. A street lamp directly above them began to flicker. They stood together, heads bent down and then in the distance a revved engine could be heard screeching towards them. In an instant, all the heads lifted up to greet a battered old car that careered at high speed, braking suddenly.

Jamie opened the front side passenger door and got in, the others bundled into the back. Without any words, Maisie Shaw put the car into gear and drove off, leaving a trail of noxious fumes behind them.

Jackie Shaw woke up and instantly knew something was wrong when she saw that her daughter wasn't lying next to her. She

jumped out of bed and went immediately into the baby's room.
When she saw that Alex was fast asleep in his cot, she sighed
in relief then went downstairs calling, 'Maisie, Maisie, love!'
There was no answer. She searched the rooms and even went
into the back garden. But when she saw that Alex's buggy had
gone, she suspected her daughter had vanished with it.

Instantly she called the SPI. 'Hello? Yes, it's my daughter,
Maisie Shaw,' she said breathlessly. 'She's gone.'

In the dawn light, Lancaster Hospital was crawling with police.
Cars with their blue lights flashing surrounded the front
entrance. Nurses and doctors were being questioned by senior
police officers. The security guard was sitting on a chair, being
stitched up by an anxious-looking young nurse.

As the family members of the missing patients came in,
they were stopped at the door and led into a side room where
the leading detective told them of the night's extraordinary
events. They were then asked several questions about their
relatives. Had they ever acted like this in the past? Were they
in communication with any strangers? Had they ever met one
another before? Each bemused relative left the room and stood
in shock in the reception area, not knowing quite what to do.
Ernest Nowell, Molly and Steve Drake, Mrs Law and Judge
Bromley's wife all looked drained. The relatives stood together,
mumbling in hushed voices, wiping tears from their eyes and
hugging each other. Eventually they were steered into a private
room by two sympathetic nurses.

CHAPTER 17

The Inspector Calls and a Witch Called Euphemia

Clovis, Tom, and Eve were all trying to enjoy their powdered eggs in the front room. They had had a much-needed sleep and were ready to get the day underway. It was lovely to know that nothing, not one ghostly entity, could follow them or visit them whilst they stayed at The Safe Haven hotel.

Tom had slept like a baby and was now ready for whatever came their way today. Clovis had taken a while to fall asleep because he'd been mulling over all the information they had uncovered. Eve had fallen asleep quickly but her dreams were somewhat dark, although she couldn't recall them and woke up startled and disorientated. Her body was shaking, and her sheets were wrapped like vines around her limbs.

Uncle Rufus came back into the room, having taken Boris outside for his morning walk.

Having already been given a full breakfast by Gerry, Boris happily slumped down in front of the fire and closed his eyes for a much-needed morning nap.

'Brrr,' shivered Uncle Rufus, rubbing his hands together.

'It's freezing out there.' He smiled at the three friends and began to unwind his long scarf from around his neck.

'What's happening today, Professor?' asked Clovis, biting into a piece of bread slathered in jam.

'Today,' replied Uncle Rufus, picking up the large brown teapot and pouring himself a welcome cup of tea, 'we are having a call with the Witchcraft department at the SPI. I've sent them all the information that we retrieved from Jennet, I also sent them images of the witch's bottle. I'm hoping they'll have some useful information for us and they might be able to tell us where exactly on Gallows Hill the witches were hanged. There's lots of other information we need to gather, too, and I want to start off with the moon phases. We'll use the computers in Albert.'

'The Witchcraft department!' cried Eve. Her eyes dazzled with sheer excitement. 'I wonder who we'll talk to? This is so cool.' She grinned to herself as she spread jam onto her bread.

'This is all brilliant, Professor,' said Clovis, bolting down the last forkful of food into his mouth. 'I can't wait to get cracking.'

'Me, too,' said Tom. 'After last night's sleep, I feel great.' He lifted his arms above his head and stretched like a cat. 'I've not slept like that in ages.'

'Good,' said Uncle Rufus. He put his cup down carefully into the saucer. 'I've got a funny feeling that today is going to be very busy. We're going to need all our energy, so finish up your breakfasts and let's get to Albert.'

'Will you be back tonight, Professor?' asked Stan as they

stood on the doorstep minutes later, with the morning cold nipping at them.

'I'm not sure,' said Uncle Rufus, looking thoughtful.

'Well, the door's always open for you, you know that,' smiled Gerry.

'Indeed, I do,' replied Uncle Rufus, hitching his rucksack onto his shoulder. 'If not tonight, I'm sure very soon.'

'Well, good luck today, whatever it is you're doing. Hush-hush, and all that,' said Stan, tapping the side of his nose. 'Careless talk cost lives,' he whispered to Eve.

Eve nodded, recognising the World War Two slogan, and copied Stan's nose tap.

Once inside Albert, Uncle Rufus started the engine to warm the place as they worked. Clovis sat at the computer console and began to look up moon phases, his hands moving quickly, swiping this way and that as images of the moon, its craters and its dark mountainous shadows whizzed past. The next image that Clovis pulled up was of a huge deep-red moon. Clovis moved his fingers, grabbed the image, swung around in his chair and brought the data into the middle of the van.

Everyone stared at the incredibly clear representation of the blood moon. It turned slowly in front of them all, in 3D, as if the moon were actually inside the van.

'That's incredible,' said Eve, staring with her mouth open.

Information began to scan upwards next to the moon. Clovis tapped on some words and the text stopped moving. 'There,' he said with confidence. 'Well, by the looks of it, the next blood moon is . . . tonight, and,' he continued, leaning back in his chair, 'it's only visible for a few hours.'

'Tonight!' said Eve, now looking very worried.

'Mmm,' sounded Uncle Rufus as he moved, never taking his eyes off the image of the moon. He sat down next to Clovis, pulled his glasses out of his coat pocket and peered closer at the information displayed in the air. Clovis was right, the next blood moon *was* indeed tonight. 'This means we have to work incredibly fast,' he said. 'Old Demdike has been working up to this one night. My guess is that something may well be about to happen with the witch trial accusers' descendants at the hospital.'

Suddenly Uncle Rufus's phone exploded in a cacophony of noise. Everyone jumped at the sound. Recognising the number, Uncle Rufus answered the video call and linked his phone to the computer screen; instantly Inspector Rutherford's face could be seen. Clovis used his thumb and forefinger and brought her image into the centre, so everyone could see her.

It was obvious that she was not at the SPI headquarters. She could be seen from her shoulders up, being buffeted about by strong winds. She had her hand on her precious velvet tasselled hat and was trying to shout over the raucous wind.

'My dears, I'm afraid to tell you that there's been an incident at the hospital. It seems all the victims have just up and left.'

'What?' exclaimed Uncle Rufus.

'It happened in the early hours of this morning, there's CCTV footage of them all leaving the hospital together. I'm sending that over to you now.'

'But where have they gone?' asked Eve.

'That I don't know, my dear,' answered Inspector Rutherford. 'If you watch the CCTV footage, you will see there is a car they get into but frustratingly, the footage cuts out before a registration plate can be seen.'

'I've got the footage now, Inspector,' said Clovis, tapping on the screen. Next to the inspector's image, video began to play of some shadowy-looking people dressed in hospital gowns moving about in the reception of the hospital.

Eve gasped in horror as she watched PC Nowell attack the poor security guard. Uncle Rufus drew his face closer to the images.

'That's definitely our chaps,' he said, shaking his head in dismay. 'But where are they going?'

Everyone was silent for a second, not sure what to make of the scene that had unfolded before them.

Inspector Rutherford interrupted the silence. 'We've got to find them and ... er ... find ... ish ...'

'Inspector, you're cutting out. Is everything all right there?' Uncle Rufus looked a little worried.

'Oh, yes, sorry,' replied the inspector, the signal back and clear, 'just a bit blustery and cold where I am at the moment.' Her hat buffeted about on top of her head. The tassels reminded Clovis of a windsock sticking out at a ninety-degree angle. The wind was obviously very brisk wherever the inspector was.

'Now then,' she shouted across the sound of the blustery weather, 'I've just heard some news about Maisie Shaw.' She peeled away a large leaf that the wind had slapped and stuck to the side of her rotund face, and carried on. 'Early this morning,' she shouted, battling against the gale, 'we heard from Maisie's mother. It seems that Maisie has disappeared too. It looks like she's definitely connected to this case and perhaps more involved than you originally thought.' Inspector Rutherford squinted, her face very serious. 'You need to bolt this one down, Rufus, my dear. I'm afraid time is against you. Do you think you'll need any assistance? Euphemia is chomping at the bit. Can you cope?'

'We'll be all right, Ruthers, we're fine here. I think tonight we'll manage to capture the souls of the witches.'

'Fascinating, dear fellow. I know you explained it to me in a text, but refresh my memory, just how are you intending to capture these souls?' Inspector Rutherford brought her face closer to the screen.

'Well, it involves the Crookes camera and some unusual powder that was given to us by Anwaar. Of course there is no way I can test it in the time we've got, but if Anwaar says it will work then I have every confidence that it will. We will take a picture of each ghost and in doing so, we will capture their very essence. I'm guessing here,' went on Uncle Rufus, scratching his chin, 'but I'm thinking once the photograph is developed, we can then burn the film and collect the ashes of that picture. The ashes are in fact the soul of the ghost. I asked in my text what kind of container you want me to put the souls into?'

'Ah, yes, I did see that question and I put it to Witchcraft department,' confirmed Inspector Rutherford. 'I know that they have been discussing the subject and I believe they have the answer and will let you know ASAP.'

'Good,' replied Uncle Rufus. 'There is a downside to my equipment, though,' he continued slowly. 'We only have a short amount of time to burn the film; I couldn't quite fix it so the soul stays inside the picture indefinitely.' Uncle Rufus was clearly disappointed with himself. 'We have to be quick, I'm guessing we'll have about a minute, otherwise the soul in the picture will be freed. Once we have captured all the souls, somehow we will hand them over to the SPI, or your good self, where it can be decided what on earth is to be done with them.'

'Capital!' shouted the inspector, clapping her gloved hands. 'Well, you know what to do if you need back-up, just flick the S.O.S. switch, and help will come straight away. I'll sign off now, keep up the good work, my friends. Euphemia will be calling you shortly and remember, it's most important that you all keep safe.'

Everyone watched as she tried to switch the phone off but struggled and in doing so revealed that all was not well.

The back of a man could be seen in the distance. Then a voice could be heard shouting, 'Inspector! We have detected a signal from the beast. We must act now!'

It was hard to hear who it could be, as the wind was howling so much. Then suddenly the picture went black and the line cut dead.

'Who was that man? Did you recognise him, Uncle?' said Eve, a little worried.

'I'm afraid I didn't hear well enough, but don't you worry, Ruthers can handle herself and she's obviously got someone with her,' Uncle Rufus said reassuringly.

'I think it could have been Anwaar,' said Clovis.

'Yeah,' agreed Tom. 'It would make sense him leaving us to go and help the inspector.'

'What's the S.O.S. switch, Professor?' asked Clovis.

'In each vehicle assigned to us by the SPI,' replied Uncle Rufus, 'there is a switch, and when it's activated, the SPI know exactly where we are and send help. After our last case with Jack the Ripper, the inspector didn't want to take any chances and so she had S.O.S. locators placed in all of our vehicles.'

'Where is it in Albert?' asked Eve, looking around and expecting to see a big red button with *S.O.S.* written on it.

Uncle Rufus put his hand under the steering wheel. 'You can't see it, but if you feel around, you'll come across a small switch.'

'Good to know,' said Tom.

'Well, I'm sure we won't need any help,' said Uncle Rufus confidently. 'Right, back to work, chaps.' He brought out his notebook and began flicking through a few pages.

'We need to find out where the descendants have gone and why,' he said, looking at his scrawled handwriting. 'So, let's say . . .' he mumbled the few words as he chewed on the end of his pencil '. . . they are all aware of the blood moon and need to be together for what Jennet called the *rising*. Where would they go to do that?' He tapped the pencil against his teeth, concentrating hard.

His thinking was interrupted by his phone ringing again.

'Ah,' he cried. 'I believe this could be the Witchcraft department. Clovis, put the image on screen please.'

Clovis tapped on the large computer screen and then pinched a blurry image with his finger and thumb and brought it into the centre of the van.

As the picture became clear, Clovis, Tom and Eve all stared at a very striking-looking woman.

'Hello, Professor, how are you?' The woman looked to be in her early thirties, she was very pretty, had a black, short bob hairstyle, and dark kohled eyes.

'Well, hello, Euphemia,' smiled Uncle Rufus. 'I don't think you've met my students; this is Eve, my niece.' Uncle Rufus brought his hand up and rested it on Eve's shoulder. 'And this is Tom.' Uncle Rufus gestured with his other hand towards a suddenly shy Tom.

He tried not to stare at the beautiful woman in front of him, but he just couldn't stop looking at her. Particularly her eyes. They were like cats' eyes, deep green and speckled with flecks of gold.

'And this is Clovis,' added Uncle Rufus. Clovis nodded back.

'Everyone, this is Euphemia Laveau, one of the many experts we have in the Witchcraft department,' said Uncle

Rufus, as he picked up his notepad and sat back down in a chair.

Everyone exchanged pleasantries and then Euphemia began.

'So, Professor, we have managed to gather quite a bit of information about the bottle you found. I gather it's still safe?'

'Indeed it is,' answered Uncle Rufus. 'It's tucked away in the glove box of Albert.'

'Good,' said Euphemia, her ruby red lips pursed into a gentle smile. 'The glass seems to originate from the early Egyptian era. In fact, this is the first one we've ever seen of this kind. And I have to tell you, we're very excited about it. There were allegedly three of these bottles made at the same time and originally, they were designed to be used for good, for protection, for peace and good luck. But after a while, each of them went missing and according to legend they were discovered by a necromancer, a being who worked for the dark lord. The necromancer used the bottles for evil; he placed blackened souls of the darkest kind inside the bottles and when the dark one needed to wreak havoc, they were set free. Many wars in that time were caused by the souls leaving the bottles and causing chaos and destruction. Two of them were eventually found and finally destroyed. Our thinking is that this bottle, the one you have in your possession, could be the last one.'

'But how on earth did Old Demdike get her hands on such a powerful tool?' whispered Uncle Rufus.

'That we do not know,' replied Euphemia.

'But this is extraordinary!' Uncle Rufus was clearly very excited and yet his face betrayed something else: fear.

'And,' continued Euphemia, 'the witch that made this binding spell was in fact very powerful too. The souls inside it have, over all these years, been building their energies, enough to possess humans and bend them to their will. We know that the souls placed inside were done so not of their own choice, but were put there under duress. But over time, their anger has grown, and they can only hear Demdike's commands. After much debate here in the department, we've decided that you must collect all the souls and place them back in the same bottle and seal it once more. Once this is done, you will bring it back to the SPI for safe keeping. We don't want those souls getting into the wrong hands. Back here, we can help the poor innocent ones go to the Veil. But Demdike, she's a whole different energy to deal with.' Euphemia smiled briefly and continued, 'Rest assured we *will* contain her.'

'Rightio,' said Uncle Rufus, his face serious, eyes down, concentrating on his notepad as he scribbled away furiously with his well-chewed pencil.

'Also, we found out some information about Alice Nutter.' Euphemia licked her lips and shuffled around in her seat. 'It seems she was a neighbour to Old Demdike and, according to her testimony, just happened to call in to Malkins Tower, Old Demdike's home, on that very same Sunday that the officials arrived. She was enquiring about sheep. She had nothing to do with witchcraft whatsoever, but was accused anyway. A terrible business.'

Uncle Rufus nodded in agreement.

'Oh, and I've spoken to Mr Fortesque,' added Euphemia.

'Ahh yes, Jack,' said Uncle Rufus, recognising the name.

'Yes,' smiled Euphemia. 'Mr Fortesque from the Reincarnation and Past Lives department. He said as soon as Maisie Shaw is found, he will come to her straight away.'

'Thanks, I appreciate that. Reincarnation is rather new to me.'

'How fascinating,' said Eve. 'To think that Maisie Shaw could once have been Alice Nutter. That poor woman, completely innocent but tortured, jeered at and then hanged in front of a mob of people. Do you know exactly where the witches were hanged?' added Eve. She was trying to remain cool and calm but inside was thrilled to be talking to a real witch. Even though no one had said the word, it was obvious that this woman was the real deal.

'After some research,' said Euphemia, 'we've managed to trace the exact location inside the perimeter of Gallows Hill where the dreadful hangings took place.' Her eyes became slits, the green and gold flashed in anger as she spat out her words. 'The place is now . . .' She paused, looked thunderously into the camera, and took a deep breath. '. . . a children's playground.'

'Of course. That makes perfect sense,' said Clovis, looking thrilled.

'What do you mean?' asked Tom.

'Well, don't you remember Old Demdike's rhyme?'

Clovis brought out his notebook and flipped through some pages in a flurry, then began to read the rhyme.

There are eleven but only five will rise,
Those who condemned us, shall be our prize,
On the night of the blood moon, where children make their
* play,*
We shall bind together, and the world you know will pay.'

'Where children make their play. That's it!' said Uncle Rufus, looking very satisfied. 'Can you send us the coordinates for the playground, Euphemia?'

'Already done, Professor,' she replied. 'I emailed them through this morning, they should be in your inbox.'

'What about the blood moon?' asked Tom, shyly. 'Why that moon phase?' He was turning a shade of dark pink.

'A blood moon is full of powerful energy for a witch,' Euphemia explained. 'Old Demdike had the sight. She was able to see into the future and knew what was going to happen to her family. She knew what she had to do. Use the bottle, hide her soul and the others' inside for hundreds of years. She bided her time, knowing that one day a little boy would free them. Only under the light and influence of this particular blood moon will she be able to take revenge by killing the descendants of the people who accused and condemned the Pendle witches to death. In committing this act, Old Demdike's revenge will be completed and once done, she will harness the descendants' souls and absorb their spirits. And in doing so, make herself a very powerful witch indeed.'

Euphemia Laveau sat back in her chair and blew out a long sigh. She drummed her long elegant ringed fingers on her desk, then leaned back in towards the camera. 'She must be stopped at all costs. I know you want to do this alone, Professor, but we are all here for you. If you get into trouble, we will come.'

Suddenly a large black cat slinked in front of Euphemia. It arched its back as the witch stroked it.

Eve, Clovis and Tom nudged each other. The cat looked into the camera, its green, gold-flecked eyes blinked slowly, then the animal simply walked out of shot, head held high, its nose rudely in the air.

'Oh, and another thing, I nearly forgot,' chimed Euphemia, sitting back in her chair and lacing her fingers together. 'The accused witch known as Chattox was an old blind woman who was the head of a rival family of Old Demdike's. The family feud was well-known in the local community. Chattox was apparently a formidable healer and some say a witch. Old Demdike didn't like the competition, as many of the locals would secretly go and see Chattox for lotions, tonics and potions to heal their afflictions, rather than her. We here at the department believe that Old Demdike took Chattox's soul without her knowing. Just imagine, when the poor woman was hanged, she found herself trapped for eternity with her worst enemy. But Old Demdike knew what she was doing, she needed power and strength and in Chattox she had that in bucketfuls.'

'That's more or less what Jennet told us,' blurted out Tom, suddenly forgetting his shyness.

Euphemia got closer to the screen, her cat-like eyes flicking upon Tom for a second.

'If you all can help these poor souls,' she said, 'and rescue the descendants, then we here at the Witchcraft department will be eternally grateful. The Pendle witch case has gone on long enough, and we need to lay their souls to rest. But remember, Professor, whenever you need us, just say the word.'

'If we get into trouble,' said Uncle Rufus, looking down at his feet, 'I promise we will be in contact. I appreciate all your help.'

Euphemia nodded and smiled.

Uncle Rufus continued, 'My plan is for us to stay out of sight and just snap away with the camera, capturing the souls. A simple operation, really, and I'm sure we'll be all right. But as any good investigator knows —' Uncle Rufus looked around at his three young ghost hunters — 'we must be prepared for anything.'

'And our job,' said Euphemia, 'begins when the bottle is given to us. We are all looking forward to working on this case and bringing it to its safe and final conclusion. Good luck to all of you.' Euphemia blinked her big eyes, smiled once more and then her image suddenly disappeared from the centre of the van.

The three friends all talked at once, excited chatter filling the van. They had just spoken to a real bonafide witch, and she had given them their starting point. The children's playground.

With a flurry of new-found excitement, the team began to research the playground, the area and its history. Clovis found images of the alleged witches. They found drawings and records of the day that they were all hanged. This case was becoming more and more fascinating as they dug deeper.

They were all shocked when they noticed the time, realising that they had been talking and researching for some hours. By the sound of Clovis's growling stomach, it was time for something to eat. The clock was now against them as it would only be a few hours before darkness fell and the blood moon shone down on them all. Tonight they somehow had to capture five souls and save the descendants.

Uncle Rufus got into the driver's seat and started Albert. Over the din of the engine he shouted, 'Everyone, seatbelts! Let's get some food first, and then go to the playground.' The engine coughed and spluttered and everyone held their breath as for a second it sounded as if Albert wasn't going to start. But suddenly an explosion rumbled through the underside of the cantankerous old vehicle, and Uncle Rufus turned around and grinned. 'Albert certainly knows how to make me nervous.'

CHAPTER 18

Paralinks and Camouflage Cream

Uncle Rufus steered Albert through the streets of Lancaster. The snow had begun to fall once more, adding to the Christmas cheer and seasonal festivities. He pulled up the old van outside a cafe, where he insisted they all went inside for something to eat from the twenty-first century. Boris was left to guard Albert.

After a large meal, lots of chatter, stomachs bursting, they made their way back into Albert and set off towards the park.

Clovis looked at his watch. Three p.m. They went slowly over a speed bump as they entered the park, on the lookout for a children's playground. Uncle Rufus had put the coordinates Euphemia had sent to him into his satellite navigation. 'It should be round here somewhere,' he called over his shoulder as he braked slowly.

'There it is!' said Tom. Swings, slides, climbing frames and roundabouts could be seen through an opening in the trees. Tom felt himself go cold; he knew in his heart that this was the place where the Pendle witches had met their end. He had felt the rope around his neck, seen the child smiling, laughing at him. He had experienced all this when he had been in Malkins Cottage. This was the place; he was positive, and this was where they would come face to face with the ghost of Old Demdike. Tom swallowed down his nerves and tried to focus on the job they would be doing in a couple of hours' time.

Uncle Rufus pulled into a car parking space, turned the engine off and stared straight ahead. 'Imagine what it must have been like to have been brought up here on the back of a cart, had a rope placed around your neck and then have the cart moved from under your feet.'

'And now, look what that space is,' said Eve, disturbed by the scene laid out before her.

They watched as a little girl and boy played on the swings. They whooped and hollered the higher their dad pushed them. Little did they know of the atrocities that had taken place here all those years ago.

'So, what's the plan?' asked Eve, climbing into the passenger seat next to her uncle.

'We wait,' said Uncle Rufus. 'If we're right, Eve, and I think we are, this is the place that Old Demdike will try to join all the spirits of the witches. It's a big, clear area, surrounded by woodland, no one to see anything, and it's the location where all the Pendle witches were hanged.'

'What if the descendants don't show up?' said Tom, joining the group at the front of the van.

'They will,' said Uncle Rufus confidently.

'We've got an hour until it gets dark,' said Clovis.

'And then,' said Uncle Rufus, 'we wait to see what they do. Remember, I have the bottle. We must keep that safe, as we need it to place the souls in and bring back to Euphemia. Anwaar has placed a seal on it, but when the time comes, we will remove it. I'm sure that tonight Old Demdike will bring the descendants here and try to kill them once she's released the witches' souls that are possessing them.'

'What better way to get revenge,' said Clovis, nodding.

'So,' said Eve. 'When do we go in?'

'I'll set Albert up now. There's a camera on the roof that will record three hundred and sixty degrees. It takes images in night vision and sound, so we won't miss anything.' Clovis, Tom and Eve watched silently as Uncle Rufus flicked the panel for the radio upwards to reveal a couple of dials and a button. He pressed this, and they could hear something moving above them. 'That's the pole with the camera on top rising up. I'll just select the measurements of the area to record.' Uncle Rufus turned the two dials and flicked the radio cover back down. 'There, all set and recording. We've got a bit of time left before darkness, then we'll get into position and wait until the victims appear.'

'And you really think Old Demdike will try to kill them?' asked Eve.

Uncle Rufus looked thoughtful and said, 'I believe what poor Tom experienced at the cottage is how Old Demdike wants the descendants to die. She wants them to feel what her family went through. But as soon as the witch's soul leaves the descendant's body, Eve and I will try to capture its spirit as quickly as possible with the Crookes camera. It won't take long for Old Demdike to realise that one by one, her family of souls is disappearing. That's why we must all stay hidden. It's imperative that no one is seen. If Old Demdike gets the slightest sniff of you, then you must get to Albert as quickly as possible. Understood?'

Everyone nodded in agreement.

'What happens then? How do we help?' asked Tom, looking incredibly nervous.

'Once the souls are out of the descendants' bodies,' said Uncle Rufus, 'no doubt the victims will be very confused and frightened. Tom, Clovis — you must do what you can to get them out of the playground, *but,* and here's the big *but,* under no circumstances must you be seen. When you have attracted the descendants' attention, drawing them out and into the cover of the trees. You and they must get to Albert before the witches have the chance to find them again.'

'But won't Old Demdike follow them here?' asked Clovis.

Uncle Rufus smiled. 'She might try, but Albert is protected, nothing can get inside it. Eve, you will be with me and help me with the Crookes camera.'

'Am I the right person to be with you, Unc? Wouldn't Clovis be better?' asked Eve, looking worried.

'I knew you'd ask me that,' said Uncle Rufus, scratching his head. 'I need to be with the camera, and *you're* going to be my assistant. You're smaller than the two boys and so we can hide more easily. I must get the camera close enough to the action. When I've taken the shot and the film comes out, you, my girl, must take the film and slip quietly, undetected, into the trees and burn it. You must pour the ashes into the witch's bottle. I've managed to construct a small copper funnel which you put into the top of the bottle, that way it will be easier for you to pour the fragments of photographs inside.'

Eve was concerned, but flattered that her uncle was entrusting her with such a big job. She didn't like the thought of burning souls though. 'Are we sure that once we've collected the souls in the bottle the SPI will release them into the Veil?'

Uncle Rufus looked warmly at his kind-hearted niece. 'I can assure you that every good soul will go to the Veil. These people who Old Demdike has trapped for all these years deserve peace and we're going to give it to them. Don't worry, Eve, all the souls that were hanged will be sent to the place that they were meant to go to. And poor Jennet will at last be able to rest too.'

Eve brightened a little. 'But what about you, Uncle? We've all seen what Old Demdike can do; she tried to strangle Tom, tried to kill him. Anwaar said that Tom, Clovis and I are protected, but what if she sees you, Uncle? What if she does the same to you?'

'I have this, remember.' Uncle Rufus pushed the sleeve of his coat up and there on his forearm was a tattoo. It was a black marking; the Eye of Horus glared back at them all. 'This will protect me from anything negative.' Uncle Rufus pulled his sleeve back down and smiled at a worried-looking Eve.

'I hope you're right,' she replied. 'The burn that the ghost of Jack the Ripper gave you was awful. I just hope that when Anwaar changed it, it really did give you protection.'

'And where do we hide until you call us?' asked Clovis quietly.

'I want you and Tom to hide in the trees directly behind wherever the descendants stand. My gut feeling is that they'll stay together. Eve and I will find a close-enough spot and hide too.'

'But what about the powder in the Crookes camera?' asked Clovis. 'When it takes a picture it makes a loud noise, and a huge cloud of white powder comes out. Old Demdike will see that a mile off.'

'Yes, Clovis,' replied Uncle Rufus. 'I thought of that too. Whilst working on the camera last night, I managed to modify the machine to be silent. I've also stopped the bright flash, so it's invisible to our eyes, but whether the ghosts will still hear or see it, I'm not sure.' Uncle Rufus rubbed his chin and made a *mmm* noise. 'Anyway,' he continued, bringing himself out of a deep scientific conundrum. 'I believe that the Crookes camera will indeed capture souls. If there are any problems and the camera doesn't work, I know there are a lot of people at the SPI on standby to assist. The most important thing to remember is that none of you are to be seen. I'm not having you in danger, understood?'

Eve, Clovis and Tom all nodded.

'Now, then,' said Uncle Rufus, looking a little excited, 'I've got some new equipment for you all.' He got up and went into the back. There he pulled out of one of the rucksacks four little round silver tins.

'These are so we can communicate without being detected,'

he said, passing a tin to each of them. They opened the small containers and discovered two translucent rubber circles inside. They were about the size of a five-pence piece and sitting on a cushion of white cotton.

'They look like buttons,' said Eve.

'What are they?' asked Tom.

'I think we put them on our face,' said Clovis excitedly.

'Well done,' said Uncle Rufus, grinning at Clovis. 'Here, let me show you all.'

Uncle Rufus took the two buttons out of their round tin and placed them on his temples. 'Now, believe it or not, I can hear everything you are all saying as long as you have your devices on too.'

'But where's the mouthpiece?' asked Clovis, sticking the circular patches on either side of his face.

'There isn't a mouthpiece, you don't need one. Let's test them, so you're all comfortable with how they work,' replied Uncle Rufus. 'Stand outside, Clovis, then tap the buttons once, that will turn them on. But take care not to be seen and then start whispering to us.'

Clovis did as Uncle Rufus asked, tapped the buttons once and then began to talk quietly. Tom and Eve were delighted to hear his voice clearly in their ears.

'How cold is it outside?' asked Eve, giggling.

'It's freezing out here,' answered Clovis, as if he were standing right there beside them all.

Clovis jumped back into the van quickly and slid the door behind him, closing out the cold air.

'What are these called, Professor?' asked Clovis.

'I haven't really thought of a name. What do *you* think we should call them?'

'What about paralinks? said Clovis.

'I like that,' said Tom.

'Paralinks it is, then,' grinned Uncle Rufus.

Clovis was thrilled with Uncle Rufus's new invention. 'What's the range on them, Professor?'

'Quite far, actually,' replied Uncle Rufus, smiling proudly. 'About ten miles, and we can use them underground too. To switch them off, just tap them twice gently. Lovely as all your voices are, I think hearing you constantly would drive me mad.' Uncle Rufus laughed when he saw Eve's hurt face. 'I'm joking, Eve, you have a gorgeous voice.'

'Yeah, in small doses,' teased Tom. 'Ow!' He jumped and rubbed his arm, having just received one of Eve's deadly arm thumps.

'It looks like that family have gone,' said Tom, looking through the windscreen.

'Good,' said Uncle Rufus. 'It's getting darker. Not long now. Are we all ready? Do you all know what you have to do?'

Everyone nodded and gathered their rucksacks, checking all their ghost-detecting equipment was there.

'Oh, I almost forgot, here . . .' He passed along three sets of small binoculars. 'These are night-vision sights. I think we may all need them tonight.'

Clovis held his binoculars as if in charge of a precious animal.

'I think he's going to explode with excitement any second

now,' sniggered Eve to Tom. The pair laughed at Clovis, who was peering through the binoculars, pointing them at various objects through the van's side window.

'Just epic,' whispered Clovis to himself.

The new pieces of equipment had seemingly taken the edge off the three friends' nerves. They all hoisted their rucksacks onto their backs; inside they each had various ghost-hunting pieces of equipment from temperature guns to EMF meters. Clovis had snuck into *his* rucksack a few cheeky snacks in case he got hungry. On the outsides of their coats, they clipped their night-vision GoPros.

'One final thing,' chuckled Uncle Rufus. He went to one of the seats at the back of the van and pulled out a drawer from under it; after rummaging around, he brought out another tin, and, grinning like a young kid, he prised it open to reveal some green gunk, which he proceeded to smear all over his face.

'Wicked!' said Tom, excitedly.

'Now this feels like special ops,' laughed Eve.

'Well, come on then, everyone, fingers in,' said Uncle Rufus, his face completely dark green with the camouflage cream.

Once everyone's face was completely covered and the giggling had died down, Uncle Rufus brought them all back to reality.

'OK, let's run through the plan again. We must all know exactly what we are doing. This must run like clockwork. There's no room for errors or mess-ups. Understood?'

The old abandoned terraced house was bare and filthy. Its windows were boarded up and covered in graffiti. Inside, it was cold and depressing. The only warmth came from four bodies, all huddled around a pitifully small fire that had been lit in a metal bucket. No one said a word, they just stared into the feeble light.

The little boy, Jamie, suddenly stood up, staring at the paint-peeled ceiling, and began to chant softly. His delicate body swayed from side to side as he whispered strange words over and over again. Soon the others followed, standing up, their hospital gowns now dirty and soiled. They held hands and joined in with Jamie's chant.

'Magoya . . . sans . . . le . . . aydo . . . free . . .' Over and over again, the words were spoken, faster and faster. They began to shout and scream like wild, rabid animals. They shook and tossed their heads from side to side.

As Maisie Shaw entered the dimly lit room, the demented shrieks, cries and chants faded in the damp air. The room fell silent. The descendants looked to Maisie and waited for her to say something. She spoke very quietly: 'It's time to go.'

Tom, Eve and Clovis watched Uncle Rufus pace up and down as they went through their plan over and over again.

After everyone was completely confident that they knew exactly what was going to happen, it was time for action.

'OK,' said Uncle Rufus. 'Wait until we get outside and then we'll switch the paralinks devices on. Remember, just tap them once. We'll sync up our EVP watches too. Hopefully we'll get some incredible voice phenomena tonight.' Uncle Rufus rubbed his gloved hands together with excitement and then pointed at the three friends. 'And don't forget to stay out of Old Demdike's way. Leave her to me. Eve, stay close to me, and Tom . . .' Uncle Rufus looked at him. 'You've done so well so far, keep it up. Only let the good ones in, no evil can penetrate your mind, you know that. Stay strong.'

Tom nodded and began to chew on his thumbnail nervously.

'What about Boris?' asked Eve. 'Should he stay here in Albert?'

'No, I want him with Tom and Clovis,' said Uncle Rufus. He pulled Boris's harness on and attached the lead, then handed it over to Clovis. 'He'll protect you both and give you any extra warning. If there are any problems, flick the S.O.S. switch and help will arrive quickly. You know where it is. Remember, Albert is protected, so if you get into any trouble, make your way back here. OK?' Uncle Rufus stared hard at his three apprentices and they nodded.

They climbed out of Albert quietly and got low to the ground, leaning their backs against the van.

The sky had turned an inky black, stars twinkling in the darkness. The odd, thin wispy cloud swept past a glorious bright red moon, the likes of which Eve, Tom and Clovis had never seen before. They all tilted their heads back, marvelling at the sight before them.

'That, my young friends, is a very powerful blood moon,' said Uncle Rufus. He was transfixed by its colour, its beauty, and he had never seen one as bright as this. No wonder Old Demdike had worked up to this night, this moon. It was an incredible sight to behold.

'Wow!' sighed Clovis.

'It's incredibly powerful,' whispered Tom. He felt his whole body tingle inside when he looked at it. What effect might it have on people or spirits that only had darkness inside of them, just like the ones they were about to face tonight?

'Now I understand why the witches want to meet under it,' whispered Uncle Rufus. 'You're right, Tom, it has incredible power, and if the right incantations are said, anything could be possible.'

'Well, let's hope we stop Old Demdike before she utters a word,' said Eve.

'Shush.' Uncle Rufus placed his forefinger over his lips.

'What can you hear?' asked Eve. Everyone had hunkered down by the side of Albert and was watching out across the park.

'It came from in the trees,' said Uncle Rufus. He looked through the night-vision binoculars. 'I can't see anything yet.'

He continued panning the binoculars around slowly. Tom, Clovis and Eve were on tenterhooks. Were the descendants here? Was it the ghost of Old Demdike?

Uncle Rufus whispered, 'It's all clear. I don't think anyone is here yet, so let's split up and get into position. Tom, Clovis, get closer to the edge of the playground but stay hidden in the trees. Eve and I will go around to face you. When they arrive, we may well have to move again, but let's start there.

Remember to keep low to the ground, crawl on your bellies if you have to.'

'Good luck,' whispered Clovis, smiling at Eve and Uncle Rufus as they set off.

'Right,' said Tom, taking in a deep breath. He pulled his rucksack straps tighter against his body and grinned at Clovis. 'Ready?' he asked.

'Ready, I'll follow you,' said Clovis quietly.

The pair made their way through the wooded area as quietly as they could. Once they could see that they were close to the edge of the playground, they slid down onto their fronts, leaned onto their elbows and began to search the grounds through their new binoculars. Boris flopped down too, smacked his chops and stared out into the red moonlit night.

CHAPTER 19

A Terrible Fog and a Sobbing Judge

The playground was eerily quiet; a gentle breeze moved the swings, just enough to make it look as if someone invisible were sitting on them. The roundabout creaked as the wind turned it slowly round.

The huge ancient oak trees swayed every so often, groaning like old men at the inconvenience of the weather's rude interruption. It was as if these deep-rooted old oaks knew that something was coming, as if they were protesting at an incoming storm.

The wind picked up and in the distance, a rumble of thunder could be heard. Tom shivered, not from the cold but from a feeling, deep within his gut, that this wasn't going to be easy. He pushed down the feeling and continued to look through the night-vision binoculars, hoping to spot something moving. The area was a massive field, really, hidden away from the main streets and roads of Lancaster. No lights from cars could be seen; it was quiet apart from the odd rustle in the undergrowth.

Clovis looked through his binoculars and could just make out what he thought was Eve and Uncle Rufus opposite them.

'Everyone in position?' whispered Uncle Rufus's voice.

'Yeah, we're here, can't see anything yet. We can see you both, though,' replied Tom, zooming the binoculars in on Eve.

'And we can see *you* both. Stay down, I believe our guests will appear any minute,' said Uncle Rufus.

Suddenly they heard the sound of a revving engine, followed by the screeching of tyres and the loud bang of a car backfiring.

'What was that?' asked Tom, looking about him with his binoculars.

'I hope it's not some guys coming to the park for a laugh,' said Eve, imagining the worst.

The car's sounds died down, and so it was just the wind, the thrashing trees and the squeaking of the swings as they jostled back and forth. The roundabout had begun to spin faster and faster, as if someone or something were pushing it.

Then a loud crash of bracken and branches came from inside the woodland.

Everyone focused their night-sights onto where they thought the noise had come from.

'I see something,' said Tom.

'Me, too,' said Eve.

'Yes,' murmured Uncle Rufus. 'Opposite us and to your left. 'It's the victims, they're here. Keep quiet and don't move, not until I tell you.'

Eve could hear the excitement in her uncle's voice and had to admit that it was infectious. Her heart was beating so fast now.

All the descendants ambled slowly towards the playground.

'Is it just me or are they walking really weird?' said Clovis.

'Yes, they're moving very strangely, it's like they're zombies or something,' said Eve.

'They're getting closer,' said Tom urgently. Using the binoculars, he zoomed in on Jamie Drake. He seemed to be the only one who wasn't walking zombie-like, in fact, he was dancing and skipping along. He twirled and jumped and was singing something.

'Jamie seems happy enough,' said Tom.

'Don't be fooled,' said Uncle Rufus.

Jamie ran from the others, across the length of the playground to the far end and over to the swings. He jumped on one, giggling and singing happily to himself and then threw his head back and howled like a crazed dog. Slowly he began to lurch himself back and forth, trying to get higher and higher.

The other three followed the boy, but all stopped at the edge of the playground. They had their heads down, their bodies unflinching, their hospital gowns fluttering in the night breeze.

'They look so weird,' said Eve.

'Hang on, who's this?' said Uncle Rufus.

Coming from the carpark and walking quite close to where Tom and Clovis were hiding, was a woman pushing a pram. She walked straight towards the group but hung back a little, keeping herself partly hidden under the trees.

'Oh my God! It's Maisie Shaw!' hissed Eve.

'It certainly seems as though her reincarnated soul, Alice

Nutter, is being manipulated by Old Demdike too,' said Uncle Rufus.

'I hope the baby's all right,' said Eve, sounding troubled.

'I'm sure the baby is fast asleep,' said Clovis, hoping to put Eve's mind at rest.

'Can you see, they've formed a semi-circle, facing Jamie?' said Uncle Rufus. 'I think we'll have to get closer to them so I can put the Crookes camera into position. I'm thinking Eve and I may need a distraction.'

'What kind of distraction?' asked Tom nervously.

'Something small, nothing dramatic, but just enough so that we can get closer. Any idea?'

'Get ready, Professor,' said Clovis. He pulled a little dog treat out from his pocket and then uttered some Arabic words. They made no sense to anyone else but they seemed to have caught Boris's attention.

The bulldog cocked his head to one side and looked at Clovis eagerly.

'Speak, Boris,' he whispered, then repeated the Arabic words again.

This time Boris understood and began to bark loudly.

'Brilliant!' hissed Tom. 'You've been listening to Anwaar and his dog training words.' He turned his head back and brought his night-vision binoculars up to his face. 'It's working,' he whispered.

The victims moved their heads slowly, all at the same time, over to where the noise was coming from. Jamie slowed down his swinging and stopped singing.

Uncle Rufus, followed closely by Eve, dashed as quickly as they could into the playground. The victims were listening to Boris's bark, and seemed totally unaware that anyone else was there.

'Keep him going, Clovis,' whispered Uncle Rufus, breathing heavily as he ran. In the middle of the playground there was a big slide and climbing frame. Uncle Rufus pointed at it to Eve, and they hunkered under the large structure.

'OK, Clovis, we're in position,' said Uncle Rufus after he'd caught his breath.

Clovis gestured for Boris to be quiet and then he gave the dog a much-appreciated doggie treat.

'Brilliant everyone,' whispered Uncle Rufus. He took the rucksack off his back and brought the Crookes camera out. Then he positioned a small tripod behind the slide and screwed the camera onto the top. Uncle Rufus managed to place it so just the lens was peeking out of the side of the slide.

'Now, we've just got to wait for Old Demdike,' murmured Uncle Rufus.

They sat patiently for another five minutes and just as Tom was about to say how cold it was, all the victims suddenly stretched their arms above their bodies. Their torsos all lit up together like little Christmas illuminations where the burn marks had been branded upon them. A pulsating hue of blue light emanated from all four bodies. Little Jamie Drake had stopped swinging on the swing. His chin rested on his chest, and he was now motionless, his body limp, his arms held high, reaching for something invisible, while his burn mark fizzed like a Catherine wheel. Then, one by one, the descendants brought their heads up and stared with wide unblinking eyes at the red blood moon. A flash of forked lightning exploded across the night sky and a clap of thunder boomed.

'This couldn't get any creepier,' said Tom.

'Yeah, I know,' said Eve. 'It's like the Devil's going to arrive in a minute.'

'What's that, coming in from the bottom of the field?' said Clovis, squinting his eyes through the binoculars.

'Is it moving?' asked Uncle Rufus. He had turned around and was also using the night-vision sights.

'This isn't good,' said Tom, his voice shaking.

A black swirling fog had rolled in from the bottom of the field, picking up momentum as it lurched towards the playground, tumbling and falling over the grass, slithering like a serpent, gobbling things up as it fell over them. The mass crept, coming close to the playground. Eve and Uncle Rufus huddled closer together. Eve scrunched her eyes shut tight, held her breath and squeezed her uncle's hand. The fog missed them and continued to move into the centre of the playground where suddenly it stopped, beginning to form a shape directly in front of the four victims.

With every second, the black mass took on the appearance of a figure, the shape of a woman becoming clearer and clearer. Then there she stood, for all to see. A huge manifestation of a truly terrifying ghost. She was the one true Pendle witch. Old Demdike. Her formidable and frightening image hovered a few feet from the ground.

'Well, that was quite an entrance! Is it me, or does she look a lot bigger and scarier than when we last saw her?' asked Clovis.

'It certainly was, and no, you're right, she does,' said Uncle Rufus. 'I think she's acquired more energy and strength. After all this time, this is the moment she's been waiting for.'

Uncle Rufus continued to whisper so quietly that everyone held their breath whilst he spoke. 'As soon as Old Demdike releases the souls of the witches, that's when we get ready to act. You know what you all have to do.'

Old Demdike's ghost looked around slowly, drinking up the atmosphere, soaking in the power of the blood moon. Her ancient face, wrinkled with time and bitterness, was lit up. The witch's bottle had done its job.

'This is where it happened,' she croaked, sniffing the air with her long thin nose. 'You were all murdered here in this place, hanged by the neck.' The ghost pointed to Jamie Drake, who was sitting watching in awe from his swing. 'Come, Elizabeth, join the others and you shall all rise up.'

Jamie Drake jumped off the swing and ran quickly to stand with the other victims. Old Demdike's evil gaze followed Jamie and, once satisfied that all the victims were standing in the right place, she began.

'Now the descendants will pay the price.' She lifted one arm above her head and with the other, she pointed at each of the victims in turn with her long bony finger. A bolt of green light rushed from the tip of her sharp nail. It was a weapon. The light fizzed as it travelled through the air, a fork of lightning striking and splintering into the judge's stomach and bringing to life the blue burn mark. It began to throb like a heart. Pumping quickly, fizzing and undulating under his skin.

'Oh my God!' cried Eve.

'It's all right, keep calm,' mouthed Uncle Rufus, gesturing for her to stay quiet.

The light then travelled from the judge to the others, one by one, binding all four victims, like an umbilical cord. Slowly and collectively their bodies began to lift off the floor. They jerked and convulsed, writhing in agony as their figures endured an enormous bolt of power.

The ghost hunters watched in horror and fascination as four ghostly souls ascended from the victims' bodies. Three women and one man floated out; the spirits stretched and moaned. But when they realised they were at last free from their hosts' bodies, their dark angry faces became joyous.

Jamie, PC Nowell, the judge and Dave Law all fell to the ground. Then slowly the adults began to stir; shaking their heads, looking around, they stood slowly, obviously confused, and not recognising where they were or why they were dressed in hospital gowns in a children's playground. Jamie's little body, though, lay still and quiet; the spirit which had been inside him hovered above. Elizabeth Device had enjoyed being in the body of a child. It had been so much fun to play, skip and run, but now it was time to get to work to help her mother.

She and the other souls looked down from high above at the scene unfolding before them.

Old Demdike's spirit levitated a little higher than the others, giving her power and the advantage. As she moved, swathes of grey and black material flapped and waved around her awful countenance. Her grey hair was pulled tightly onto the top of her head, revealing a face that was thin and painful to look at, the skin covered in huge warts and wiry hairs. Her eyes were like black stones, dead and lifeless, the lips spiteful, twisted and thin.

This ancient old spirit was fizzing with energy and hatred. Just to know that these pathetic creatures could see and hear her and were about to be made to understand what their kind did to hers, was pure ecstasy. She watched as their confusion changed to horror. Dave Law and Judge Bromley stared in terror as their eyes locked onto the hideous sight that was now hovering in front of them. Neither of them noticed the other apparitions who were hanging above them all. Their attention was firmly fixed on the thing moving right before their eyes. Were they dreaming? Had they died and gone to Hell? What was happening and who were these other people standing next to them?

PC Rachel Nowell rubbed her eyes and then screamed at the apparition hanging in the night sky. It stared deep into her very being. She had never seen or felt anything so terrifying in her life. She turned and tried to run but fear had got the better of her and her shaking, weakened legs wouldn't move. She turned back round to face the horrific entity that now seemed to be moving closer towards them all.

'Shush, shush,' cooed Old Demdike's ghost as she floated quickly towards the now-crying policewoman. 'Oh deary, deary me. Scared, are we?' The hideous old ghost brought a bony finger up to the policewoman's face and pulled a strand of hair away.

PC Nowell flinched, covering her face with her hand.

Old Demdike laughed. She had her audience now. 'You can't run, you can't hide. I will always find you,' she sang excitedly.

Dave Law tried to make an escape too but to everyone's horror was hit with what looked like a green bolt of lightning from the ghost's hands. He rolled around on the wet ground, moaning and shaking. PC Nowell grabbed him and cradled him in her arms.

Satisfied that her victims were not going anywhere, Old Demdike began her tirade. 'Your ancestors accused us, jailed us and executed my kind. I was put in a dungeon and left to rot. I starved to death because of *you*.' Her form rushed up close to the judge. In shock, the man screamed in terror. Old Demdike placed her wizened, wrinkled old hand under his chin and tipped his head back.

'Do you know what your ancestor did to us?'

The judge scrunched his eyes shut tight and shook his head, hoping that this nightmare would end.

'*No?*' Old Demdike's reply was sarcastic. 'I'll tell you, shall I?' she spat, bubbling over with the poison of hundreds of years of anger and fury. The judge and his companions had no idea what was happening: why were they here and what was going on? Wide-eyed and shaking with total terror, they watched on.

Old Demdike moved effortlessly around them all. As she glided and floated, she purged her ancient, twisted feelings out onto her poor confused prey.

'Your ancestor,' she shouted to Judge Bromley, 'was a judge like you. And there he sat on his throne, passing judgement on my kin.' Her voice was getting louder now, venom spewing from her cold, cracked lips. 'You are just the same, aren't you? A pathetic judge. Well, soon, oh great judge —' the ancient ghost grinned spitefully like a vicious cat — 'soon you will experience exactly what my family went through. You will feel the rope around your neck, and I will love watching you choke and grunt like the pig you are.' She stared at each of the victims in turn. 'Quite a fitting death. Don't you think?'

The judge had begun to weep.

Old Demdike pushed her horrendous face close to his and asked in a whisper, 'Well, answer me, isn't this a fitting end, judge?' All the man could do was nod. The ghost laughed even harder and moved onto the police officer. '*Your* ancestor was Nowell. He had something to prove, didn't he, eh? He was on a witch hunt and didn't give up. You're just like him, aren't you? Think you're a do-gooder? Well . . . ?' Old Demdike took a step back and screamed in PC Nowell's face: '*YOU'RE NOT!* I'm in charge now, and I've hunted you down. I've hunted you all down and now I'll have the pleasure of watching you all die.'

Demdike slid along to Dave Law. She looked the market trader up and down and chortled. 'And . . . what about Mr

Law?' She drew her long finger across her neck slowly, smacking her lips.

Dave Law stood quivering, looking back and forth between the others and the ghost. He questioned his sanity, but thought he could try to talk his way out of whatever this was.

'I've done nothing wrong, love,' he said nervously. 'I just sell stuff, that's all, you know, on the markets. I don't want any trouble. Look, whatever prank this is, I won't tell anyone, if you just let us go, all right?'

'Let you go?' sizzled Old Demdike. 'I think my granddaughter would like to have a word with you. Your ancestor brought our whole world crashing down, Mr Law.'

Taking her cue, the ghost of Alizon Device floated down and faced Dave, the man whose body she'd been possessing for the last few days.

Poor Dave, he didn't know where to look. His legs buckled at the sight of a second ghost.

The ghost of Alizon Device circled the man shaking, now on his knees. *Now* he knew what she had felt all that time ago.

She began to talk, her voice just audible. 'I said I was sorry,' she said, 'sorry I cursed your ancestor. But no one listened. He was a pedlar, just like you. I hanged because of your blood. Well, now it's time for you to hang, right here where we all met *our* deaths.' Dave squeezed his eyes shut, desperately trying to rid himself of the image of the ghost. He opened his eyes again, but the appalling sight was still there, so close to his face. Dave had never been a religious man, but right now he needed all the help he could get, and so he brought his hands up to together and began to pray over and over again.

Meanwhile, Uncle Rufus was switching the various lenses around at the front of the Crookes camera. He needed to get as close as possible to the action. At last he settled on the lens that could get a clear shot of the ghosts from where he and Eve were positioned. He placed it over the front of the camera and began to follow the soul of Alizon Device. With his thumb poised over the button of the Crookes camera, he waited for the whole of her image to appear in the viewfinder. *There* she was. Uncle Rufus pressed the button, the camera made a tiny snuffling noise. Meanwhile, Eve was set, like a sprinter at the starting blocks. She knew what she had to do.

The picture shot out of the camera and Eve grabbed it. Uncle Rufus signalled for her to go. She got down low and scrabbled quietly on all fours across the short distance from the slide into the trees. There she took out the witch's bottle, pulled Anwaar's seal off the top and positioned it on the snowy ground with the copper funnel. She flicked the lighter on and began to burn the corner of the film. Charred flakes of the smouldering image of an ancient dead teenager began to fall into the funnel, tumbling down into the bottom of the blue bottle.

Tom, Clovis and Uncle Rufus watched in delight and amazement as the ghost of Alizon Device began to fade.

'It works! The powder works! One down, four to go,' whispered Uncle Rufus, relieved and delighted. 'I think now is the time for our main distraction. Old Demdike is going to notice any second now that Alizon's soul has disappeared. Are you ready, Tom?'

'Yep,' said Tom. He took a deep breath, got up slowly and carefully, turned around and, keeping low to the ground, moved over to a huge oak tree and closed his eyes. He'd never done this before but, according to the professor, because of the connection he had made with this one particular entity and her willingness to help, it should work.

Tom concentrated and began to picture the ghost of Jennet Device in his mind's eye. He called out for her, over and over again. Suddenly his stomach flipped, and his head went all fuzzy. He knew then that he wasn't alone. He knew that she had come.

Meanwhile, Uncle Rufus was having a bit of trouble trying to get Elizabeth Device's soul in shot. Her spirit was incredibly lively, but unlike the others, she wasn't teasing or taunting Jamie, her host. Perhaps that was because Jamie wasn't the descendant of someone who'd done her wrong. He was just the boy who'd opened the bottle. The boy who'd set her free.

'Clovis,' whispered Uncle Rufus. 'When Tom brings in the distraction, it's time for you to go in and get Jamie out.'

'I'll try,' said Clovis. 'Oh God,' he said to himself nervously, forgetting that everyone could hear him. 'Don't mess this up.'

'You won't,' said Eve, encouraging her friend over the paralinks.

Uncle Rufus decided to concentrate on another of the witches. He moved the camera's eye over to Old Demdike and thought, *Let's see*. But every time he tried to look at her image through the viewfinder, the picture that came out was black. *Not good,* he thought. He realised with dread that Old Demdike wasn't going to be so easy to capture. Her energy must be too powerful.

Tom was still concentrating. Eyes closed, breathing relaxed. Suddenly he knew that Jennet was close, and then he heard her. 'Tom?'

He turned round, searching for the whereabouts of the voice, and stumbled around the tree's trunk, coming face to face with the poor spirit of Jennet Device. Her scraggy face, the empty soulless eyes, her bony body and her swirling black cloak.

'It's time, Tom,' she said.

Tom gulped and nodded.

The ghost of Jennet rose up off the ground and without any warning passed right through Tom. Tom caught his breath and felt as though he had been punched in the stomach. He realised that along with the icy cold feeling in his torso, he could feel the anger, the rage and the determination. Jennet was on the war path.

CHAPTER 20

A Distraction and a Purge

Uncle Rufus was still trying to capture Elizabeth's soul but was finding it almost impossible. Old Demdike hadn't noticed that Alizon had gone, or if she had, she hadn't reacted.

Now the ghost of another Pendle witch hovered over the judge's head. She looked down on the body that she had been inhabiting all this time, and felt no pity for the pathetic, jabbering wreck laid out before her. This ghost was similar in looks to Old Demdike: in her clothing, filth and her general demeanour. In life, Chattox had been a mean old woman and hadn't changed in death. She had been Old Demdike's enemy and yet here she was, joined to her old rival like gum stuck to a shoe. Judge Bromley yelled out as his eyes locked onto the image of another, nightmarish old ghost hanging just inches above his head.

Chattox began to cackle with laughter. It was infectious, and soon Old Demdike joined in, as did all the other ghosts. The noise was horrendous. The terrified descendants placed their hands over their ears and winced in pain.

Uncle Rufus was aiming the camera slightly above the judge's head. He sucked in a sharp breath as he moved it upwards, taking in the awful image that had manifested from the poor judge's body. He knew this was Chattox. He lined up the camera, making sure he had all of the ghost in frame and then pressed the button. As soon as the machine captured the soul on film, Eve made off with the image into the safety of the woods. There, she took the lighter and condemned another Pendle witch back into the bottle.

Everyone could see the apparition of Chattox begin to fade. 'Two down, three to go,' whispered Eve with relief and satisfaction.

Next Uncle Rufus trained the Crookes camera on the ghost of James Device, who was hovering above his whimpering host, PC Nowell.

'You look just like him,' observed the ghost. He was inches away from the police officer's face. He had been a handsome young man once but now his image was one of sorrow and hate, his eyes dead and black.

'I didn't do anything,' cried PC Nowell. 'We can't be held responsible for the things our ancestors did.'

Old Demdike and James began to laugh. They looked to each other, both clearly enjoying the pitiful cries of their prisoners, and oblivious to the disappearance of their ghostly companions.

'I can't wait to see you hang,' said James, looking spitefully at PC Nowell. He said no more, simply turning around and floating up above his host's body.

Suddenly Old Demdike and James were distracted by something rushing towards them.

'Oh my God,' whispered Eve.

'This is going to be interesting,' murmured Clovis, not quite believing what he was seeing.

Jennet's ghost tore towards the centre of the playground and faced her grandmother, Old Demdike.

'Well, well, if it isn't the Pendle witch child. All grown up, I see,' laughed Old Demdike.

'Leave James alone, he never wanted a part of this, he always hated you,' whispered Jennet, looking sadly over at the apparition of her brother.

'James is very happy being here with me, aren't you, my lad?' hissed Old Demdike.

The ghost of James Device nodded back at his grandmother.

'One thing I do know, my dear Jennet,' continued Old Demdike, 'is he knows how to be loyal. He loves his old granny.'

Jennet stared at the pitiful spirit of her brother whom she herself at the age of nine had accused of witchcraft.

'James, it's me, Jennet.' Jennet moved over towards him. She tried to talk to his ghost, but one look from her brother's spirit said it all.

'Get away from me! You killed me — you killed us all.' James tipped his head forward and began to sob. And in that moment, Uncle Rufus pressed the button, the camera whirred and Uncle Rufus handed the picture to Eve. Seconds later, the smoking image of a young man fell from the copper funnel into the bottom of the witch's bottle.

Jamie Drake woke up suddenly and sat up, rubbing his

tired eyes and looking about him. PC Nowell moved over to the little boy.

'It's all right, love,' she whispered.

'Where's my mummy and daddy?' asked Jamie, who was clearly very confused.

Jennet's ghost was now face to face with her granny and mother Elizabeth.

'You're bullies, that's all you are,' said Jennet. 'I'm a good person and I always have been. It's you two who treated me badly. I've lived hundreds of years feeling terrible for what I did — but I don't any more. If I'd felt love from either of you two maybe, just maybe, I would never have been told to do what I did by a complete stranger. I was a little girl. *Your* little girl, and you didn't love me enough, if at all. But now I'm free of your curse, free from both of you.'

Jennet smiled at her mother and grandmother and whispered, 'You don't frighten me any more. You are the ones who should be frightened. I know where you're going, Granny, and from what I've been told, it's pure hell.'

'Little Jennet,' squawked her mother, Elizabeth. 'You were always useless, weren't you? A waste of my time and your grandmother's. You were a cursed child, one I would like to forget.'

'Your words can't hurt me any more,' said Jennet. She turned away and began to fade. But just as she was about to completely disappear, she spun back and said: 'I'm going to a beautiful place, I'm released from my bonds. Now I'm free at last.' From out of the deep redness of the sky a brilliant thin shaft of light dropped down and engulfed Jennet's spirit. The skeletal image was no more, it was only replaced by the spirit of a little girl.

The ghost hunters watched on as the spirit of a once-tortured soul was now, after hundreds of painful years, finally set free. Eve wiped away her tears, knowing that if everything else failed tonight they had all done at least one amazing thing. They had helped Jennet Device cross over to the Veil.

'You come back here, don't turn your back on me!' screamed Old Demdike.

The brilliant white splinter of light closed, and the sky darkened once more. The wind had died down completely, but rain had begun to fall with intensity, and puddles formed on the concrete, like mirrors reflecting the inflamed sky and the full blood moon.

Old Demdike wasn't happy. She sniffed the air once more and to her horror noticed that apart from Elizabeth, all her companions had disappeared.

'Nooooo!' she screamed, and twisted, this way and that. 'Where are they? What's happening?' she shrieked.

'Everyone stay still, and low,' said Uncle Rufus.

Clovis and Tom were kneeling under a large bush and had been trying very hard to attract the attention of Jamie. Clovis didn't dare call out his name, as he didn't want Old Demdike and Elizabeth to hear him. Tom picked up a tiny stone and threw it over, hoping it would land near Jamie. To Clovis's and Tom's elation, the stone landed on the boy's bare foot. Jamie jumped and looked up, catching two sets of eyes blinking in the darkness. He squinted, and stared as the strange teenage boys waved him to come over. Jamie released himself from the police officer's embrace, and she too turned around.

Clovis and Tom motioned for them both to come over. Clovis placed his finger over his lips and both boys began to walk backwards, hoping that the police officer and Jamie would follow.

By now Old Demdike was apoplectic with rage at the disappearance of her accomplices and began to scream at Elizabeth. Uncle Rufus took his chance, as this had been the only time so far that Elizabeth had kept still. He focused the camera and took the shot. *Click.* The Crookes camera whirred softly, and then out of the front, like a tongue jutting from a mouth, a square picture popped out once again. Uncle Rufus pulled it from the machine and passed it to Eve, who then ran back to her hidden spot and began to burn the terrible ghostly image of Elizabeth Device.

Tom and Clovis had now managed to get Jamie and PC Nowell into Albert. They explained who they were and that they were here to help. 'You're safe now,' said Tom. 'Don't leave the van, though. If you do, she might find you.'

Jamie looked terrified. 'Don't worry,' said Clovis smoothly. 'Nothing horrid can get inside here.' Young Jamie nodded and PC Nowell hugged the boy close to her.

'Now,' said Tom, gesturing for them both to sit down, 'we're going back for the others.' Clovis rummaged around under one of the seats and brought out a thick blanket and placed it over them both. 'We'll be back soon and then we can get you back to your families.'

'But what's happening and what the hell is that out there?' asked PC Nowell, her eyes wide with distress.

'We'll explain when we get back,' said Tom.

Outside they instructed Boris to stay and guard. Boris watched as his two friends retreated back into the darkness of the woods. The dog sniffed the cold night air, farted and waited for their return.

'Jamie and PC Nowell are safe inside Albert, and we've left Boris guarding them,' whispered Clovis over the paralinks. Then he and Tom hunkered back down in their original positions.

'Brilliant,' said Uncle Rufus. 'Well done, and I've captured Elizabeth. That just leaves Old Demdike. Stand by, boys, to get the others out.'

Old Demdike turned around and began to call out for her daughter. If she weren't so evil, it would have been a pitiful sight. 'Elizabeth, where are you? Elizabeth? Please, Elizabeth, I can't do this without you.' Old Demdike's face eventually dissolved into a frenzy of crazed fury and hatred. She screamed and swore, roared and raged. Then she turned to Dave Law and Judge Bromley, as if noticing them for the first time. She came down to their level and moved her ghostly figure towards them.

'What happened to the woman and the boy?' her voice thundered.

Eve, Uncle Rufus, Tom and Clovis knew that both men

were now in terrible danger. Uncle Rufus spoke quietly to his apprentices. 'Tom, go back to Albert and press the S.O.S. switch. I don't want any harm to come to those men, and I think she's going to kill them. I've tried to capture her soul, but for some reason, perhaps her energy is far too strong, the camera won't take her image. Quickly, do it now . . . run.'

'I'll try and reason with her,' said Tom, moving forward out of the trees.

'You'll do no such thing. Get to Albert and flick the S.O.S. switch,' commanded Uncle Rufus. 'I'll deal with her.' Tom stood still and watched in open-mouthed terror as the ghost witch lifted her arms, her hands pointing directly at Dave Law and the judge. The two men cowered, holding onto each other in total, abject fear. He set off towards the Albert as quickly and as quietly as he could.

Old Demdike pushed her long bony fingers straight at the two terrified men and, from their tips, thin lines of green light flew out and began to wrap slowly around the men's necks. She roared with delight as she watched her two final victims beginning to panic. They kicked and gurgled, trying desperately to breathe. They clutched at their necks, struggling in vain to grab at the thing that was restricting their breathing. They clawed at their skin, now desperate, eyes bulging, staring wildly about them, not quite believing this was happening to them.

Suddenly a girl's voice bellowed from the centre of the playground.

'You old hag!' Eve stood tall, her face thunderous and enraged.

'Eve!' shouted Uncle Rufus, but it was too late.

In her hands, held high above her head, was the witch's bottle. The little white figures tied to the neck tinkled against the blue glass.

'Guess what's inside here?' said Eve, shaking in her boots. She hoped that this was a good distraction so the others could help the judge and Dave Law. 'I have the souls of Alizon, Elizabeth, James and Chattox inside. If you want them back, you have to let the judge and Mr Law go. If you don't, I will smash this bottle on the ground and your precious souls will be caught up in the wind, never to be seen again.'

Old Demdike sniffed the air and her apparition thundered towards Eve and the bottle. The horrific ghost stood much taller than Eve, bristling with fury. She brought her atrocious face close to the bottle and sniffed the top of it. Slowly she brought her head up, realising that the girl was speaking the truth. Inside her blackened soul, the witch boiled with ferocity. She would have to play this one carefully. One wrong move and the girl could drop the valuable bottle, and its precious cargo would be lost for all eternity.

'So, you have my bottle,' the old witch whispered to Eve. 'Are *you* giving *me* an ultimatum?'

Eve took a deep breath and knew she'd have to do her best acting. She put on her most determined, stubborn face, her eyes flashing menacingly.

Old Demdike weighed up the situation. The girl didn't appear to be scared. She needed that bottle back, she *had* to get the bottle back. In that moment, the ghost's bony face turned dark with rage. 'Give it to me!' she screeched, her fingers twitching, ready to strike at Eve.

Uncle Rufus picked up the tripod and Crookes camera. To avoid being seen, he sped into the woods and began to run round the outer edge of the playground. He hunched down as he ran, using the trees and bushes as cover. Once opposite Eve, his plan was to run in and grab her.

'I'm coming, Eve,' he whispered.

He scrambled through the trees but in one quick movement, he stumbled over a fallen tree trunk. Pain shot through his knee; he fell to the ground, clutching at his leg. Silently he cried out, the agony ricocheting through his body. Desperately he tried to get up but fell again, this time hitting his skull on a tree stump. He felt his head explode with pain and then everything went black.

'What the hell's going on?' asked Tom. Through the paralinks he had heard Eve confront Old Demdike and now Uncle Rufus wasn't answering. He began to panic. He opened Albert's door and dashed over to the steering wheel, there he moved his hands underneath it, desperately searching for the S.O.S. switch. There it was! He flicked it, made sure that Jamie and PC Nowell were all right, then as quietly as he could, he made his way back to join Clovis. His friend was lying flat on the ground, resting on his elbows, panning the night-vision binoculars from left to right. Clovis whispered over the paralinks to the professor.

'Professor, can you hear me?'

Tom could see that the professor hadn't got Eve out of there. What had she done and where was their mentor?

'Professor?' whispered Tom urgently.

Still no response.

Clovis moved the night-sights slowly, trying to see if he could locate the professor. He zoomed in on the wooded area opposite them, then saw a leg sticking out of a bush. It was the professor's, and it wasn't moving.

'Bloody hell, Tom, the professor's hurt. I can see him on the ground. I'll go to him. You stay here.'

Before Tom could answer, Clovis was off, keeping low to the ground and running as fast and quietly as he could. He mumbled to himself as he moved, knowing that both his friends could hear him. Panic was bubbling up inside him. What had happened? Why was the professor lying on the ground and not responding to their calls? As he got closer, he could see that the professor was indeed out for the count on the cold wet ground. He rushed towards his hero and lifted his head gently.

'Professor, are you all right? It's me, it's Clovis.'

Uncle Rufus slowly blinked open his eyes.

'Clovis, I've taken a little tumble,' croaked Uncle Rufus. 'Quick, take the Crookes camera and try to capture Old Demdike's soul. I dropped it when I fell. I hope it's not damaged.'

Clovis checked that the camera wasn't broken. 'It seems fine, Professor,' he said with relief.

'Good, now listen to me, Clovis,' said Uncle Rufus, grimacing with pain. 'Some of Old Demdike's power might have diminished now that we've recaptured the other souls. So it might make it possible for the camera to work its magic.' Uncle Rufus paused, clutching the side of his head and then let out a small moan. 'I'm afraid all I can see is stars at the moment. If the camera fails in capturing her soul, we'll have to wait for the SPI to arrive. I take it Tom sent the S.O.S.?'

Clovis nodded and looked down at Uncle Rufus's pale face. 'But, Professor, I can't leave you here.'

'Of course you can. I'll be all right in a moment. But we must help Eve. She's placed herself in danger. I was running to help her and then this tree got in my way.'

'Yes, I can hear her now, she's playing for time, I think,' said Clovis.

'All right then, off you go. Hide behind the slide and take the damn picture as quickly as you can. I'll go straight to Eve and pull her out . . .' Uncle Rufus smiled weakly and tried to lift his head, but quickly lay down again. '. . . when the world stops spinning,' he said, closing his eyes.

It slowly dawned on Eve that she'd done something really stupid. But she couldn't just stand by and watch someone else get hurt. She was sure what she had chosen to do would get her into trouble with her uncle. But if she could just give him, Clovis and Tom more time to try to extinguish this vile ghost, then it would be worth it. She was really worried now; she had heard Clovis talking over the paralinks to her uncle and realised that he was injured. That did it for her. Eve was ready for a fight, she just hoped Clovis could take the shot in time. She stuck her stubborn chin out and pushed the bottle higher into the air. 'Come any closer, and I promise you I'll smash it.' Eve hoped the old witch wouldn't detect her bluff. Or would she? Eve squeezed her eyes shut and hoped for the best. The last thing she wanted to do was smash the bottle and release all the souls again.

But Eve's determined face seemed to do the trick, as Old Demdike stopped in her tracks. But then she smiled and laughed a terrible wicked laugh. 'You're a feisty little thing, aren't you?'

Eve ignored the ghost and battled on. 'As I said, I want you to leave Mr Law and the judge alone. Let them go free.' She was trying to disguise the fear in her voice and stood even taller. 'I'll give you the bottle if you let them go.'

Old Demdike was beaten; her plans had all failed. Now she stood alone in a place that held nothing but hatred and death. Oh, how she had wanted her revenge, but she hadn't got it. Fury raged within her ice-cold soul. Her spirit shuddered and she could feel the power begin to ebb away. She consoled herself, knowing that she could try again, come back and take the revenge she so desperately needed. This was not the last they would hear of Old Demdike. Knowing that her time was short, the ghost decided to at least take the bottle back and its precious cargo. She smiled slyly and nodded to the girl.

'Agreed,' grinned the witch.

'Let me see them go first,' said Eve.

Old Demdike's black eyes seemed to glow red as she stared

longingly at the bottle, her prized possession. Without turning round, the ghostly witch gave a flick of her hand, signalling that the two men could leave. The green threads disappeared, leaving the judge and Dave Law to fall to the ground. They coughed and gasped, trying desperately to get some air into their lungs. It was Tom who ran in quickly and collected the very shaken casualties — and in doing so blew his own cover.

Seeing that the judge and Mr Law were free, Eve held her nerve and slowly lowered the bottle.

'And who might this be?' hissed Old Demdike, homing in on Tom.

Tom knew what was about to happen; he shouted to Dave Law and the judge: 'Run, get to the van. Go now . . . run!'

The two men didn't have to be told twice. They ran as fast as their shaking legs could carry them, through the trees and towards Albert.

Tom ran and grabbed hold of Eve. 'Are you all right?' he asked.

Eve trembled and nodded. If she spoke to her friend now, she would crumble.

Tom whispered, close to her ear. 'Did you hear? Clovis is going to try again with the camera. We must keep her here.'

'Now,' said Old Demdike, she was clearly delighted at having a fresh victim. But something told her deep down that the girl was the one she had seen in her visions. She must spare her. Old Demdike knew they would meet again. The ghost bent forwards, bringing her grotesque face close to Eve and Tom.

'You, girl, step away and be gone. But, little witch, be warned, I've not finished with you. I like to have fun with new members of my coven. You *will* fight the urge now, you won't even know of its power yet, but one day when you do, I'll be waiting in the shadows to come and collect you.' Old Demdike laughed even harder and rolled her scraggy head from side to side. With a flick of her hand, she pointed at something moving in the woods and chanted something under her foul stinking breath.

'Run, Eve!' whispered Tom.

Both Tom and Eve sprinted away from the centre of the playground, aiming for the cover of the trees in the distance. Just as they reached the boundary of the forest, Eve fell. Tom made a grab for her, but as he did so, the blue witch's bottle fell from Eve's pocket. He snatched it up and cried out again to his friend. 'Get to the van, Eve!' Eve didn't look back, but carried on running through the branches and bushes.

She didn't notice that the blazing green viper-like tendrils of Old Demdike's had twisted themselves around Tom's body, pulling him back towards the old ghost.

Eve finally stopped running and looked around for Tom, but he wasn't there. Suddenly she felt something grab hold of her ankle. She screamed out, falling down onto the bracken and sodden earth. Looking down, she could make out a hand holding onto her ankle. In the darkness, she couldn't see who it was grasping at her. Eve kicked out with her other leg, desperate to get free. Suddenly she felt a vicelike grip around her other foot. She cried out again and saw Maisie Shaw lying on her side, holding tightly onto her. Eve tried to move away but found she couldn't. Maisie's grip was strong and the look on her face was so evil.

'Get off me, Maisie!' cried Eve, struggling to get free. Kicking and wriggling, she eventually pulled her leg away from Maisie's grip and jumped up. Suddenly she felt an excruciating pain in her stomach. Eve looked down and saw to her horror that Masisie was now sitting up — in one hand she held a creepy-looking doll, and in the other, a huge black needle.

'Naughty girl,' sang Maisie in a croaking voice. 'Don't look so scared, Eve. If you say yes, you can join us, it doesn't have to hurt. I knew when I saw you in the house that you were once a witch, I can smell it on you. We always like to test our witches with the dolls. Are you a strong little witch or are you weak? Let's play.'

Maisie laughed manically and then suddenly plunged the needle deep into one of the doll's legs. Instantly Eve screamed out and fell back down to the floor. She clutched at her thigh, trying to find a breath as all the air seemed to have left her body. After a second or two, the pain thankfully disappeared. Eve sat up and watched as Maisie walked around her, with the doll lying limply in her hand and the black needle held high in the other. In an instant, Eve found her strength and leaped up, grabbing Maisie around the legs, bringing her down onto the wet, cold ground.

The two rolled around on the slushy floor. Eve was desperately trying to get the voodoo doll out of Maisie's hands.

She now realised what it was and that if she didn't get rid of it, Maisie would always be able to harm her.

But Maisie was too strong for her and managed to get on top of Eve once more. The doll was firmly gripped in her tightly fisted hands. Eve looked up and, through the drizzling rain, could see nothing but pure venom in Maisie's coal-black eyes.

Clovis was hearing all this terrifying commotion through the paralinks. He wanted to run and help his friend but knew that he had to take this picture of Old Demdike first. He got the camera in position behind the slide, placed it carefully on top of the tripod and began to find the correct lens, just as the professor had done earlier. Once he was happy that he could take the shot, he took a deep soul-searching breath, wiped the rain from his glasses and looked through the lens. He watched on in horror as he saw Tom being tormented by Old Demdike, like a cat playing with a trapped mouse.

'So,' Old Demdike chortled, sniffing Tom's face. 'You are a curious one. I can sense you have the gift . . . could be useful to me, but then again . . .' The old witch leaned back and instantly swished her calloused, wizened old finger, bringing about the electrifying light that began to coil like a green serpent around Tom's neck.

Clovis took a sharp intake of breath. 'Oh my God, Tom!' Clovis started to panic. What could he do?

Suddenly Tom's voice whispered quietly in his head. 'It's all right, I'm protected, remember. I can't feel a thing. I'll keep her thinking that she's winning, but, Clovis, please hurry up.'

Tom was incredibly relieved to see that Anwaar's protection spell was doing the trick, as all he could feel was an icy blast of cold air around his throat. But this time he felt no pain, no strangulation and he could breathe very easily.

Tom began to put on a bit of a show for the old witch. He gasped and clawed at his throat, struggling and fighting, much to Old Demdike's delight.

CHAPTER 21

Bowler Hats and a Voodoo Doll

Uncle Rufus opened his eyes to see what appeared to be a well-dressed gentleman leaning over him and peering down close to his face. 'Hello,' said a posh voice.

Uncle Rufus rubbed his head and began to sit up slowly, thinking that perhaps he was hallucinating.

'Poor chap, he can't see us,' said another voice.

'There's two of you?' said Uncle Rufus staring widely into the darkness. 'I'm seeing double,' he moaned.

'Hello, there. I think he's coming round now.'

Uncle Rufus rubbed his eyes and then massaged his knee, the pain was excruciating. As his eyes adjusted to the darkness, he could make out, standing next to each other, two very smartly dressed gentlemen. Both wearing black business suits and bowler hats and holding briefcases and umbrellas.

'Percival?' asked Uncle Rufus.

'Indeed, indeed.' Percival smiled warmly and peered closer at his earthly friend. 'Looks like you've been doing an outstanding job, Professor,' he said. He raised himself slightly off the ground to take a look at what was occurring in the playground. 'And Tom seems to have captured Old Demdike's attention.'

'What!' gasped Uncle Rufus, getting up too quickly and stumbling forwards.

'Steady on, old fellow,' said the other man, grabbing hold of Uncle Rufus's arm. 'Oh, I'm Reginald, by the way, another guardian. I'm very pleased to make your acquaintance.' The other smartly dressed gentleman tipped his bowler hat at Uncle Rufus.

'Thank goodness,' said Uncle Rufus. 'You've arrived just in time. I think Old Demdike is about to blow a gasket. The guardians are just what we need right now. Thank you. I think I'll be all right in a moment. I just need to catch my breath.'

Uncle Rufus stumbled again; his head was banging, he put his hand up to where the pain was radiating and felt hot, wet, sticky blood.

'It seems Tom is auditioning for the lead role in an amateur dramatics play. He's doing a grand job with Old Demdike,' said Percival, proudly.

'What's the lad doing?' Uncle Rufus brought his fingers up to his temples and felt for the paralinks but to his horror, they were no longer there. They had obviously fallen off when he hit his head.

Suddenly he heard a scream. He didn't need paralinks for that! Realising it was Eve, he staggered to his feet and limped in her direction.

Eve screamed again as Maisie thrust the needle into the doll's right hand.

'Say yes!' Maisie hissed.

Eve shook her head. 'No, I won't, I'll never join you.' She grabbed her hand, trying to lessen the pain by squeezing it.

Maisie had moved from sitting on top of her victim, and now was relishing complete power as she stood opposite her. Eve decided to use a different tack and try reasoning. Would it work? She didn't know, but hopefully it would give her some time and her friends or her uncle would come to her rescue.

'Oh, Maisie, please come with me,' said Eve, standing up. She offered her hand out to the young woman, who was standing an arm's length away from her. 'Come on, Maisie, you must wake up. Don't listen to Alice, she's not you. She's not even herself. Maisie! Alice! Listen to me, this isn't you. It's old Demdike, she's bewitched you, making you do things you don't want to do. Think of your mum, Maisie. Think of baby Alex . . . Argh!' Eve screamed in agony and dropped to the floor once more.

Maisie walked over to where poor Eve was now writhing about on the ground. She loomed over her victim, and with one twist of the large black needle, she slowly plunged it further into the small ragdoll.

'Naughty girl,' she hissed.

Eve clutched at her left thigh. The hot searing pain ran all the way down her leg.

Just then, Uncle Rufus managed to reach Eve. He grabbed her and held her close. 'It's all right, Eve, I'm here.'

'She's got a voodoo doll, Uncle,' whimpered Eve. 'She keeps stabbing it and it's . . .'

In her trance-like state, Maisie brought the large pin out of the doll's leg and then stabbed it with renewed vigour into the doll's face.

Eve screamed again, bringing her hands up to her head.

Uncle Rufus tried to move Eve out of harm's way, but she was in too much pain. He was just about to try to get the doll off Maisie when something shot past him, flying quickly through the air.

Boris landed on top of Maisie. They thrashed around on the wet muddy ground. The dog managed to knock the doll from her hands, and after another struggle he overpowered her. Maisie suddenly stopped fighting and just lay there. Had she given up the fight? Boris was standing over her, his growls rumbling deep in his chest, his teeth bared and saliva dripping down onto his prey's face. Maisie didn't move.

Eve and Uncle Rufus began to panic. Had Boris hurt her? She didn't stir, didn't try to get away, she just lay there, eyes wide open, staring up at the blood red moon.

'It's all right, Eve,' said Uncle Rufus. 'Come, Boris, good boy.' He patted the bulldog and whispered to Eve. 'We must hurry, it's time to wrap this case up.' He grabbed Eve's hand, picked up the strange doll and kneeled next to Maisie. He checked to make sure she was breathing, took his coat off and laid it over her. Then he walked over to the pram, expecting to see a baby inside — but there was nothing, just a crumpled blanket.

'There's no baby,' said Uncle Rufus, looking worried and confused. 'I'll come back for Maisie in a moment. She's still too dangerous to take with us. Come on,' he urged, 'the guardians are here now. They will search for the baby and finish the job. Let's get you to Albert.'

Once Eve and Boris were inside the van and Uncle Rufus had made sure all the descendants were OK, he nodded at Eve and jumped back out.

Eve slid the door open again. 'Where are you going?'

'First, I must check on Maisie, and then I have to help Tom,' said Uncle Rufus, rubbing his knee. The weather was awful now, the rain lashing down. Uncle Rufus looked like a drowned rat. 'But, Uncle, I can help,' protested Eve.

'No, Eve, you've done enough, and after dealing with Maisie, I think you need to rest now.' Uncle Rufus's tone was one that Eve knew shouldn't be questioned or argued with. She began to slide the door shut but before she did fully, she said, 'Be careful, Unc.'

Clovis was trying so hard to get a clear shot of the ghost, but she kept moving too close to Tom.

'For God's sake, stay still, you old bag,' he whispered under his breath.

'Take the bloody shot, will you,' said Tom, now sounding very tired.

Bizarrely Clovis suddenly felt a very odd, cold sensation

behind him. He turned around quickly and saw two ghosts standing close by.

Uncle Rufus was keeping low and running up behind them.

'All right, Clovis?' he whispered as he moved around the two strange-looking ghosts and kneeled down. 'Right,' he said to Clovis, 'ready to try and capture this annoying witch's soul? Oh, and of course you must remember the guardian, Percival, and this is Reginald, he's a new addition to the team.'

Clovis nodded and grinned nervously up at the two spirits. He never, in a thousand years, would have thought that he'd ever be making pleasantries with two ghosts.

Percival tipped his bowler hat at Clovis and beamed happily.

'Right,' said Reginald, 'let's get rid of the old girl. Is the camera ready?'

Clovis nodded and put his eye up to the lens. He hoped his glasses wouldn't steam up, as he needed a really clear shot.

'I did try and take her picture before,' whispered Uncle Rufus, looking back over his shoulder at his two ghostly companions, 'but her image just went black. I'm rather worried in case it happens again.'

'As you know,' said Percival, 'it's all down to energy, and we are under the impression that the old girl is quite pooped . . . exhausted . . . kaput! She's used nearly all her energy and the last of it she's spending on Tom, who we have to say, is rather brave, isn't he?'

'Yes,' whispered Tom over the paralinks. 'But if you could

all just cut the polite chit-chat and hurry up and take the bloody shot, please!'

'Yes,' mused Reginald, as if he could hear Tom too. 'Have another go at taking the old witch's picture, and you'll see it will work this time.'

Clovis turned to Uncle Rufus and asked, 'Do you want to do it?'

Uncle Rufus shook his head 'No, I want you to do it, Clovis.'

'Will somebody please do it!' shouted Tom.

Clovis looked again through the lens, and moved the camera slightly to the right, just missing Tom out of shot. The old witch was laughing manically as she witnessed what she thought were Tom's final breaths.

Clovis pushed the button down. The Crookes camera whirred, and a small puffing sound came from the perspex box at the back. Everyone waited a few seconds and then the contraption vomited out the picture.

'Quick, let's see,' said Uncle Rufus, going to the front of the camera. He pulled the picture away and saw with absolute pleasure, the image of Old Demdike.

'Yes!' he hissed. 'Now quickly, we need to burn the film,' said Uncle Rufus. 'Where's the bottle?'

Clovis put his hands over his face and said quietly, 'Tom has it, I can see it in his back pocket. We'll never get him out in time.'

Uncle Rufus and Clovis watched on, feeling defeated. They should have been elated as they saw the ghost of Old Demdike start to fade and the thin strands of green fizzing electricity uncoiled themselves from Tom's neck. The old witch was captured, but unless they could place her in the bottle within the next minute, her soul might escape.

'Quick, let's burn the photo,' said Uncle Rufus urgently.

He got out a lighter and lit the corner of the polaroid film. They all watched in satisfaction as the image began to curl and blacken, falling into Clovis's cupped hands.

Suddenly, out of nowhere and to everyone's horror, Eve ran across the playground, through the fading ghost of Old Demdike. She slid under the ghost's vanishing manifestation, grazing her side as she flung herself towards Tom, who had just found his feet.

'Run, Tom! She'll try and take the bottle.' Eve had heard through the paralinks that they hadn't got much time before Old Demdike's image was lost. She suspected that the devious old witch could try one last attempt to take the bottle with her.

Tom realised what Eve was doing and followed quickly behind her. Old Demdike's ghost was diminishing fast, but not fast enough. She flicked both hands out towards Eve and Tom. Green and black tentacles shot from out of her fingers, slithering like serpents towards them both. Tom looked back and side-stepped out of the way, but Eve's foot was caught. The green and black fizzing cords wrapped tightly around her ankle. With one jolt she was pulled down with a heavy thud. Screaming and kicking, she turned onto her back as she slid across the icy ground. And in that moment she knew that she was about to come face to face once again with the ghost of Old Demdike.

Eve shrieked as the cord around her ankle pulled tighter. She opened her eyes and could see that the ghost was hardly there any more. But she heard her vile voice: 'You're coming with me, little witch!'

Eve slid further towards the ghost, yelling, 'Help me, Uncle! Help me!'

Suddenly, an enormous, bright white light bolted into the red night sky and enveloped Eve. The bonds wrapped around her ankle dissolved into nothingness and instantly all her fear and pain disappeared. The light moved swiftly over to the fading ghost of Old Demdike.

Standing behind the light, Eve could just make out the shadows of two men, both were holding something high above their heads. Who they were, she didn't know.

Eve was exhausted, but managed to pull herself up and rush over to the safety of her uncle and friends. She flopped into her uncle's arms and said quietly, 'That was close, I thought I was gonna die.'

Tom quickly passed the witch's bottle to Uncle Rufus, and the ashes that had been caught in Clovis's hands were then carefully placed inside it. Uncle Rufus placed a strange silver cap over the top of the bottle and they all sighed with utter and total relief. At last, they had managed to capture the lost souls of the Pendle witches. They had done it. They had won.

Everyone watched on from beneath the slide. They could see that the guardians had put their umbrellas up over their heads; from the tips of each one, a fizz of beautiful white light was converging outwards to make an arc.

The ghost hunters were spellbound. They watched from their hiding place as the light began to slowly diminish, and with it, they could just make out the rolling, twisting black fog they had seen earlier, when Old Demdike had first made her appearance.

Once the light had gone, the two guardians folded their umbrellas back into place and walked with purpose back towards them all.

'You'll have no more trouble with her,' said Reginald, checking the time on his silver fob watch.

'Thank you so much, gentlemen,' said Uncle Rufus.

'It was a pleasure and an honour to work with you and your very capable and brave students,' said Reginald.

'Well,' said Percival. 'We must dash, got another case to see to. Cheerio to you all.'

The two guardians tipped their bowler hats, turned around and walked off with a spring in their step. Just before they faded completely out of sight, they could be seen tipping their hats again to something, a shadow, coming towards them.

'Hello, who's this?' said Uncle Rufus, straining his eyes through the rain.

Everyone looked harder into the distance and watched mesmerised as the figure of a woman began to materialise. As she took one step after the other, her identity was unveiled. A staggeringly beautiful woman with white alabaster skin, green gold-flecked large eyes, and a silky black bobbed hairstyle strutted towards the group.

'Euphemia!' cried Uncle Rufus.

'Hello all,' nodded Euphemia.

'As you can see, Euphemia, we've completed our task and wrapped up the case, although we did need help in the end from the guardians,' said Uncle Rufus.

Euphemia looked Tom, Eve and Clovis up and down, one by one. 'We are so proud of you all. And may I say, the whole of the SPI is abuzz about you young students. But I've been instructed by the inspector to personally take the bottle back with me, so we can begin our work with the souls straight away.'

'You will be kind to the innocent ones, won't you?' blurted out Eve.

'The only soul here who is going to the Abyss is that of Old Demdike,' said Euphemia confidently, 'where I'm sure she'll fit in quite nicely. Now,' said the witch, tucking some hair behind a very heavily pierced ear, 'I mustn't delay. I must fly, old Mafdet needs his dinner.'

Euphemia took the witch's bottle out of Uncle Rufus's hands, nodded and smiled. As she bounced away back into the darkness, she turned around briefly and winked.

How Euphemia Laveau had arrived and how she returned, the three friends couldn't tell.

'Did she say "fly"?' asked Tom. 'And who's Mafdet?'

'It's her cat,' replied Clovis, and to everyone's surprise, for the first time ever, he was just too weary to give a full explanation.

'Well, I have to say I'm very proud of you all too,' said Uncle Rufus, smiling. 'Well done. Come on, let's go and see if Maisie is all right — and then let's get out of here.'

They all made their way back through the forest of trees and bracken to where they had last seen Maisie.

'She's not here,' said Eve, feeling very worried.

'Don't panic, Eve, I've got the doll, she can't hurt you any more,' soothed Uncle Rufus.

'Your coat's still here, Professor,' said Clovis, picking it up and placing it over his arm.

'And so is the pram,' said Tom.

'Where the hell, is she?' muttered Uncle Rufus. 'And more importantly, where's the baby?'

'I don't think the baby was with her,' said Eve. 'I think she had the voodoo doll in the pram, not Alex.'

'Well, we need to check,' said Uncle Rufus. 'I'll have to phone Maisie's mother.'

Uncle Rufus wandered off to make the call and minutes later returned. 'Well, at least that's something,' he said with relief. 'Baby Alex is fast asleep in his cot. But Maisie hasn't been in touch with her mum.'

'Maybe she went back to the van,' said Eve, starting to walk in that direction.

Uncle Rufus and the others wandered through the bracken and ferns, calling Maisie's name as they went. Uncle Rufus was worried. Where had the girl got to? He picked up his pace, still limping, and with each step he took, a bolt of pain shot through his leg. Tom, Eve and Clovis followed closely behind.

'We've got to get those other poor people back to the hospital,' Uncle Rufus muttered, more to himself than the others. 'If Maisie's not in the van, I'll alert the police and get them searching for her, she can't have got far.'

Everyone climbed on board Albert, but there was no sign of Maisie. 'We can't keep looking. We've got to go,' said Uncle Rufus, shaking his head in frustration. 'I need to get these people back to the hospital.' Everyone sighed with relief as the unpredictable vehicle started straight away. Uncle Rufus patted the steering wheel, and smiled, saying, 'Thank you, Albert, I think you know we're all very tired.'

With all the victims safely onboard, Uncle Rufus drove Albert back to the hospital, where the descendants were returned to their wards, much to the relief of their families.

All the victims seemed dazed and confused. Uncle Rufus assured them that in time the memories of their terror-filled night would fade. He knew that sooner rather than later, some members of the SPI would come and visit the victims and help them to get better. They would ensure to take the bad memories away and of course erase the horrific blue burn marks.

It was too late to get the train back to London and so it was that a very happy Gerry and Stan welcomed them all back to The Safe Haven hotel.

Stan and Gerry thought from their dirty faces and exhausted demeanours that they must all have been caught in another air raid. After much fussing and a hot drink of milk, everyone went gratefully to bed. They all slept peacefully and woke up with a spring in their step. They'd wrapped up a phenomenal case — and to top it all, it was now Christmas Eve and time to go home.

❈❖❈

After breakfast, they shouted their goodbyes from the back seat of Albert, and watched on as Gerry and Stan waved happily at the retreating orange camper van.

At the station, Uncle Rufus parked Albert up and placed the key under the front wheel arch. Thinking no one was watching, he patted the front of Albert and whispered something, but when he came round to the side of the van he saw the young ghost hunters all staring and grinning at him.

'Just saying thank you and goodbye,' said Uncle Rufus, looking embarrassed.

The long train journey was filled with excitement. Talk of Christmas, favourite food, TV programmes and of course presents, passed the time as the train sped through the countryside.

Eventually it began to crawl past large buildings and houses all crushed together. They had at last reached London, and Clovis, Tom and Eve were already standing at the doors in eagerness to get home.

CHAPTER 22

A Christmas Star and a Ghost Called Florence

As soon as the taxi pulled up outside her home, Eve ran through the open gate, put her keys in the lock and pushed open the old heavy door. Inside, what she and the others saw took their breath away, for there at the bottom of the stairs was the biggest Christmas tree they had ever had.

Standing by it were Tom's parents, Clovis's mum Claudette and his brother Jahmeel.

'You're back,' said Tom's mum, Ange, clearly delighted at seeing her son. She went over and kissed Tom's face all over and squeezed him hard.

'Mum,' said Tom, embarrassed by his mother's affection.

'Have you done this?' asked Eve, her mouth still gaping open.

'We certainly have,' said Claudette. 'I hope you like it. Your uncle gave us some instructions and we were told to leave the star at the top, as it's something you both like to do together.'

'It looks amazing! Thank you so much,' said Eve, tears glimmering in her eyes.

'Yes, thank you,' said Uncle Rufus. 'The research work took

so much longer than I initially anticipated, so thank you, I don't think we would have got a tree up in time if it wasn't for your help.'

'Our pleasure,' said Claudette.

'Now, Eve,' said Uncle Rufus, 'Shall we?' He held out a silver star. Eve smiled and took the decoration from him and then turned to face the tree. Uncle Rufus brought a chair from the kitchen for her to stand on and she popped the star onto the top of the tree. Now Christmas could begin.

'Big boobs!'

Everyone turned around to see Mr Pig the parrot swoop over from his perch in the front room to sit on a branch of the Christmas tree. The baubles and decorations quivered with the weight of the colourful bird. Boris barked and growled at the parrot, to which the bird replied, 'Arse crack!'

After everyone had finished laughing, they discussed timings and details for tomorrow's celebrations over cups of tea and some of Claudette's homemade mince pies.

'Until tomorrow, then,' said Tom's dad as Uncle Rufus and Eve finally waved their friends off.

As soon as the front door was shut, Uncle Rufus turned to Eve. 'Can you message Tom and Clovis?'

'What? They've only just left.'

'I know, but I couldn't tell you all with their parents there.'

'Tell us what?'

'Tomorrow, after our Christmas feast, I've arranged for you to go back to The Bow Bells Pub and finish that investigation. But you're to go on your own. It will be your first official lone investigation. The SPI have just confirmed it.' Uncle Rufus looked at her stunned face.

'Really? And can we take all the equipment?'

'Yes, it's all yours,' said Uncle Rufus.

Eve hugged her uncle. 'Thanks, Unc, that's just brilliant. Our first solo mission.'

Uncle Rufus laughed at her reaction.

'But what will the others tell their parents?' said Eve, looking a little concerned. 'They'll never let us leave on Christmas day.'

'Don't worry about that,' said Uncle Rufus. 'You will be taking some Christmas dinner over to the pub, as Geoff the landlord is a friend of mine and is feeling a little low. But of course, in return he's agreed that you can finish the investigation. Meanwhile,' winked Uncle Rufus, 'I will remain here in this wonderful house, eat more food and watch movies on the TV with my good friends.'

The next morning, Eve suddenly remembered what day it was and leaped out of bed quickly, nearly falling over Boris in the process. She flung her dressing gown and slippers on and ran down the old winding staircase.

The smell of fresh coffee and cinnamon wafted into her nostrils as she walked into the kitchen to find her uncle drinking coffee and eating pancakes.

'Merry Christmas, my darling girl,' said Uncle Rufus.

'Merry Christmas, Unc.'

'Your main present's under the tree. Look for a small box,' he instructed.

Eve ran into the hallway and began to rummage amongst the presents under the tree. Eventually she found it. It was a small square gift, wrapped perfectly in Christmassy paper and ribbon.

'Well, open it,' laughed Uncle Rufus.

'Open it!' squawked Mr Pig, dancing beside her on the floor.

Eve tore it open. Inside was a beautiful turquoise oval stone. Eve delicately pulled it from the box, revealing that it was a ring.

'Oh, Uncle, this is beautiful.' She slid it onto her finger and held her hand out to admire it from afar.

'It was your aunt's,' whispered Uncle Rufus. 'I had it resized and now it's yours. It's turquoise, it helps with connecting to the spirit world. I think you've earned it, Eve,' he added fondly.

Eve stood up and hugged Uncle Rufus for a long time, and when they pulled apart, both were crying.

'You little monkey,' laughed Uncle Rufus. 'You always can make me emotional.'

'Sorry, Unc,' laughed Eve, wiping away her happy tears. 'I'll never take it off,' she said.

The rest of the morning was spent working together, setting the table in the dining room, eating, drinking and playing music. Soon the others began to turn up, bringing more presents, heaps of food and lots of cheer and merriment.

Claudette Gayle immediately took over the kitchen and began to boss everyone about. She instructed Clovis, his brother Jahmeel, Eve and Tom to pass her various ingredients and kitchen utensils. All the while she danced to the Christmas music around the large kitchen as she prepared a feast fit for the gods.

Before long everyone was sitting around the table and tucking into the delicious spread. Gifts were opened, crackers were pulled, and bad jokes were told.

As the dinner drew to a close and all the plates and pots had been cleared up, Uncle Rufus winked slyly at Eve and said: 'I think you need to set off to give Geoff his dinner now.'

'Oh, right,' said Eve, realising that it was time to go to The Bow Bells Pub. The young ghost hunters gathered together their rucksacks, packed with equipment and set off excitedly on their bikes.

After a short ride, they arrived at the pub. Clovis knocked at the door and eventually it creaked open to reveal Geoff, the landlord.

'Oh, thank God you're here. I'm bloody starving. In you come, then.' Geoff greedily took the covered plate Eve had brought, and made his way to his flat above the pub. He looked back over his shoulder and shouted: 'It's all yours! And merry Christmas.'

Clovis, Tom and Eve got straight to it. They opened the door to the ladies' toilets.

'Right,' said Eve, pulling the night-vision camera out of her bag. 'I don't think we should put the lights on, we had such great phenomena last time when we were in the dark. You guys agree?'

Clovis and Tom approved happily and so Eve set up a camera by the sink. 'This angle is great,' she said, positioning the camera on a tripod. 'We can get most of the room in with this wide shot.'

'Yeah,' agreed Clovis. He delved into the bag and brought out the night-vision GoPros and passed one each to Tom and Eve.

'Let's press record and synchronise the EVP watches,' said Tom.

'Eve, do you want to do the honours?' asked Clovis, pointing to the toilet in one of the cubicles.

'OK, but promise you won't laugh? Especially you, Tom.'

Tom didn't answer, he had gone quiet and closed his eyes.

'Someone's coming,' he whispered.

'I hope she shows herself,' said Clovis, peering intently at the space where Eve was now sitting.

Suddenly the room seemed to drop in temperature dramatically, signalling that Tom was indeed right, a soul from the spirit realm had joined them.

Tom's head began to fizz, his stomach doing a somersault.

Then one toilet after another began to flush, causing Eve to jump up in alarm. She'd forgotten to put the lid down. 'Really, on my new jeans!'

Clovis couldn't help but laugh as Eve tried to survey her

own behind, and the huge wet patch that had begun to seep through the denim.

'Can you smell smoke?' asked Tom, sniffing the air. 'It's like cigars.'

'Yes, this ghost liked to smoke,' whispered Eve.

Suddenly, the fuzzy outline of a woman began to form right in front of Clovis. He couldn't believe his luck. He took his glasses off and gave them a quick clean, eager not to miss any details of the apparition that had materialised so close to him. Her attire was Victorian, a long black dress with a white apron over the top, on her head she wore a white mob cap. Her hair was greying and bits of it had fallen out from underneath her cap. But the most fascinating sight was the cigar which clung onto the edge of her lip as if stuck on with glue.

Tom heard the woman's voice in his head. 'I died here,' she whispered. Tom conveyed the words to Eve and Clovis. The ghost continued to talk quietly through Tom. 'I was cleaning and suddenly, I felt a tightness across my chest. I grabbed onto the chain of the toilet to try to stay upright but it didn't do the trick and I was found dead as you like, on the floor.'

Clovis reached his hand out and wondered what it would feel like to put his hand through her image. Feeling brave, he pushed his hand forward, watching in amazement as it completely disappeared. He noted that it was much colder inside the apparition, in fact his hand was starting to freeze.

'Do you mind, young man, that is most uncomfortable.' Tom sniggered and relayed the message.

Clovis could tell she wasn't happy with him by the look of disgust on her exhausted face.

'What's your name?' asked Eve gently. 'And why haven't you moved on? Surely you don't want to be here for eternity?'

Tom waited for the response and then told Eve and Clovis what she was saying.

'She says her name's Florence, and that she's scared. She hasn't been the most honest of folk, had her fingers in the till on more than one occasion, and thinks that she might go to Hell.'

'I think you being here for over a hundred years has been enough of a punishment. You're not going to Hell, Florence. It's time for you to leave,' said Eve.

'No! I don't want to! I'm scared,' shouted the ghost.

Again, the toilets all flushed at the same time. Clovis, Tom and Eve watched her as she flew around the toilet cubicles pulling all the chains as quickly as she could.

Eve was losing her patience and stood by the main exit, placed her hands on her hips and said loudly and very clearly: 'Stop! Now, Florence, listen to me, it's time to go.'

CHAPTER 23

A Drinky-poo and a Reunion

Back at Uncle Rufus's house, the guests had left and Uncle Rufus was sitting quietly by the fire, enjoying a brandy and the company of Mr Pig and Boris. The poor bulldog had begrudgingly given in to the bird's grooming routine. Mr Pig was sitting on the dog's back, pecking and picking away at Boris's brown fur. Bizarrely enough, the bulldog was obviously enjoying the feeling and was very relaxed. He stretched his back legs out, yawned and let off a steaming puff of a fart.

Suddenly a barrage of noise exploded from the hallway as Eve, Clovis and Tom burst in through the front door.

'That was fabulous!' cried Clovis, clearly exhilarated by the evening's ghost-hunting events.

'Yeah,' added Tom, 'and when she said to me, "You're a nice young chap", I didn't know what to think!'

'She fancied you! A Victorian ghost fancied you,' laughed Eve. 'I'm so pleased we managed to send her to the Veil.'

'Yeah,' chimed in Clovis. 'If it wasn't for you, Tom, and your calming voice, I think we would have ended up calling a plumber. At one point while she was arguing with Eve, I thought she was going to make the toilets explode!'

The friends were now howling with laughter.

'Well done, Tom,' sighed Eve, grinning. 'You were brilliant.'

'I see you've all had a great time,' said Uncle Rufus, watching the three young friends in the doorway of the front room.

Their happy chatter was interrupted by a loud and purposeful knocking at the door.

Uncle Rufus went and pulled open the heavy door: there stood a very bedraggled-looking Inspector Rutherford and an incredibly tired Anwaar.

'Good grief, chaps. Come in, come in,' fussed Uncle Rufus, leading his friends into the warmth of the front room. 'Boris, Mr Pig, off there.' Uncle Rufus gently shooed the animals off the sofa and the tired guests gratefully sank back into it.

'You look like you've had a time of it,' said Uncle Rufus. 'Are you both all right?'

'First, a drinky-poo, I think,' said the inspector, unravelling her cloak and taking off her gloves. 'How about a sherry, my dear man?' The inspector clicked her tongue and winked at Uncle Rufus. 'If you would be so kind,' she said breathlessly.

'Anwaar?' asked Uncle Rufus.

'Just a cup of tea for me,' said Anwaar.

Uncle Rufus rushed into the kitchen whilst Eve, Clovis and Tom bombarded the inspector with questions about where they had been. Had Anwaar been helping her all this time and had she heard about their case?

When Uncle Rufus came into the room with the drinks, the inspector began to answer some of their questions.

'Yes, we have been on a case in Bodmin, Cornwall,' said the inspector, holding on tight to a dainty sherry glass, 'and it's certainly not been an easy one at that. Unfortunately, we couldn't close the case, and so we will have to rethink that one.' She took off her hat, which was slightly out of shape, one of the tassels looked rather weedy and limp. Her hair was messy, and Eve nearly burst out laughing when she noticed a small spiky thorn twig sticking out of her grey curls.

'And, Anwaar, were you there too?' asked Tom.

'Yes, I was,' said Anwaar, pushing his long dark hair behind one ear, revealing another strange-looking tattoo, 'and unfortunately, it's a case that's proving to be rather frustrating.'

'But I hear *your* case went rather well,' said Inspector Rutherford, sipping her drink. 'We've been hearing all about it from our sources and we are fully briefed.'

'It was brilliant!' said Clovis, unable to contain his excitement.

'But scary,' said Tom. 'Especially when Eve nearly got dragged away. But then the guardians came in and then we met . . .'

'Euphemia Laveau,' said Eve. 'She's a real witch, isn't she?'

'But of course,' replied the inspector, laughing. 'Who else is going to run the Witchcraft department?'

'I've already sent all the files and EVP recordings over to you, Inspector,' said Uncle Rufus, changing the subject and sounding serious for a moment. 'Oh, and one thing I must give to Euphemia is this — hang on, I'll get it.' Uncle Rufus made quickly out of the room and returned with the ragdoll and black needle.

'It was stuffed with a handkerchief that had Eve's blood on it,' said Uncle Rufus, sitting back down.

'I had a nosebleed when we went to see Maisie Shaw, I must have dropped it there,' said Eve.

'This shall be destroyed back at headquarters,' said the inspector, looking carefully at the doll, 'and you must burn the handkerchief, Professor.'

'Already done,' said Uncle Rufus nodding at the crackling fire.

'These things, as you now know,' said Anwaar, looking at Eve, 'are incredibly dangerous. Voodoo dolls or poppets have been around for centuries. Many healers made them to cure the sick, whether it be of the mind or the body, but others used them to cause pain and havoc to a person's life.' Anwaar looked down, clearly troubled. If anything had happened to these young ghost hunters, he would never have forgiven himself. 'Only when a doll is filled with the victim's hair,' continued Anwaar, 'or nails or blood, and then enchanted with a curse, can the doll work. You were very lucky, Eve. Maisie Shaw could have killed you.'

'But why? Why did Maisie have that doll? And why did she become so violent and vicious? I thought you said she was Alice Nutter reincarnated, and that Alice was innocent and not a witch. But if that's true, why did she speak through Maisie as if she was?' asked Eve. The questions had been burning inside her all the time they'd been travelling home.

Anwaar leaned forward on the sofa and spoke quietly. 'It seems that Old Demdike sensed that you were perhaps once a witch. And it's possible that in another life many hundreds of years ago, you may well have been.'

'Oh, wow!' breathed Eve, not quite believing what she was hearing.

'My guess,' continued Anwaar, 'in fact it's more than a guess, is that you were a white witch, quite a powerful one too. Old Demdike could sense that and wanted you to join her. According to the Witchcraft department, before a new witch is invited into a coven they are put through their paces and pain.'

'That's a lot to take in, Eve,' said Uncle Rufus carefully.

'It's fascinating!' cried Clovis. 'Old Demdike was trying to convert her or bring out what she once was.'

'I always knew you were a bit freaky,' joked Tom.

Eve replied by pinching her friend playfully on the arm.

'And to answer your second question as to why Alice did this, when she was apparently innocent of being a witch?' chimed in the inspector. Her eyes suddenly widened as she whispered to an enraptured audience: 'We believe what happened was a paranormal rarity. We call it "Spiritus Entare", which is when a spirit is aggressively possessed by a stronger, more formidable entity . . .' The inspector pursed her lips and folded her arms under her bosom. She spoke so quietly that everyone leaned closer to hear.

'Let me put it plainly,' she said in a hushed tone. 'We believe that Maisie is Alice Nutter reincarnated, however, through

"Spiritus Entare", Alice has become something darker and increasingly more sinister. And so possibly has Maisie. What that something is, we do not know.'

'This all sounds very ominous,' said Uncle Rufus, 'and it's something I've only ever heard of, never seen, until now.'

'It does indeed, but it's nothing we can't handle,' reassured Inspector Rutherford. 'We need to find Maisie and get to the bottom of who or what is controlling her mind. We're very worried about her and want to help her as soon as possible. Her house is under twenty-four hour surveillance. The police are looking for her all over the country, and I've been assured that she will be found and soon. The good news is that her baby was never taken out of the house. He's safe and sound with Maisie's mother.'

'Yes, that was such a relief!' exclaimed Uncle Rufus. 'Hopefully, when Maisie does come home, she can return to her normal and happy life and be reunited with her son. You'll let us know as soon as you hear anything, won't you?'

'Of course, Professor. Try to relax, it's all in hand,' said Inspector Rutherford.

'One thing that is worrying me,' said Eve very quietly, 'is that Old Demdike said she would come and find me. Can she . . . can she get to me?'

'My dear girl,' said the inspector. 'It isn't possible for that old witch to bother you. She's in a place that she can never leave. I can assure you, you are incredibly safe and sound.'

Eve visibly relaxed.

'In fact, that's the other reason we're here: to tell you all officially that Old Demdike has been sent into the Abyss. And all the other souls have gone to the Veil.'

'Yes!' hissed Clovis.

'Get in!' shouted Tom as if he'd just scored a hat-trick.

Eve just smiled, her eyes gleaming in the firelight. She was so happy and relieved.

'Myself and Anwaar,' continued the inspector, 'were on our way home and thought we would bring you the good news in person and congratulate you all for closing the case. So, well done to all of you.' The inspector raised her glass in the air but her face soon fell as she realised she had drunk the last of her sherry. 'Oh dear, this will never do. Now, Professor, my dear friend, could I trouble you for a refill?' And she jiggled her glass up and down, beaming like a Cheshire cat.

The young ghost hunters smiled. Who knew what the following year had in store for the three friends? But whatever it was, they were ready for it. Ready for more ghostly, spooky adventures.

CHAPTER 24

Maylum and Some Carols

Maisie had abandoned the old car; it had eventually coughed its last toxic breath about a mile away. The journey had been a long and arduous one. By some strange propelling force, she had travelled through the night and now she was nearly at the end. She walked along the cold, dark streets. Huddling further down into her thin coat, she tried to keep warm. It had been a very tiring and exhausting few days and now all she wanted to do was rest.

She had known where to go, it had been shown to her in dreams. Images of a dimly lit street, a row of Victorian houses all standing upright like soldiers, waiting for a command. She was to look for a house called Maylum. What that was, she didn't know, but she had been told that once inside she would never have to suffer, never need or want for anything in her life again.

Burrowing further into the neck of her winter coat, she stopped directly outside one of the houses. Anyone watching would have seen a lone woman standing and staring at a grimy stone wall. What was she looking at?

Her eyes fixed on the darkened, dirty windows, saw the

small metal black sign swinging slowly back and forth in the gentle night breeze. The sign squeaked; it was the only sound that could be heard in the dark street. The young woman looked around her. A rustle in a bush opposite disturbed her thoughts. Was she being watched?

She looked back at the creaking sign and saw that it was the name she had been looking for. '*Maylum*,' she whispered.

She looked harder at the sign and noticed underneath the letters was a small insignia. It was nothing more than a figure of eight on its side with a straight line going up from its centre, and another two lines crossing it horizontally. *What does that mean?* she thought.

Suddenly she saw a dark shadow move across the upstairs window. She knew now that they were waiting for her. Sucking in her breath, she looked at her mud-covered shoes and felt compelled once again to walk forward.

The voice in her head had changed now: it wasn't a woman any more, it was something else. It was darker, more sinister and much stronger. Swallowing her fear down, she walked up the steps and brought her hand up to take hold of an enormous black metal door knocker. A grotesque, contorted head that she guessed to be a goat, with large, curled horns stared back. It almost seemed to be mocking her. Dare she make her presence known?

She took another deep breath and placed her hand on the face of the devilish goat figure. She brought the knocker up and then bashed it down with a false sense of bravery.

It was too late to turn back now.

Heavy footsteps could be heard walking towards the door from the other side. The wooden portal slowly creaked open, and nothing but darkness could be seen. There was only a voice, a chocolatey smooth voice: 'Hello, Maisie, we've been waiting for you.'

Percival and Reginald watched from the security of the holly bush across the street. They both witnessed Maisie Shaw disappear into the building.

'Well, well,' sighed Percival. 'The inspector was right.'

'Indeed, she was,' replied Reginald. 'She's not going to like this, not one little bit. Shall we report it to the SPI now?' he asked, looking very concerned.

'Let's do it first thing in the morning,' said Percival. 'Let them all enjoy their Christmas.'

ACKNOWLEDGEMENTS

Thank you to all at Andersen Press, you're just the best!

Also, to my friends and family, who have supported and stuck by me. I love you too x

Yvette Fielding was the youngest ever *Blue Peter* presenter at age eighteen, and she's since gone on to host and produce *Ghosthunting With . . .* and *Most Haunted*. After years of studying ghosts, she's become television's 'first lady' of the paranormal. She lives with her husband and two children in Cheshire.

Yvette's experience of the paranormal . . .

In 2004, I took the *Most Haunted* team to Pendle Hill. We were there to broadcast a live television show for Halloween and investigate various locations associated with the Pendle witches. One of those locations was Tynedale Farm House. Allegedly this little cottage was home to two of the Pendle witches: Anne Whittle, also known as 'Chattox', and her daughter Anne Redferne.

I remember being very nervous all day about the night's coming investigation and I wasn't alone. The rest of my team were quiet and withdrawn. When I asked if they were all right, they replied that they were a little worried. This made me more on edge, as whenever we all felt nervous about a certain location, invariably things tended to get a little testing, shall we say.

As darkness fell over the Lancashire countryside, it was time to go. We made the journey in two minibuses, and drove slowly down a muddy track. We were in the middle of nowhere and when we arrived at the farm house, the hairs on the back of my neck shot up like needles. We all looked at the ominous building, its dark windows staring back at us. Who was in there? Something wasn't right about this place, I could feel it. In that moment I knew we were in trouble, and we hadn't even walked through the door yet.

There were two big broadcast trucks sitting outside the house and inside were lots of technicians making sure we got on air. Many of the tech team were sceptical about ghosts and paranormal activity, that is, until this night.

My team and I were all cabled up and ready to go. I was given the signal that we were on air and so our investigation began.

I opened the door into the cottage and we all gingerly made our way into the small hallway. As soon as we were inside, we heard a woman's laughter. That unnerved us, as it wasn't a pleasant sound at all. It was a cackle, and it was menacing.

A member of the team pointed to the electrical unit on the wall and noticed that the counter was turning very quickly.

'How odd,' they said.

'Why?' I asked, shining my torch at the box.

'The house isn't connected to the mains supply.'

Dumbfounded by this discovery, I moved the team into the main living room, where I thought it would be a good idea to do a Ouija board session. The Ouija board was set up and we sat around the large square board, placing our fingers lightly on the glass.

As the glass began to move rapidly around and around in a circle, I noticed an odd squeaking noise coming from underneath the table. I looked under it and pointed my torch to where I thought the noise was coming from. What I saw took my breath away: the screws holding the metal legs in place were being unwound. By what? I don't know, but they were definitely rotating and slowly unscrewing themselves.

The camera operators went under the table and caught the screws moving and the sound they made as they came away. Suddenly the table began to move and shudder on its own and then the whole thing collapsed.

As you can imagine, we were all in shock and some of us began to panic. I couldn't, because I had to keep the show going. The next thing I witnessed was one of the crew desperately trying to catch his breath.

'Oh my God! What's wrong?' I shouted. The cameraman had his back against the wall and began to claw at his neck. He was trying to pull something away.

Immediately our security officer came into the room and carried him out. I turned to the other camera and tried to explain what was happening to everyone watching at home, but halfway through, another crew member began to choke too, then another and another, and another! It was terrifying and I felt helpless.

Outside on the grass in front of the house, my team were all lying down, being attended to by the paramedics. Some of the crew were being given oxygen, others were in shock. I'll never forget the looks on the paramedics' faces as they inspected the unusual red marks around the necks of some of the team. What they thought was going on, I'll never know.

The director of the show was now screaming for a shot as the camera was lying unattended on the floor inside the cottage. I remember the poor floor manager Sally replying 'There's nobody left!' It was at this point that Sally had to take the camera and provide the closing shots of the investigation. My close-up filled the screen, to reveal tears rolling down my shocked face.

I and two other members of the team were the only ones out of nine crew members that were unaffected by the activity in the house. Why not us?

The technical team had come out of the trucks to see if they could help and were astonished by the scene they had just witnessed. And so had the whole country, as the event was all over the news the next day. It was the first time that a paranormal live TV show had shocked a nation. And if you ever ask a *Most Haunted* fan which is their most memorable moment, most will always say 'Pendle Hill'.

It took me a long time to get over that investigation. I really did have nightmares, reliving that event at Tynedale Farm. And I wasn't alone. Many of the *Most Haunted* crew suffered too and some of the sceptical tech team had to question their beliefs. It was a night that will remain with all of us forever.

I'll never forget seeing the panic in my friends' faces, their bulging eyes, as they gasped for breath, and then finding the red rope marks around their necks. How can you explain that? My only explanation is that it was paranormal, and the two

Pendle witches were the ones responsible. I really believe that the spirits of Chattox and her daughter were in that house and wanted us to feel their pain, their last breaths, as they died on Gallows Hill.

THE HOUSE IN THE WOODS

YVETTE FIELDING

When Clovis, Eve and Tom decide to play with a ouija board in an old abandoned house on Halloween, none of them foresees the horrors they're about to unleash. What starts out as a bit of fun, soon transcends into something far more terrifying when a distressed and determined spirit follows them home. Before long the friends are caught up in a series of events beyond their wildest imaginings and their journey as ghost hunters begins . . .

'When I grow up I wanna be a ghost hunter!'
KEITH LEMON

'If you're reading this scary book in bed then it might be wise to leave the landing light on'
PAUL O'GRADY